CHRISTO
DEAD MAN TWICE

CHRISTOPHER BUSH was born Charlie Christmas Bush in Norfolk in 1885. His father was a farm labourer and his mother a milliner. In the early years of his childhood he lived with his aunt and uncle in London before returning to Norfolk aged seven, later winning a scholarship to Thetford Grammar School.

As an adult, Bush worked as a schoolmaster for 27 years, pausing only to fight in World War One, until retiring aged 46 in 1931 to be a full-time novelist. His first novel featuring the eccentric Ludovic Travers was published in 1926, and was followed by 62 additional Travers mysteries. These are all to be republished by Dean Street Press.

Christopher Bush fought again in World War Two, and was elected a member of the prestigious Detection Club. He died in 1973.

By Christopher Bush

CHRISTOPHER BUSH

DEAD MAN TWICE

With an introduction
by Curtis Evans

DEAN STREET PRESS

TO

JOAN AND TONY AND PETER,

The only people in the world who think me wonderful. That is because they are very, very young.

"I believe as much as I can and God Almighty, I am sure, will pardon me if I have not the digestion of an ostrich."

LORD HALIFAX TO BISHOP BURNET

The thing is, of course, utterly incredible ... and yet one wonders. Could the Bishop have written a detective story?

INTRODUCTION

THAT ONCE vast and mighty legion of bright young (and youngish) British crime writers who began publishing their ingenious tales of mystery and imagination during what is known as the Golden Age of detective fiction (traditionally dated from 1920 to 1939) had greatly diminished by the iconoclastic decade of the Sixties, many of these writers having become casualties of time. Of the 38 authors who during the Golden Age had belonged to the Detection Club, a London-based group which included within its ranks many of the finest writers of detective fiction then plying the craft in the United Kingdom, just over a third remained among the living by the second half of the 1960s, while merely seven—Agatha Christie, Anthony Gilbert, Gladys Mitchell, Margery Allingham, John Dickson Carr, Nicholas Blake and Christopher Bush—were still penning crime fiction.

In 1966--a year that saw the sad demise, at the too young age of 62, of Margery Allingham--an executive with the English book publishing firm Macdonald reflected on the continued popularity of the author who today is the least well known among this tiny but accomplished crime writing cohort: Christopher Bush (1885-1973), whose first of his three score and three series detective novels, *The Plumley Inheritance*, had appeared fully four decades earlier, in 1926. "He has a considerable public, a 'steady Bush public,' a public that has endured through many years," the executive boasted of Bush. "He never presents any problem to his publisher, who knows exactly how many copies of a title may be safely printed for the loyal Bush fans; the number is a healthy one too." Yet in 1968, just a couple of years after the Macdonald editor's affirmation of Bush's notable popular duration as a crime writer, the author, now in his 83rd year, bade farewell to mystery fiction with a final detective novel, *The Case of the Prodigal Daughter*, in which, like in Agatha Christie's *Third Girl* (1966), copious references are made, none too favorably, to youthful sex, drugs and rock and roll. Afterwards, outside of the reprinting in the UK in the early 1970s of a scattering of classic Bush titles from the Golden Age, Bush's books, in contrast with those of Christie, Carr, Allingham and Blake, disappeared from mass circulation in both the UK and the US, becoming fervently sought (and ever more unobtainable) treasures by collectors and connoisseurs of classic crime fiction. Now, in one of the signal developments in vintage mystery publishing, Dean Street Press is reprinting all 63 Christopher Bush detective novels. These will be published over a period of months, beginning with the release of books 1 to 10 in the series.

Few Golden Age British mystery writers had backgrounds as humble yet simultaneously mysterious, dotted with omissions and evasions, as Christopher Bush, who was born Charlie Christmas Bush on the day of the Nativity in 1885 in the Norfolk village of Great Hockham, to Charles Walter Bush and his second wife, Eva Margaret Long. While the father of Christopher Bush's Detection Club colleague and near exact contemporary Henry Wade (the pseudonym of Henry Lancelot Aubrey-Fletcher) was a baronet who lived in an elegant Georgian mansion and claimed extensive ownership of fertile English fields, Christopher's father resided in a cramped cottage and toiled in fields as a farm laborer, a term that in the late Victorian and Edwardian era, his son lamented many years afterward, "had in it something of contempt....There was something almost of serfdom about it."

Charles Walter Bush was a canny though mercurial individual, his only learning, his son recalled, having been "acquired at the Sunday school." A man of parts, Charles was a tenant farmer of three acres, a thatcher, bricklayer and carpenter (fittingly for the father of a detective novelist, coffins were his specialty), a village radical and a most adept poacher. After a flight from Great Hockham, possibly on account of his poaching activities, Charles, a widower with a baby son whom he had left in the care of his mother, resided in London, where he worked for a firm of spice importers. At a dance in the city, Charles met Christopher's mother, Eva Long, a lovely and sweet-natured pompous, blustering man," over a political election, he lost all of the banker's business, much to his mother's distress. Yet against all odds and adversities, Christopher's life greatly diverged from settled norms in Great Hockham, incidentally producing one of the most distinguished detective novelists from the Golden Age of detective fiction.

Although Christopher Bush was born in Great Hockham, he spent his earliest years in London living with his mother's much older sister, Elizabeth, and her husband, a fur dealer by the name of James Streeter, the couple having no children of their own. Almost certainly of illegitimate birth, Eva had been raised by the Long family from her infancy. She once told her youngest daughter how she recalled the Longs being visited, when she was a child, by a "fine lady in a carriage," whom she believed was her birth mother. Or is it possible that the "fine lady in a carriage" was simply an imaginary figment, like the aristocratic fantasies of Philippa Palfrey in P.D. James's *Innocent Blood* (1980), and that Eva's "sister" Elizabeth was in fact her mother?

The Streeters were a comfortably circumstanced couple at the time they took custody of Christopher. Their household included two maids and a governess for the young boy, whose doting but dutiful "Aunt Lizzie" devoted much of her time to the performance of "good works among the East End poor." When Christopher was seven years old, however, drastically straightened financial circumstances compelled the Streeters to return the boy to his birth parents in Great Hockham.

Fortunately the cause of the education of Christopher, who was not only a capable village cricketer but a precocious reader and scholar, was taken up both by his determined and devoted mother and an idealistic local elementary school headmaster. In his teens Christopher secured a scholarship to Norfolk's Thetford Grammar School, one of England's oldest educational institutions, where Thomas Paine had studied a cen ry-and-a-half earlier. He left Thetford in 1904 to take a position as a junior schoolmaster, missing a chance to go to Cambridge University on yet another scholarship. (Later he proclaimed himself thankful for this turn of events, sardonically speculating

young milliner and bonnet maker, sweeping her off her feet ˈ
a combination of "good looks and a certain plausibility." A
their marriage the couple left London to live in a tiny ren
cottage in Great Hockham, where Eva over the next eight
years gave birth to three sons and five daughters and perfo
learned the challenging ways of rural domestic economy.

Decades later an octogenarian Christopher Bush, in]
memoir *Winter Harvest: A Norfolk Boyhood* (1967), characteriz
Great Hockham as a rustic rural redoubt where many of tl
words that fell from the tongues of the native inhabitants "we
those of Shakespeare, Milton and the Authorised Version.
Still in general use were words that were standard in Chaucer
time, but had since lost a certain respectability." Christophe
amusingly recalled as a young boy telling his mother that
respectable neighbor woman had used profanity, explaining tha
in his hearing she had told her husband, "George, wipe you that
shit off that pig's arse, do you'll datty your trousers," to which his
mother had responded that although that particular usage of a
four-letter word had not really been *swearing*, he was not to give
vent to such language himself.

Great Hockham, which in Christopher Bush's youth had
a population of about four hundred souls, was composed of a
score or so of cottages, three public houses, a post-office, five
shops, a couple of forges and a pair of churches, All Saint's and
the Primitive Methodist Chapel, where the Bush family rather
vocally worshipped. "The village lived by farming, and most of
its men were labourers," Christopher recollected. "Most of the
children left school as soon as the law permitted: boys to be
absorbed somehow into the land and the girls to go into domestic
service." There were three large farms and four smaller ones,
and, in something of an anomaly, not one but two squires--the
original squire, dubbed "Finch" by Christopher, having let the
shooting rights at Little Hockham Hall to one "Green," a wealthy
international banker, making the latter man a squire by courtesy.
Finch owned most of the local houses and farms, in traditional
form receiving rents for them personally on Michaelmas; and
when Christopher's father fell out with Green, "a red-faced,

that had he received a Cambridge degree he "might have become an exceedingly minor don or something as staid and static and respectable as a publisher.") Christopher would teach English in schools for the next twenty-seven years, retiring at the age of 46 in 1931, after he had established a successful career as a detective novelist.

Christopher's romantic relationships proved far rockier than his career path, not to mention every bit as murky as his mother's familial antecedents. In 1911, when Christopher was teaching in Wood Green School, a co-educational institution in Oxfordshire, he wed county council schoolteacher Ella Maria Pinner, a daughter of a baker neighbor of the Bushes in Great Hockham. The two appear never actually to have lived together, however, and in 1914, when Christopher at the age of 29 headed to war in the 16th (Public Schools) Battalion of the Middlesex Regiment, he falsely claimed in his attestation papers, under penalty of two years' imprisonment with hard labor, to be unmarried.

After four years of service in the Great War, including a year-long stint in Egypt, Christopher returned in 1919 to his position at Wood Green School, where he became involved in another romantic relationship, from which he soon desired to extricate himself. (A photo of the future author, taken at this time in Egypt, shows a rather dashing, thin-mustached man in uniform and is signed "Chris," suggesting that he had dispensed with "Charlie" and taken in its place a diminutive drawn from his middle name.) The next year Winifred Chart, a mathematics teacher at Wood Green, gave birth to a son, whom she named Geoffrey Bush. Christopher was the father of Geoffrey, who later in life became a noted English composer, though for reasons best known to himself Christopher never acknowledged his son. (A letter Geoffrey once sent him was returned unopened.) Winifred claimed that she and Christopher had married but separated, but she refused to speak of her purported spouse forever after and she destroyed all of his letters and other mementos, with the exception of a book of poetry that he had written for her during what she termed their engagement.

Christopher's true mate in life, though with her he had no children, was Florence Marjorie Barclay, the daughter of a draper from Ballymena, Northern Ireland, and, like Ella Pinner and Winifred Chart, a schoolteacher. Christopher and Marjorie likely had become romantically involved by 1929, when Christopher dedicated to her his second detective novel, *The Perfect Murder Case*; and they lived together as man and wife from the 1930s until her death in 1968 (after which, probably not coincidentally, Christopher stopped publishing novels). Christopher returned with Marjorie to the vicinity of Great Hockham when his writing career took flight, purchasing two adjoining cottages and commissioning his father and a stepbrother to build an extension consisting of a kitchen, two bedrooms and a new staircase. (The now sprawling structure, which Christopher called "Home Cottage," is now a bed and breakfast grandiloquently dubbed "Home Hall.") After a falling-out with his father, presumably over the conduct of Christopher's personal life, he and Marjorie in 1932 moved to Beckley, Sussex, where they purchased Horsepen, a lovely Tudor plaster and timber-framed house. In 1953 the couple settled at their final home, The Great House, a centuries-old structure (now a boutique hotel) in Lavenham, Suffolk.

From these three houses Christopher maintained a lucrative and critically esteemed career as a novelist, publishing both detective novels as Christopher Bush and, commencing in 1933 with the acclaimed book *Return* (in the UK, *God and the Rabbit*, 1934), regional novels purposefully drawing on his own life experience, under the pen name Michael Home. (During the 1940s he also published espionage novels under the Michael Home pseudonym.) Although his first detective novel, *The Plumley Inheritance*, made a limited impact, with his second, *The Perfect Murder Case*, Christopher struck gold. The latter novel, a big seller in both the UK and the US, was published in the former country by the prestigious Heinemann, soon to become the publisher of the detective novels of Margery Allingham and Carter Dickson (John Dickson Carr), and in the latter country by the Crime Club imprint of Doubleday, Doran, one of the most important publishers of mystery fiction in the United States.

Over the decade of the 1930s Christopher Bush published, in both the UK and the US as well as other countries around the world, some of the finest detective fiction of the Golden Age, prompting the brilliant Thirties crime fiction reviewer, author and Oxford University Press editor Charles Williams to avow: "Mr. Bush writes of as thoroughly enjoyable murders as any I know." (More recently, mystery genre authority B.A. Pike dubbed these novels by Bush, whom he praised as "one of the most reliable and resourceful of true detective writers", "Golden Age baroque, rendered remarkable by some extraordinary flights of fancy.") In 1937 Christopher Bush became, along with Nicholas Blake, E.C.R. Lorac and Newton Gayle (the writing team of Muna Lee and Maurice West Guinness), one of the final authors initiated into the Detection Club before the outbreak of the Second World War and with it the demise of the Golden Age. Afterward he continued publishing a detective novel or more a year, with his final book in 1968 reaching a total of 63, all of them detailing the investigative adventures of lanky and bespectacled gentleman amateur detective Ludovic Travers. Concurring as I do with the encomia of Charles Williams and B.A. Pike, I will end this introduction by thanking Avril MacArthur for providing invaluable biographical information on her great uncle, and simply wishing fans of classic crime fiction good times as they discover (or rediscover), with this latest splendid series of Dean Street Press classic crime fiction reissues, Christopher Bush's Ludovic Travers detective novels. May a new "Bush public" yet arise!

Curtis Evans

DEAD MAN TWICE (1930)

AFTER THE tremendous success in 1929 of Christopher Bush's inspired detective novel *The Perfect Murder Case*—boldly trumpeted by Charles Seddon Evans, chairman of Heinemann, publisher of the novel, as "one of the best detective stories of our generation"--the British journal *T.P.'s Weekly* confided to the mystery reading public later in the year that the author's "second detective novel will be *The Death of Cosmo Revere*." In actuality *The Perfect Murder Case* already was Christopher Bush's second detective novel, Jarrolds having published that which was the author's first detective novel, the rather obscure *The Plumley Inheritance*, three years earlier, in 1926. Yet there remains a question today, based on the respective publication histories of the novels in the United Kingdom and the United States, as to whether it is *The Death of Cosmo Revere* (*Murder in Fenwold* in the UK) or *Dead Man Twice* that should be seen as Christopher Bush's third detective novel.

Most, though not all, secondary sources--one of the major exceptions is the massive 1980 reference guide *Twentieth-Century Crime and Mystery Writers*--list *Dead Man Twice* as the Christopher Bush detective novel that immediately followed *The Perfect Murder Case*, yet the contemporary notice in *T.P.'s Weekly* makes clear that *Murder in Fenwold*, under the title *The Death of Cosmo Revere*, was originally intended to be Bush's follow-up detective novel. In the United States this plan was followed in 1930, with *The Death of Cosmo Revere* seeing publication in the country in May and *Dead Man Twice* five months later in October. However, in the United Kingdom, this order was reversed, apparently in contravention of the author's intent. *The Death of Cosmo Revere/Murder in Fenwold* contains references to *The Perfect Murder Case* which seem clearly to indicate that there was no intervening case between the two.

Where *The Death of Cosmo Revere/Murder in Fenwold* concerns an independent investigation into a country house slaying made by the lanky and bespectacled Ludovic "Ludo" Travers, author of the bestselling *The Economics of a Spendthrift*, and his ex-CID friend and colleague John Franklin, both of whom are affiliated with the renowned inquiry, advertising and publicity firm of Durangos Limited, in *Dead Man Twice* Travers and Franklin reunite with the Scotland Yard team from *The Perfect Murder Case*--Superintendent George "the General" Wharton, "blinking and wiping the moisture off his heavy moustache and looking more like a steady-going old paterfamilias than ever" (though those old duffer looks are mightily deceptive), and his attendants Inspector Norris and Doctor Menzies—to solve the bizarre problem of the twin demises of a butler and his master, boxing champion Michael France. Butlers normally were not bumped off in Golden Age detective fiction, particularly in the lead murder, if you will, although in 1933 Georgette Heyer did just that in her mystery *Why Shoot a Butler?* and in 1941 Miles Burton (Cecil John Charles Street) used the murder of a butler to lead his readers *Up the Garden Path*. Christopher Bush anticipated both authors in this respect with *Dead Man Twice*. "Even in these democratic days it is hardly the thing for a butler, as in *Dead Man Twice*, to be lying poisoned on top of his master's own confession of suicide, the master at the same time lying shot in the room overhead," complained the distinguished crime fiction reviewer, author and editor Charles Williams, his tongue firmly in cheek. "Servants ought not to get above themselves like that." Similarly, members of the boxing profession made unusual murder fare in mysteries, though Philip Macdonald slew a pugilist three years after the publication of *Dead Man Twice* in *Death on My Left*.

We learn in *Dead Man Twice* that Superintendent Wharton has "intense admiration" and respect for the immensely talented dilettante Travers, but, although Wharton allows in on his murder investigation both Travers and Franklin (the latter of whom had already been investigating the matter of Michael France's receipt of certain threatening letters), the superintendent has no intention of losing control of it to a bright amateur and his private detective friend. Wharton is in fact, one of the better realized policemen in Golden Age detective fiction--smart, capable and realistically portrayed, in contrast with the broadly-drawn bumblers of the period. In *Dead Man Twice* Wharton needs all his capacities, as well as those of Travers and Franklin, in dealing with one of the thorniest murder problems Christopher Bush ever set down on paper. (Diagrams and floorplans are included to aid readers intent on solving the problem for themeslves.) At just whose hands "gentleman boxer" Michael France ("He was at one of the big public schools, sir," explains Travers's man Palmer, who, unlike his master, is rather a fan of fisticuffs. "Eton, I believe—and at Cambridge, sir, and then went in for boxing as a profession....his uncle I think it was, lost all his money in that big smash....") and his butler, Soames, met their respective deaths in France's townhouse in St. John's Wood is a question that implicates the boxer's friend and factotum, thriller writer Kenneth Hayles ("definitely the best public school type"); Peter Claire, the well-heeled, aristocratic racing motorist and chief backer of France ("Did you hear how he spoke? 'Evenin', Wharton." As if I was a bloody footman!"); Claire's "remarkably attractive" and "sporting" wife, Dorothy ("She was Dorothy Pleasance, you know—one of the Berkshire Pleasances. Lord Faxton's her uncle...."); an enigmatical valet named Usher; and the unknown blonde who left stray hairs behind her on Michael France's settee. (States Wharton bluntly of Michael France's florid bedroom, "It's the show room of a super-brothel.")

At one point in the novel, Ludo Travers--a fan of mystery fiction, but only the quality stuff, don't you know—vigorously denounces one of Kenneth boxing champion Michael France Hayle's hackneyed thrillers as a hodgepodge of "All the preposterous and creaking machinery from every shocker ever written! All the clichés and outworn flourishes! We get rooms that descend bodily, sliding panels, a vanishing corpse, dope dealers, an opium den, a mysterious poison, a Chinese villain, and a heroine...who's abducted and rescued. The Chinaman turns out to be a detective in disguise...."

Travers's amusing anti-thriller diatribe reflected the then-ascendant credo in British mystery of the true detective fiction writer, as embodied in Ronald Knox's recent *Detective Fiction Decalogue* (which, among other things, frowned on secret passages and included an absolute prohibition on "Chinamen") and the oath of the Detection Club, an organization formed at the beginning of 1930 whose membership included such accomplished authors of true detective fiction as Agatha Christie, Dorothy L. Sayers, G.K. Chesterton, E.C. Bentley and Freeman Wills Crofts. Christopher Bush would join their distinguished company seven years later, but with *Dead Man Twice* following fast upon the heels of *The Perfect Murder Case* (and, in America, *The Death of Cosmo Revere*), the schoolmaster turned detective novelist had already proven himself an exceptionally distinguished practitioner of a most difficult craft.

CHAPTER I
THE MAN WHO TOLD A LIE

IT IS EASY, as Wharton told Franklin when he wished to rap him over the knuckles, to be wise after the event. In spite of that truism, there had to be arguments and the consequent differences of opinion, and in those Franklin and Wharton for once in their lives were of the same mind. As they put it, those events that preceded the tragedy of No. 23, Regent View, had precious little bearing on its elucidation. That would have been merely a question of time. Patient inquiry would have led them to the end of the same road and with the same certainty.

Ludovic Travers thought differently—a rather strange point of view for one who was never in the case except at third hand, whatever part he may have taken in the elucidation. According to him, those preliminary events revealed subtleties of motive and conduct that no inquiry could either have revealed or appreciated, especially considering the nice restrictions placed nowadays on the taking of evidence, and, at the other end of the scale, the loquacious pitfalls of coroners' courts.

As for the remaining interested party—Chief Inspector Norris—he was already immersed to the neck in another job, and being a person who derived little satisfaction from argumentative inquests, thought a lot and said little, leaving events and outcome to settle the matter for themselves.

* * * * *

As Ludovic Travers wandered along the Hampstead Road, he wondered why on earth a fellow like Churton—French Correspondent of the *Financial Adviser*—should have chosen that particular district for the flat which he so rarely had the opportunity of occupying; quite a long way from Fleet Street really, and yet not so far as to escape noise or claim any compensatory amenities. As a matter of fact there was nothing wrong at all with Churton's *pied-à-terre;* it was Travers himself who was disgruntled.

When in his capacity of financial adviser to Durangos Limited, he had heard Churton was in town and had rung him about those Moroccan concessions, he had been only too delighted to accept the other's invitation to come along to the flat and talk the whole thing out over a cup of tea. "Hundred and thirty-seven, Hampstead Road," came Churton's voice airily over the phone. "You can't miss it. Over Scarlett's the photographer's—you know, chap who does all the actresses!"

So far so good. Then Travers forgot where the numbers commenced and having tramped all the way along Tottenham Court Road, found himself with a goodish stretch of crowded pavement still to negotiate. A quarter of a mile of that produced no sign whatever of a photographer's or any shop of the name of Scarlett. On the way back he did what he should have done at the outset—looked for the numbers above the side doors of shops; even then No. 137, when he found it, wasn't a shop at all but one of those mushroom Schools of Languages that appear from time to time, students and all complete.

Travers polished his glasses and had a good look at the notices that occupied the centre of the plate-glass window—

THE MAESTRO SCHOOL OF LANGUAGES
(As advertised)

FRENCH. GERMAN. ITALIAN. SPANISH.
RUSSIAN. TURKISH.

DIRECT METHOD

PROFICIENCY GUARANTEED IN TWELVE
LESSONS.

and flanking these, matter much more insinuating—posters of a too obvious Englishman, gesturing before a whiskered and as obviously delighted foreigner, with the explanatory slogan

"Why shouldn't he be you?"

and secondly an alert young man, exuding vitality in the presence of a managing director who was saying—

"Mr. Maestro, we have decided to make you our foreign correspondent at £800 a year!"

and, of course, the slogan repeated. Travers winced as if in pain, rubbed his glasses again and opened the side door. At the top of the stairs was a corridor with more doors; on the first—MAESTRO SCHOOL OF LANGUAGES—and below, in unmistakable figures, No. 157.

Thereupon Travers cursed the insufficient light, his own eyesight and everything else that seemed relevant. Outside on the pavement again he set off with a warier eye on the fanlights, and it was then that the peculiar event occurred.

Imagine its taking place in a matter of seconds—a man whom he was sure he knew, coming along on the window side of the pavement; the definite recognition of the slight figure with its short, almost mincing steps; the lighting of his own features into the first wrinklings of a smile; then as he drew abreast, the "Hallo, Hayles! What are you..." and finally the inexplicable thing— the overwhelming certainty that the other had recognised his name, and yet the quick turn away to the windows; then a rapid step or two and the man was lost among the crowd!

Travers peered after him, wondering what had happened and, as he suddenly realised, looking very much of a fool. Had he been cut dead? and if so, why? Or had it been a mistake and wasn't the fellow Hayles after all? But it couldn't have been a mistake; there was no possibility of error about a chap like Hayles with his mournful face and its thin line of moustache that began at the nostrils and wisped its way to the drooping corners of the mouth. Travers shook his head perplexedly, shrugged his shoulders and moved on.

Above a side door was what really looked like 137 and he went gingerly up the dim stairs. As he stumbled at the top a door in front of him was opened and Churton came out.

"Hallo, Travers! That you?"

"It's me all right!" said Travers and dusted his knees ruefully. "You've certainly got up in the world since I saw you last."

The other laughed. "Come along in! It's a weird neighbourhood, but I've got an affection for it. My old rooms used to be here when I was a student."

"And what's happened to Scarlett's?" asked Travers as the other drew back for him to enter.

"I say, I'm awfully sorry about that. I rang you up to warn you but you'd already gone. I knew Scarlett's were leaving for new quarters—Bond Street, I believe—but I didn't know they were going to-day. Let me take your coat...."

* * * * *

Two hours later as Travers descended the ill-lighted stairs, he suddenly recalled that inexplicable affair of Hayles and, thinking the matter over, was inclined to put it down either to absent-mindedness or some sudden idiosyncrasy. Further thought made him moreover of the opinion that Hayles knew he was going to be recognised and to avoid it, had chosen an adroit turn of the head rather than the more usual look that goes right on into space. *Kenneth* Hayles, wasn't it? He'd run across him first at the Scriveners' Club—new member wandering round like the proverbial lost soul—and had promptly acted the paternal ancient and got him settled. And he'd seen him since—heaps of times—and spoken to him; rather decent sort of chap, nicely mannered, well-bred and all that. Rather on the shy side, perhaps, and not a bad thing either nowadays. And what exactly had he written? Shockers of some sort, wasn't it? Then that avoidance of recognition might have meant that he was none too anxious to be seen on his way to the purlieus of Soho in search of local colour! Travers smiled, then a dawdling taxi caught his eye and by the time he'd got in, the whole incident had left his mind.

Probably too he'd have forgotten it completely if something else hadn't turned up in the very same context. After dinner that night at the Scriveners', he strolled into the reading room to look at the latest prices. There'd be no more than a couple of other members in at the time, both buried in saddle-bags and backs towards him, and in a matter of seconds his own back was to the light and his head among the financial pages. A few minutes later, he was vaguely aware that one occupant of the room was leaving it, and a few moments later was unmistakably aware that a newcomer was about to enter. Feet padded along the corridor and the door was jerked open. Travers, squinting over the top of his *Evening Record recognised Ballard of the Messenger*.

"Hallo Hayles! They told me I'd find you here." He lowered his voice at the sight of Travers legs. "I've been chasing you all the afternoon and evening."

"Sorry! Why didn't you ring me up?"

"I did! I rang up about half-past four and they said you'd gone out."

"Gone out!" The voice was incredulous. "You sure you're right about the time?"

"Dead certain. About half-past four. I said, 'Is that twenty-three, Regent View?' and the old boy—"

"Somers?"

"That's it. He said, 'Yes,' and I said could I speak to you and he told me to hang on a minute and then he came back and said you'd just gone out."

"Funny! He must have made a mistake. I've been in the whole damn day till an hour ago." He changed the subject, rather abruptly it seemed to Travers. "Something urgent you wanted?"

The conversation became a murmur, with one word alone that was continually audible—a word that sounded like "Fransse." Travers, between the upper millstone of polite disregard and the lower of what had become perfectly natural curiosity, found concentration impossible and quietly sidled from the room. Ten minutes later he was picking up his own papers in his rooms at St. Martin's chambers. On the front page of the *Evening Record,* in splash headlines only previously missed because he had begun at the other end of the paper, was something that seemed to be of considerable importance.

BRITAIN TO REGAIN HEAVY-WEIGHT TITLE?

FRANCE TO MEET FERRONI IN NEW YORK.

SPECIAL INTERVIEW

then a big centre-page picture and three columns of letter-press. He gave his glasses a preliminary clean, had another look, then smiled. That word "Fransse" that he'd heard at the club was apparently a man's name—the Michael France of the picture. But what did it all mean? Travers, completely out of his depth, settled into his chair and waded meticulously through the lot.

What he gathered was that Al Shepherd, described as the greatest promoter America had ever known, had by cable obtained the agreement of Michael France, described as the idol of the British public, whether boxing or not, to terms offered by him for a meeting with Toni Ferroni, described as the Cleveland Cyclone; that the contest would be recognised by the British and American Commissions as being for the heavyweight championship of the world and that the articles of the fight would be signed in London within a week. Everything seemed colossal— dollars in hundreds of thousands, hundreds of thousands more for cinema rights; even the men themselves—six foot five of Ferroni and two inches less of the other man. Then if the papers were to be believed, for a matter of two months the whole world would be in a state approaching frenzy. Already that afternoon the audience at the Paliceum, where France was doing a show, had risen and cheered for five solid minutes when the news had been specially flashed on the screen.

Travers let the paper fall to his knees and thought things over. Michael France. Now what did he know about Michael France? Then it trickled slowly back—pictures in the papers, news items on the screen, casual remarks and chatter at the club. And what else? Travers shook his head.

If you knew Ludovic Travers or could have followed his self-examination as he sat there looking into the fire, you would have been certain that whatever his attitude there was nothing superior or highbrow about it. If anything there was a considerable amount of condemnation. The event, for instance, was an important one, or a paper like the *Record* would never have rushed into splash headlines and superlatives; moreover, if the male population of two continents was already in a state of excitement, how was it that he himself was unaware of the events leading to it, and so remote from the feelings of the man in the street? The name, as far as he was concerned, was merely a name; casually registered in the background of his mind. For that, however, there was some excuse. The sporting pages had no interest for him whatever, except perhaps occasional events at Brooklands—and of course the Derby or something like a Schneider Trophy which one couldn't very well avoid. Then he smiled to himself and pushed the bell.

Palmer came in, or rather glided in, with his patriarchal, silver hair and impeccable manner.

"Oh, sit down, Palmer, will you," said Travers. "You seen the papers to-night?"

Palmer balanced himself respectfully on the very edge of the saddle-bag. "Well sir, I have... and I haven't."

"I see." He passed over the three papers. "What's all this excitement about boxing? Who's this Michael France exactly?"

"France? Oh, you mean France, sir."

"I see. Sort of rhymes with—er—romance."

"I beg your pardon, sir. I didn't mean of course to correct you, sir—but—well, he's a gentleman boxer, sir."

"You mean a sort of rough diamond."

"Oh no, sir! He was at one of the big public schools, sir—Eton, I believe—and at Cambridge, sir, and then he went in for boxing as a profession."

Travers raised his eyebrows. "What in heaven's name did he do that for?"

"Well, sir, his uncle I think it was, lost all his money in that big smash—"

Travers made a quick movement. "Oh, France and Jesperson! Old France was his uncle, was he?"

"That's it, sir. This France—the boxer, sir—was amateur heavyweight champion at the time and so he went in for the professional game as a living; much against his friends' advice, I believe, sir."

Travers smiled. "I expect so. And he's done pretty well out of it?"

Palmer was enthusiastic. "He beat the lot of 'em, sir! Went through 'em like a knife through hot butter—Rawson, Joe Griggs, Kid Levine, that Frenchman Valiant, Fred Dunally, all the lot of 'em, sir. He's never lost a fight!"

"Really! Then why isn't he the champion of the world—if that's what they call it?"

Palmer shook his head knowingly. "They've kept him out, sir! Champion of Europe, that's what he is officially, only those Americans won't let anybody in. They've turned him down and side-tracked him and made a regular fool of him, sir, and now they find they've made such laughing stocks of themselves that they can't wriggle out of it any longer. They've *had* to give him his chance, sir."

"And he's got a chance to win?"

"Chance, sir! I wouldn't mind laying—I mean to say, sir, it's ten to one on him. Ferroni can't live in the same street."

"Really! Then he's what you might call a world beater."

Palmer nodded convincingly. "He's a wonder, sir! Moves like lightning—and a wicked punch, sir! I saw the other day where someone in the papers said he was Dempsey and Driscoll and Jimmy Wilde rolled into one. There's only one fault in him, sir; he will play with his man. He knows he's got 'em beat, sir, and he just won't finish 'em till he feels inclined—so to speak."

"Cat and mouse business, what?"

"That's just about it, sir, only some say he likes to show off." Then Palmer lowered his voice. "And they do say he's the very— he's a rare one for the ladies, sir!"

Travers whistled sympathetically. "Really! But surely the two don't go very well together? I mean you can't keep fit and go in for that sort of thing?"

"I expect that's *after* his fights, sir. When he's training, he trains, sir—so to speak."

"I see," said Travers and laughed gently. "But how is it you know all this, Palmer? I didn't know you were a boxing fan."

Palmer settled back in his chair. "Well, sir, I used to do a bit that way myself when I was younger. Also, this is a national affair, sir—so to speak. It's a good many years, sir, since an Englishman was the world's champion—not like it used to be, sir, when I was younger."

Travers poured himself out a drink and pushed another across to his man. "Well, here's good luck to him anyway!"

Then he smiled whimsically. "It's really chastening, you know, Palmer, when you come to think of it. I suppose I'm one of the few people who find it difficult to get really excited about all this." He picked up one of the papers and glanced at a paragraph. "What's he doing at the Paliceum? France, I mean."

"Music hall turn, sir. Sparring with partners or shadow boxing or punchball and so on, sir. They say he gets a thousand a week!"

"The devil he does! And the fair ladies! No wonder you said he rhymed with romance!... You seen him, by the way?"

"I thought of going to-morrow, sir," said Palmer, rather apologetically. "As I shall be free, sir, I took the precaution of ringing up for a seat for the special matinée, sir. I knew there'd be a crush, sir—so to speak."

"Very sound forethought!" smiled Travers, and Palmer, sensing the end of the interview, melted away. In a couple of minutes, however, he was back with a book.

"Excuse me, sir, but I thought you might be interested in this—er—volume, sir. A present, sir—from a nephew of mine."

Travers took it languidly. *Two Years in the Ring. Michael France and Kenneth Hayles.*" He frowned slightly. "Thank you, Palmer. I would rather like to run an eye over it."

But first of all he had a good look at the picture on the front page of the nearest newspaper—a naked bust, topped by a head from which a pair of rather supercilious eyes looked out and whose jaw looked decidedly unfriendly. Rather a fine face on the whole—full of character and with quite a lot of the thoroughbred about it. Indeed, the more he looked at it, the more intriguing he found it. As for the book, that was far more fascinating than he could ever have imagined and half an hour later he was still reading steadily, his own manuscript untouched on the desk beside him.

All that, by the way, was on the Monday.

CHAPTER II
TRAVERS JOINS THE SWIM

ON THE THURSDAY evening, John Franklin, head of the Detective Bureau of Durangos Limited, was working in his private room at Durango House. Just as the telephone bell rang he was wrestling with a set of accounts and for some minutes young Cresswold, his personal assistant, had been looking anxiously at the clock which was just short of six. With his eye still on the foolscap pages Franklin picked up the receiver and mechanically moved a scribbling pad into position.

"Yes... speaking... Most decidedly! Very pleased indeed." Then a laugh. "Oh, that doesn't matter! I shall be here a couple of hours yet... Quite!... Very good, Mr. Hayles... Good-bye!"

He glanced at the clock. "You in a hurry, Cresswold?"

Cresswold was, but he didn't feel like saying so.

"Then slip along to Central Information and get all the data on a—" he consulted the pad—"a K. W. Hayles. Hurry 'em up!"

As the door shut he reached out for the reference stand-bys and, finding nothing, settled again to his figures till Cresswold came back with the clip of papers.

"Hm! Malbury... John's, Cambridge... Secretary to Michael Rutlish France." He whistled as he recognised the name. "Co-author of *Two Years in the Ring* (Parry, 1929). Other books— *The Madison Gardens Mystery* (Parry, 1930), *The Fighting Chance* (Parry, 1931)." He flicked over the other cuttings. "Hm! Padding! Sort of stuff they *would* send up." Then he turned to Cresswold.

"You read either of those novels? They sound rather in your line."

"I read the Madison Gardens one, sir. All about boxing."

"I rather gathered that," said Franklin, not too unkindly. "What'd you think of it? Pretty good?"

"Well, sort of medium, sir."

"Know anything else about him?"

"No, sir, I don't," and Franklin caught a quick look at the clock.

"All right, Cresswold. I shan't want you any more."

Franklin himself was decidedly curious. The reference to France had started him going; indeed it had given him the very next thing to a thrill: Wonderful chap France! All the clichés came into his head—perfect fighting machine, punch like the kick of a mule, sudden death in each hand, greased lightning and all the rest of them. For a minute or two Franklin became the average Englishman, sporting mad. He was in an imaginary ring, his shoulders hunched and his eyes narrowed in the presence of an equally imaginary Ferroni. A moment more and he'd have been doing a left lead or settling Ferroni's business with an uppercut but—the waiting-room bell rang.

His impressions of Kenneth Hayles during the first five minutes he was in the room were excellent ones. He was definitely the best public school type—exquisitely mannered without a trace of effort and reserved in a refreshingly unusual way without being aloof. The striking thing about him was his plaintive-looking face with the enormous brown eyes that were oddly luminous; there was something of the spaniel about them which the charm of his smile strangely enough accentuated. He was frailish too in physique in spite of the five foot nine at which Franklin assessed him; altogether one might have imagined him a tentative or embryo poet and most decidedly not a writer of thrillers. What his qualifications were for the general factotumship of Michael France, Franklin was vaguely wondering as he placed the chair and passed over the cigarettes.

"Thanks very much," said Hayles and as he blew out his first ring, gazed round the well-fitted, reticent room. Then he caught Franklin's eye and—actually blushed.

"You won't think me rude, Mr. Franklin, but all this is so different from what I expected. I mean this office, and—er—yourself."

Franklin smiled. "You mean the detective's den."

The other smiled too. "Well—er—yes; and the detective. You see one imagines a—er—sort of ruthless, efficient—I say, I beg your pardon—super-efficient sort of policeman person, boring his eyes into you and so on."

"There's plenty of time for that," said Franklin—and waited. The other coughed slightly and began what certainly sounded like a prepared speech.

"As I told you over the phone, Mr. Franklin, I haven't come here to see you actually on business; I mean I don't want to consult you on crime or anything like that. I've read about your cases, as everybody else has, and being myself in a very minor way a writer of what one calls thrillers, thought I'd venture to come and see you with a most unusual request. I—er—don't mind saying now that I'm actually here, that I feel a great deal less bold than I did over the phone. As a matter of fact, I'm ashamed to ask you."

"Carry on, Mr. Hayles! Don't worry about that."

Again the melancholy smile. "Right-ho, then! Here goes! First of all, may I say I'm naturally prepared to pay anything you like for the favour or favours. The thing is, I'm engaged at the moment on a book which requires as a main character the head of a department like your own, and what I was wondering therefore was if you'd be good enough to let me use your office—and possibly yourself—as models, and also if you'd act—in a purely private capacity of course—as critic or colleague in the technical parts. Naturally." he added hastily, "I, or we, could camouflage the whole thing so that there was nothing personal about it." The look he gave was as much anxious as apologetic.

"I see," said Franklin and nodded his head thoughtfully. For a moment or two he sat tapping his teeth with the stem of his pipe, then made his decision.

"It's an attractive proposition, Mr. Hayles, and something I've often thought I'd like to have a shot at... but I'm afraid there's a snag in the way. Considering the nature of my agreement with the firm, I don't think I'd like to approach them for permission—as I'd certainly have to. But I'll tell you what I will do. If ever you're in doubt as to procedure, or what you call technicalities, come and see me at—" he took a card from his case and passed it over—"my private address and I'll be only too pleased to do everything I can, provided of course it's all anonymous."

"I say, that's splendid of you!" Hayles really looked amazingly relieved as he put the card in his own case. "You people really have no idea what a nuisance all this question of colour is."

Franklin laughed. "Oh yes we have—if we're conscientious workmen. No! don't go, Mr. Hayles!" as the other made as if to rise. The prospect of losing his caller had made Franklin realise that at that very moment he himself was in a heaven-sent position for information of quite another kind, and Franklin, when he chose, could be as charming and as disarmingly insinuating as the best of 'em.

"Do have another cigarette! It's so rarely that one talks anything in this room but shop—and pretty sordid at that sometimes."

Hayles dropped back in the seat. "If you're sure you're not in a hurry yourself?"

"No hurry whatever." He passed over the lighter and put the question casually. "I suppose like everybody else you're frightfully excited about the big fight?"

Hayles took a long while lighting that cigarette before he answered. "Yes... in a way... it is rather wonderful."

"You think he'll win?"

Hayles gave a non-committal sort of smile. "I'm afraid that's a secret, but—er—between ourselves, I don't see how he can possibly lose."

Franklin smashed his fist into the palm of his hand and gave a jaunty toss of the head. "That's the stuff we want! That'll show 'em what we're made of! I'd like to see him knock about fifteen kinds of hell out of Ferroni!" Then the head of the Detective Bureau of Durangos Limited, having ceased for a moment to exist, appeared to catch himself out in the act of becoming enthusiastic—and sobered down. "He must be a wonderful chap—France! You've known him a good while, Mr. Hayles?"

"Practically all my life."

Franklin nodded in a subtly gratified kind of way. "And now you're his chronicler—or historian."

Hayles gave a deprecating shrug. "His set of bumpers—fore and aft—would be more like it. He hates cheap publicity and all that sort of thing; letters, autograph albums, photos—you know, all the Hollywood stuff."

"I know. Flappers and hero worship. Still, you get your compensations, Mr. Hayles. You get a free front pew at all the big fights—"

"Don't you believe it!" said Hayles, shaking his head. "I don't believe there's anybody in the world less of a pugilist than myself. I simply loathe all that side of it; the smell, crowds, gladiator business and so on. But for the love of heaven don't tell anybody I said so!"

His expression was so genuinely apprehensive that the other had to laugh. Then, "What about your book—*Two Years in the Ring?*"

"Bread and butter. Would you like to live everything you hear in this office?"

"God forbid!" said Franklin hastily. "Still, as a friend of mine often puts it, it's always the other fellow's job that's romantic. And I know I'd give a good-sized hunk out of a quarter's salary to be at the ringside in Jersey City when that fight comes off."

Hayles nodded. Then suddenly he seemed to have an idea.

"Have you met him?—France?"

"I haven't—but I'd jolly well like to!"

The other thought for a moment. "I think I can fix that for you, purely privately of course. Tell you what I'll do. If I can arrange it, shall I ring you up?" and he rose to go.

"I say, that'd be frightfully good of you!" stammered Franklin.

"Don't you believe it. And don't forget you're going to give me more than a *quid pro quo* over my book!"

Extraordinary good chap, thought Franklin as he stoked up his pipe preparatory to getting down once again to those figures.

One of those deceptive fellows too—absolutely competent, no doubt, or he couldn't handle all that stuff of France's; and yet not two pennorth of side. Awfully attractive face too, and that diffident manner of his—very appealing. And fancy him—John Franklin—about to meet the great Michael France! Why, there wasn't a man, a real full-blooded Englishman, who wouldn't rather shake hands with Michael France than—well, than dine at Buckingham Palace. Lord, what a man! Beaten all the pro.'s at their own game—and kept his hands clean—and kept his caste as well! And what about having a look through the evening papers to see if there was any later news, before starting work?

In other words, Franklin, in common with the great majority of his countrymen, was being shaken on his perch and having his normal outlook considerably affected by one of those sporadic, sporting events which—whether Test matches or Cup finals—puzzle the superior of us and rejoice the hearts of circulation managers.

* * * * *

At practically that same moment something else was happening. As Hayles stepped out of the lift, Ludovic Travers—also working later than usual—was waiting to step into it. This time Hayles couldn't avoid him; not that he showed any disposition to, because he didn't. His smile was lugubriously effusive.

"Hallo, Travers! What are you doing here?"

Travers smiled. "Just earning a living. Like Ahab, hunting out the profits."

Hayles hesitated for a moment, trying to see the point of the joke, and the other, in a mischievous moment decided to take his revenge.

"By the way, you're a mighty important person nowadays?"

"I! How's that?"

"Well, I looked you straight in the eye in the Hampstead Road the other afternoon and you cut me dead."

"I did! When was that?"

"Last Monday—about four-thirty."

Hayles looked puzzled. "You saw me last Monday afternoon!" He shook his head and smiled. "Sorry! You must have made a mistake. I don't think I've been in the Hampstead Road for years."

"Must have been your brother then."

"Haven't got any!"

Travers laughed. "Splendid! That being so I'll accept your apology."

All the same, that second meeting with Hayles put into his head the suggestion of an idea that had been floating around for days. What about going round to the Paliceum and seeing the great Michael France in the flesh? In five minutes he was phoning up—and securing, by a phenomenal stroke of luck as the clerk assured him, a stall that hadn't been taken up.

At eight o'clock he was in it—half a guinea's worth and five rows back from the front. He hadn't been carried off his feet by the masculine hysteria over France; nothing of the sort—at least that was what he assured himself. The reason he was there was for filling in a gap in the general education and necessary background of an economist. No man moreover should be altogether remote from those impulses, patriotic and sporting, which were an essential part of the life of every civilised community—and so on.

As a matter of fact he was mildly excited. In the intervals between the turns, the conversation around him seemed to be of nothing but France. He heard names that he dimly remembered and found himself cocking an ear all round. His left hand neighbour was demanding of her husband whether France was really such an Adonis as the papers made out, while the flapper on his right was announcing that she simply adored boxers. Trivial, all that, but necessary as a prelude to what was to come. Moreover, during a lull in those conversations, Travers had a brain wave— he thought he knew why Hayles had told Ballard that yarn about not going out. He'd simply known that people would ring him up, pestering for news about the contract for the fight and he'd therefore given the butler chap the tip to say he was out. Perfectly easy when you came to think of it, except—and then he frowned—that it didn't explain why he himself had been cut.

As the curtain fell on the turn that preceded that of France, the excitement, even in the stalls, got really noticeable. The great building began to hum like a hornets' nest and in the heights of the gallery clapping had already started. The rise of the curtain seemed deliberately delayed and as the orchestra struck up the swinging strains of "You've Got 'em Going, Baby!" the upper peaks of gallery and circle joined in and soon the whole of the packed audience appeared to be singing. Mob hysteria, Travers self-consciously assured himself, but it was uncommonly thrilling for all that.

The vast interior seemed already to be in total darkness but yet more lights were lowered till the footlights made a white clamour. Then the curtain swung back disclosing the ring against a background of further darkness. The audience hushed. A figure in evening dress came forward to the footlights and began an announcement.

"Ladies and gentlemen! we have the honour to present to you for a few moments this evening, Michael France, the heavyweight champion of Europe—"

A voice shrilled stridently from somewhere above, "The WORLD!" and then a huge shout burst from the audience with round after round of applause. The announcer bowed and smiled, then raised his hand and the crowd hushed dramatically. "As you say, ladies and gentlemen, most likely heavyweight champion of the world!"

That brought pandemonium. Roar after roar of applause burst out, then came clapping, and up above the gallery began to sing again. "Damn good staff work!" thought Travers, but better was to follow. Just when the hall seemed all one vast roar, a figure in a dressing gown appeared from the wings. The orchestra crashed into "See the conquering hero comes!" and the crowd went really mad. Even Travers found himself clapping furiously. Two minutes of that and the announcer withdrew; the sparring partner appeared; the timekeeper took his seat by the gong; the dressing gown was slipped off and the sham fight began. In a second the roar of the crowd became an intense hush.

Travers was fascinated. France seemed to move like a lithe and enormous cat but his speed was deceptive. There would be a wicked flash from the other man's glove but he wasn't there. The great, muscled body was elusive as quicksilver. Back he would go to the ropes and you'd wait for the thud of the blow he couldn't possibly avoid and then all at once he'd be somewhere else and out would shoot that wicked left of his and back would go the other fellow's head with a jolt and he'd be away again. Then he'd close in and they'd go at it, toe to toe—thud! thud! grunt! thud!—and then he'd give a sort of laugh, a jab of that long left and away he'd go again, the audience laughing and cheering like mad. Once the other man rocked him with a quick uppercut and Travers saw him stiffen, then cut in with a lightning left and right. The gong sounded. The first round was over!

When finally France had come again and again to the footlights and the curtain was rung down, Travers' education was almost complete. He knew something of the reason for the frenzy the papers had prophesied. France *was* a wonder; a genius—unique! He'd made that other chap—who was he by the way? He consulted his programme—Fred Dunally, ex-heavyweight champion of England, look like a novice. Pre-arranged of course, a lot of it, but not all. You couldn't arrange that six foot three of perfect development, the play of the muscles, the incredible gracefulness, the uncanny speed of the footwork and the devastating certainty of that wonderful left hand. A thousand a week—and by jove! he was worth every penny of it!

Half an hour later he got restless. The rest of the programme was very much in the nature of an anti-climax—the comedian far too obvious to be funny and the drawing-room playlet too primly decorous, and as his seat was handy for the gangway he made an unobtrusive exit towards the side. He passed through the swing doors and after a few yards of steps and stone corridor, found himself with a choice of two ways and no indication as to which was the right one. The one he did take brought him to a further corridor at right angles and almost into a collision with a man whose silk hat made his height even more pronounced. Without appearing to notice Travers he passed straight on, whilst Travers—who had recognised the famous France—fell in behind at a suitable interval, judging from the top hat and the dark overcoat that the boxer was bound for the outside air.

The door, when he got to it, seemed to be a private one—at least it was not a public entrance or a stage door. There was no sign, for instance, of a crowd waiting to acclaim the hero; all there was was a limousine with a chauffeur and all complete. One of the theatre attendants was closing the door and beyond the profile of the boxer, Travers caught the merest glimpse of a woman, leaning suddenly forward as if to adjust a rug about her knees.

Travers moved on, then saw something else. Twenty yards or so behind, a taxi was drawn up at the kerb and as he passed, the fare leaned forward and tapped to the driver with a motion to the limousine in front. Travers looked back. The limousine was already in motion and the taxi was following it. But the really strange thing had been the occupant of that taxi. In the fraction of a second in which Travers had seen him and in spite of the immense horn-rims the man had been wearing, he was sure it was no other than Hayles.

Not that Travers scented a mystery—nothing of the sort. It was just the coincidence that puzzled him. What a curious sort of bloke Hayles seemed to be—always popping up of late at odd moments under romantic circumstances! *Did* he wear glasses usually? They seemed to strike one as a trifle odd. And what had he been doing in Durango House that afternoon? And why wasn't he in the car with France? The woman—the fair lady—that'd be it; two's company and so on! She and France and Hayles and the private door to avoid the crowd.

But *was* there a crowd? That could soon be settled. He turned in his tracks and wandered round to the stage door—at least he gathered it was the stage door. A couple of policeman were already making a way for traffic. Travers approached a sporting-looking gentleman who was craning his neck over the sea of heads.

"Would you mind telling me what all the crowd's for?"

"Michael France!" said the other, and went on craning.

* * * * *

Somewhere about ten-thirty that night, Travers, rather bored with his own company, strolled along the vestibule to Franklin's quarters at No. 21. Franklin was in front of the fire, reading a book.

"Hallo!" said Travers, picking up the tobacco pouch, sniffing the contents, then filling his pipe. "How's crime?"

"Not too bad. Have some tobacco!"

"Thanks!" said Travers, drawing up a chair and holding his hand out for the matches.

Franklin squinted at him. "Why the—er—beautiful garments?"

"These? Oh! been to a show—Paliceum—this chap France everybody's talking about. Wonderful fellow! And damn good looking by the way. Regular patrician profile and all that."

That started Franklin off and he had to hear all about the show. And he had an interesting contribution to make.

"That patrician profile you were mentioning, is rather funny. Do you know he's had his nose smashed in?"

"Has he, by jove! Who did it?"

"That chap he was sparring with to-night—Dunally. It's all in this book —*Two Years in the Ring*. France was messing about the way they always say he does and all at once this chap Dunally gives him an awful tonk on the smeller. Ten seconds later, France knocked him out. It didn't happen to be a championship fight, by the way."

"And what happened to the nose?"

"Some big Harley Street bloke set it. They say it's a damn sight prettier than it was before—only he can't smell very well. It's all in this book."

"Price tuppence!" added Travers flippantly. "Can't smell, eh? Damn good chap to murder!"

"As how?"

"Turn the gas on in his bedroom! That reminds me—Pass the matches!"

"Very brainy," said Franklin. "By the way do you know a chap called Hayles?"

"Oh rather! Saw him at Durango House this evening. Wonder what he was doing there?"

Franklin told him. Travers nodded his head at the climax, then gave his old, whimsical smile.

"So you're likely to see the great Michael France in person! Why the devil aren't I a detective?"

"Because you didn't start young enough," said Franklin. "But it isn't 'likely'—it's 'definitely.' Hayles rang me up a few moments ago and asked me if I'd go out to dinner with him at a chap's called Claire, where France is coming on after his show's over."

Travers sat up. "Claire? You mean Peter Claire?"

"That's the chap. The racing motorist and so on."

Travers nodded. "I know him rather well. Curious sort of fellow. Met him at Brooklands a lot. Know his missis pretty well too—vivacious little person but not very stimulating. What's he got to do with France?"

"Good Lord!" exclaimed Franklin. "Where the devil were you dragged up? Take this book along and learn something! Claire's his backer—the chap who's been behind him all through!"

Travers cast a languid eye over the book. "I *have* read it—or some of it; only I seem to have forgotten all the parts that are important." He handed it back. "About your friend Hayles who has a passion for colour. I know you're fond of scandal. What do you make of these three occurrences?"

Franklin made nothing, that is to say he was fertile in excuses. Moreover, as he insisted, Hayles was a thundering good fellow. Travers was gratified to hear it. After that for another hour it was France—and France all the way; and the enthusiasm by no means one-sided.

CHAPTER III
FRANKLIN IN THE CLOUDS

IT WAS ROUND about midday on the Friday that the fog began moving over London. An hour later, a screen of whitish grey had settled over everything and by the middle of the afternoon it was a regular old-time "pea-souper"; filthily yellow, almost palpable and so dense as to make invisible the fingers at the end of your arm. Franklin first of all smelt it, then tasted it, and a peep out of the lighted office told its own tale. Then, shortly after five, Hayles rang up and suggested meeting at St. John's Wood Station instead of Piccadilly as arranged.

Luckily, No. 3, Regent View, was only a couple of hundred yards away and Hayles knew every inch of the road.

"You know Claire, I suppose?" he asked, as they moved cautiously along the pavement through the unnatural light.

"Only by reputation. I've never actually spoken to him."

"You'll find him a very good chap," said Hayles. "He doesn't chatter a lot but he's an awfully good sort. Mrs. Claire's simply delightful!"

His tone was so enthusiastic that Franklin shot a look at him, and so dense was the fog that he saw only the blurred outline for his pains.

"Is she young?" he asked.

"About my own age—or younger. She was Dorothy Pleasance, you know—one of the Berkshire Pleasances. Lord Faxton's her uncle."

Franklin uttered to himself two pious wishes—that she wouldn't be too standoffish and that the fates would remove from his reach any bricks that were capable of being dropped. That brought them to the house and what it was like was impossible to judge in that damnable gloom, except that it was a large one. Inside, however, things were at least visible; the spacious lounge hall, for instance, bristling with heads and antlers that told where Claire had spent a good many months of his thirty years.

"Will you come into the drawing-room, sir?" asked the footman. "Mr. Claire will be down in a moment, sir."

"All right, Archer," said Hayles. "And bring in a couple of cocktails, will you," and he led Franklin off through the door.

On the heels of the drinks came Claire, beefy and sleepy looking but quite agreeable for all that. Franklin put him at six foot and fourteen stone. And he'd certainly spent a good deal of his time out in the weather, for beneath his hair—blond almost to whiteness—his face was a study in reds and browns. The eyes were narrowed and peering like those of a man who habitually faces the wind, and the little wrinkles at the corners gave a general impression of good nature—a careless, satisfied sort of good nature that comes from a comfortable and natural indolence, though that and a man with the reputation of Peter Claire seemed hardly in keeping. His voice was the last thing you'd expect. True the drawl was there, but with it went a curious directness. It was the sort of voice that could remain almost inaudible and yet be positively insulting.

"Hallo, Kinky! And this is Mr. Franklin. How'd you do," and he thrust out a huge fist. Then before Franklin could say a word—"They've got you a drink then? Get Franklin off his pins, Kinky! What's it like outside?"

"Hellish!"

"Hm! Going to last?"

"Well—er—I can't say." Hayles's voice was very reedy in comparison. "You can never tell, you know, with these fogs. Will it—er—upset your plans for to-morrow?"

"Oh lord, no! It won't be all over the country, will it?"

"The weather report—in the papers to-night—is pretty bad," and he glanced at Franklin.

But Franklin at the moment was catching Claire's eyes fixed on him with an intensity that was rather unsettling. The eyes dropped at once and Claire took a sip of the short drink.

"Well, happy days! fog or no fog."

"Here you all are then!" came a voice. Mrs. Claire stood framed in the doorway. Franklin got up; Claire lumbered to his feet; Hayles sprang up, his face beaming.

As soon as Franklin saw her he thought of one of those pleasantly mannered boys one meets on holidays. Her jet-black hair was close cropped and the black curve of the eyebrows gave the eyes an expression of interest and interrogation that was Puckish. The lips were smiling and the eyes were smiling. Franklin, at his old game of lightning registration, thought of "alluring," then changed it to "roguish," then discarded that. Not exactly a beautiful woman but a remarkably attractive one—a man's woman and a jolly good sort. Sporting probably to the last inch of her; breeding in every line, and five foot two of fascination and good fun. Topping gown she had on too—all shimmers and yellow fluffiness.

He found himself bowing awkwardly and then in a couple of minutes perfectly at ease. Claire rather dropped out of things, but the other two chattered away and seemed to be taking him for granted. Hayles appeared to be a kind of young brother— laughed at and called "little man" and "Kinky"; all quite good fun, with Dorothy Claire deceptively on the quiet side but friendly and jolly as anything. Hayles didn't seem to be able to keep his eyes off her. Awfully attractive that gorgeous little laugh of hers too, as Claire shrugged his beefy shoulders at some remark of hers.

Dinner was a very unpretentious affair in spite of the fluttering attentions of the butler and a couple of footmen. The food was good and though he was the worst thing in connoisseurs, Franklin knew the wine was good too. Then, too, as far as conversation was concerned, he might have been a stockbroker or a man-about-town for all the allusion to his profession. Hayles and Mrs. Claire kept up a chatter that was almost hectic, on subjects that flitted from plays to contract bridge. Claire, at the head of the table, seemed to lean forward with hunched, immense shoulders over his plate as if he were guarding it and now and then Franklin saw the suspicion of a frown come over his face as if he were an elder in the company of two children whose jollity threatened to become too uproarious.

"What are you really doing to-morrow, Peter?" Hayles asked during a rare pause.

Claire kept his eyes on his plate where he was wrestling with the tough foundation of a savoury. "As arranged. Going to Lingfield, then back to Royston with Utley. Why don't you come to Lingfield yourself and make a bit?"

"Well—er—I'd like to, but I'm going down to Martlesham on that job of work."

Claire grunted. "Sorry! I forgot." Then he turned to Franklin. "Horse of mine going to-morrow at Lingfield. Kampinbolo. Don't know if you've heard of it?"

"I haven't," said Franklin. "Queer sort of name, isn't it? Sounds like an absconding Greek!"

Claire pushed out his lower lip to the semblance of a smile "Does rather! Place in Africa, as a matter of fact, where I once had a bit of trouble with some porters. I think he'll win."

Dorothy Claire's voice cut in like a silver bell—"Oh, darling!"—then stopped. It was as though she'd realised in a flash some mistake she was going to make. Then she went on, with all the enthusiasm gone. "I do hope he wins! But what about Parson's Pride?"

Claire lowered his eyes to his plate and his voice was so final as to be curt.

"Rogers is riding. If I start him he'll win."

She leaned over to Hayles. "What shall we have on him, little man?" Then to her husband, very timidly, though that may have been a pose—"Darling, I do so want a new coupé!"

Claire made a gesture of resignation, an indifferent rather than a humorous one, and on the chatter went again. He and Franklin went on discussing big game shooting and it was not till they had moved off to the drawing-room that something struck Franklin as unusual. Not once during the evening had France's name been mentioned! Twice, at least, they'd seemed on the point of coming to it and once Franklin himself had made a leading question, but Claire had skirted round it. Perhaps there were simply enough reasons for it but yet it was strange, considering that Hayles had brought a guest for the one ostensible reason, that Hayles was his general factotum and Claire the man who had financed him. Perhaps that was the reason. Those two had long since taken France as a matter of course.

The mention, when it did come, was by Claire about half an hour later, and that would be about nine-thirty, plumb in the middle of an argument between Hayles and his partner in some card game *à deux* they were playing over by the fire. Claire himself and Franklin, like two seniors in a nursery, were yarning away by themselves when Claire butted in.

"What time's the Midge coming, Kinky?"

Dorothy Claire looked up as if startled. Hayles's mournful face with its streak of moustache and plaintive eyes, went scarlet. He fumbled with the cards. "After the show, I—er—rather gathered." He glanced at the clock and went on more fluently. "He ought to be round in a minute or so, unless the fog—er—holds him up."

"Well, come over here, you two," said Claire in his blunt way. "Cheer Mr. Franklin up a bit!"

"That's a libel on yourself," protested Franklin as the others came across. Hayles sidled into a chair. Dorothy Claire took the end of the settee, spread the gown over her knees and sat primly.

"Well, what are we going to do?"

"I know!" suggested Hayles. "Let's tell Bates to bring the gong in, and when the Midge comes we'll give it a wallop!"

Claire narrowed his eyes and looked at him. "What a baby you are, Kinky!" and Franklin couldn't tell if he were serious or not. Dorothy Claire got up quickly and began rearranging the chrysanthemums in the bowl on the side table and Hayles laughed rather inanely. For the first time that evening, the four of them had become separate and detached individuals. A jarring note seemed to have been struck, at least Franklin felt so in his bones. He was wondering just what to say, or when the unnatural silence was going to break—then voices were heard and the door opened.

"Hallo, Dorothy! Hallo, Peter! And the little feller here too! And"—France stopped before Franklin and smiled—the jolly smile of a man who feels on good terms with himself and all the world. Claire did the introduction business, then clapped Franklin on the back.

"Get the Midge a tot! And look after your own!"

Franklin set about the job. France said when. Hayles had the merest spot and Claire had a long one. Franklin, wondering whether he were putting his flat foot clean in it, smiled across.

"The tiniest spot for you, Mrs. Claire?"

She made a face. "Perfectly horrible stuff! Just some soda, please!"

He took it over, then freshened up his own drink. The three of them grouped round the fire.

"Well, here's how!" said France and held the glass to the light. He took a pull at it, then smiled round the circle. "Two more of those chaps and my number's up."

"You're starting on Monday?" drawled Claire.

"On Monday as ever was!" His voice was very friendly, and jolly as his smile. "Same old game. Got about a stone to get rid of. I've got Dunally, by the way. He signed along the dotted line this afternoon."

Claire didn't seem surprised. "I thought you would. He'll probably keep you on the move. Has Spider Fletcher been cabled to, Kinky?"

"Two days ago—I told you so yesterday," said Hayles aggrievedly.

Claire grunted. "And you'll want another good man, not counting amateurs."

"What about yourself?" The question was obviously flippant.

Claire looked round at Franklin. "Don't know. I rather fancy both Mr. Franklin here—and myself—could land a hefty wallop. We could look after ourselves, eh?"

As Franklin smiled and shook his head he sensed somewhere a subtle aggression—some hidden reason for the sneer that lay behind the remark. France took it all seriously. "I expect you would, old chap. And Mr. Franklin." Then he laughed. "Do you remember that chap Miles—how he sailed into me at that charity exhibition? Bored me to the ropes before I knew where I was!"

"What about the little fellow?" drawled Claire, and this time there seemed affection rather than malice. "You going along, Kinky?"

"Kinky's staying... to put the autographs in!"

"I think it's disgraceful!" broke in Dorothy Claire. She explained to Franklin. "Midge actually makes Kinky sign up all the autograph albums!"

Franklin looked suitably amused, then Claire's voice came in again.

"What are you doing to-morrow, Midge?"

"Doing? My God! he asks me what I'm doing!" and he laughed. "Playing touch with Dunally—matinée and evening. Oh, and watching another bloke eat at the Girandole before the evening show. Then I'm going out of town for the week-end— seeing a bloke about a little dog." He looked round at Claire and beamed, then thought of something quite different. "I say, what do you think happened to-night? That chap Forbes actually had the damn nerve to suggest that I should come on later to-morrow night—sort of spectacular wind-up to the contract!"

"What'd you say?"

"I didn't! I just looked at him!"

"Did you now!" said Claire, leaning back in the settee corner and running his arms along the top. "And what about your public? Haven't they got to be attended to?"

France refused to be ruffled. "Of course they have, old chap! I'm attending to them all right—only just a bit earlier."

Claire nodded and smiled. "And what's the big idea about all the hurry to-morrow night?"

France didn't look at him. He got to his feet, yawned and stretched, then remarked casually, "Cussedness, old chap! Just cussedness!" He moved over to the tray and put the glass down. "Kampinbolo going to-morrow?"

"If the fog holds off. I'm going down in any case—and that reminds me. I mayn't be back till after you've gone on Monday. Still, I'll slip round to-morrow and see you about that." He, too, got to his feet and moved over to the tray. "What about you, darling, if the fog's like this?"

She hesitated for a moment. "I don't think I'll go—after all... Or perhaps I may." Then she laughed and sprang to her feet. "Do you know we're talking all this about ourselves and poor Mr. Franklin is looking dreadfully out of it!"

She smiled round at them. "Let's play something! What shall it be? I know! Vingty—for pennies!"

"Splendid!" said France. "Get the chips, Peter, you lazy devil!"

Claire balanced his drink carefully and resumed his corner. "Count me out. You four play. I'm too devilish sleepy to keep my eyes open."

In five minutes everything was going with a swing and Franklin had never felt more at home in his life. Everybody was in great form. All sorts of side shows were introduced to keep the ball rolling. Even Hayles showed a vein of unrelieved hilarity and altogether it was a very juvenile evening and the best fun in the world. France himself was perfectly charming—topping face and not the least bit of side; more like a moneyed dilettante than anything else he could think of, though of course, as Franklin assured himself, he wasn't a boxer really; that was merely force of circumstances and so on, and in any case, what the devil did it matter if he was? He, and Claire, and Hayles reminded him of the Three Musketeers; nobody coming into that room could ever guess the real relationships in which they stood. France was perhaps a bit cynical at times, and Claire the least bit irritable, and poor little Hayles got badgered unmercifully, but what a thundering good lot they all were! Even Claire looked benevolence personified as he lounged with closed eyes in the settee corner.

It was just after midnight when the party broke up. If anything the fog seemed less dense but you couldn't see the width of the drive. At the main gate the three stopped for a last word.

"Kinky'll see you as far as the station," said France. "It's all on his way."

"And what about you?" asked Franklin.

"Oh, I'm all right!" He pointed away up the left-hand blackness. "Couple of hundred yards and I'm there."

Franklin, the last cheerio said, sat reviewing in the train what had really been one of the jolliest evenings he had ever known. Perfectly wonderful, he thought, the number of wholly delightful people there were in the world, waiting to be known. Take little Hayles for instance—awfully good chap; intensely loyal type and—Franklin frowned slightly—obviously worshipping the ground Dorothy Claire walked on, though there was no harm in that. Then there was Claire—with that blasé, irritable pose of his—just the fellow, with his nerves of steel wire, to have at your back in a crisis. And his wife—awfully pretty woman! jolly and friendly as could be; a thoroughbred to the fingertips and without an ounce of affectation. What had Travers said about her? "Vivacious without being stimulating." Well, he ventured to disagree. She was just the sort of woman Ludo ought to marry.

As for France, Franklin was complacently gratified. His had been the grand manner, the natural assurance of the aristocrat and that perfect merging into surroundings that paradoxically made him conspicuous. The hero had turned out to be even more heroic because he had been so essentially human. In short, as John Franklin was drowsing off to sleep, his last ideas on life were, as you may gather, that it was great—not only for its experiences but for its delightful possibilities.

CHAPTER IV
FRANKLIN COMES DOWN TO EARTH

FOR ONCE in a way Franklin's morning reflections were not at variance with his overnight, and presumably over-coloured, impressions. More than once in the middle of routine work in his office, he would feel a sudden, inward gratification. After all, in one evening he had met the most popular man in England and another whose name was almost as well known. Not only that, he had met them on equal terms and as one of themselves. Then he suddenly remembered that in the general exuberance just before they'd left the house, he'd asked Claire to put a couple of pounds for him on that horse of his. What was the name exactly? He consulted the paper and found it in the list of probables for the 2.30.

Kampinbolo (Mr. P. Claire)...... Bowing. 8st. 61 b.

That alone was a delightfully thrilling continuation of the adventure, especially for one whose yearly flutter was on the Derby—and then a matter of shillings. What had France had on it? A tenner, that was it, and Dorothy Claire another. Perfectly wonderful if it won! Ten to one for instance! Lord! he'd have to send Mrs. Claire a bunch of flowers as big as a house!

Then young Cresswold came in with more papers to be looked over and Franklin really got down to it, though the whole unusual experience was making a pleasant and optimistic background, in spite of the gloom outside and the trying artificial light. One o'clock and he yawned.

"I think you might go now, Cresswold. What's it like outside?"

Cresswold had a look. "Perfectly ghastly again, sir. I thought it was going to clear up about an hour ago. You can't see a chimney, sir."

Franklin, thinking of possible winnings, clicked his tongue in annoyance. And he was not so interested as he might have been when Cresswold all at once remembered something and burst out excitedly—"Talking about the fog, sir, rather funny thing happened yesterday!"

Franklin nodded politely.

"You know my brother's in the Air Ministry—Meteorological Office, sir; well, yesterday afternoon just before four he happened to be on the ground floor—you know, sir, right against the lift—when he saw an American chap sort of wandering round and this chap came up and asked him where he could get a weather report. Tom said he didn't feel like being sarcastic as this chap looked a decent sort—gentleman and all that—so he told him where it was posted up, and then this chap says, 'It's a mighty important thing to me, so isn't there any way to find out what the weather'll be like right over the week-end?' Tom told him where he'd find the week-end forecast, then he says, 'Oh! I've seen that—Dense fog over London and South Coast—but is it reliable?' Tom says he kept on badgering him about it and at last he says, 'See here! I'm open to pay anything you like for the information, but what chance is there of an aeroplane leaving the Hendon Aerodrome to-morrow afternoon?' 'It can leave all right,' says Tom, 'but the fun'll start when it tries to land again. Where's it going?' The chap looks round, then sort of whispers it confidentially. 'Across the Atlantic—and there's a mighty lot of money hanging to it!' Tom says he was absolutely flabbergasted when he heard that."

"You mean it wasn't a feasible proposition?"

Cresswold laughed with the scorn of the partially initiated who apes the expert. "Absolute suicide, sir. Weather over the Atlantic's been simply ghastly and, as Tom said, if he was doing anything as important as that, why didn't he get in touch with the big pots?"

"Probably something illegal... and he wanted to keep it secret."

Cresswold nodded knowingly. "That's just what I thought, sir, when Tom told me—and that's why I thought you'd like to know about it. And the really funny thing was, sir, that one of the senior officials happened to come along at that very moment and this American chap sort of mumbled something and moved off. Then when Tom was telling me about last night, sir, I suggested we should ring up the *Record*—in case there was anything in it—and give them the confidential tip."

"What'd they say?"

"The chap they put us on to laughed like blazes, sir. He seemed to think we were pulling his leg—but he took Tom's name in case anything came out of it; all in strict confidence of course, sir."

But what Franklin had been seeing was the unprofessional side of the episode. "Your brother had better be careful," he said dryly. "It might be a risky business for a person employed in a government office to go telling tales—and nobody should know that better than you." A word in season, moreover, wouldn't be amiss. "Remember that, Cresswold," he went on. "The slightest leakage of anything from this office—"

"But you know I'd never do anything like that, sir!"

Franklin had no intention of rubbing it in. All the same, he knew the reminder could do no harm, while an occasional ticking-off did youngsters like Cresswold all the good in the world.

"And what *is* the weather going to be like?" he asked more kindly.

Cresswold still looked rather injured. "What I told you, sir. Dense fog over London and local mist else-where. They say it's one of those blanket fogs, sir—absolutely clear up above."

Franklin attempted a jocular ending. "Well, you'd better buy a pair of stilts! Oh! what about the midday post, by the way? See to it, will you, on your way down?"

He pulled out his pipe and drew in a chair. No use going to lunch till that correspondence had been gone through. Then as he sat there his thoughts naturally went back to that wonderful evening. Extraordinary handy for those three, living all of a heap, as it were. And jolly handy for the Tube Station, in spite of the modern use of cars. Funny little chap, Hayles! Then he smiled. How desperately anxious he'd been on that short walk, through the fog to the station, to explain away all that badgering he'd had to put up with! The one concern in his mind seemed to be that he should be regarded as quite a different fellow, in reality, from the sort of humorous mascot which he'd been during the evening. He'd mentioned—quite casually of course—his various responsibilities and one or two things he'd done.

A tap at the door put an end to Franklin's ruminations and in came the commissionaire with the letters.

"Very late to-day, sir! Expect it's the fog, sir."

Franklin agreed. He ran through the small assortment and put his own on one side. Only one looked at all promising—a foolscap envelope marked "Personal," and inside which was a smaller envelope marked "Strictly confidential," by no means an unusual thing for that office. But he got the surprise of his life when he saw the signature at the bottom of the sheet of greyish notepaper.

tel. Primrose 003023, Regent View, W.
Saturday.

Dear Franklin,

Would you be so good as to look through the enclosed and tell me what you make of them. Personally I find them, after certain inquiries I have made for myself, absolutely inexplicable.

I have further enclosed three specimens of handwriting and on these I should like your opinion in strictest confidence.

Will you drop in and see me privately to-morrow Sunday) at about 2.30, when I shall be alone. Do not trouble to answer, except to phone me up at the Paliceum his evening if you are NOT able to come. Many thanks,

Yours sincerely,

Michael France.

The enclosures were three half sheets of cheap paper; at the top left hand corner of each a pencilled letter, and the one marked (c) bearing that day's date.

(a) I have just got back to England and found out what you done you dirty swine. Unless you are out of the country in three days you are for it.

LUCY.

(b) As you don't think there's anything to it, this is your final notice to quit. In 24 hours your for it.

LUCY.

(c) Michal *(sic)* France your numbers up. I'm coming for you and coming quick.

LUCY.

Franklin smiled—he really couldn't help it. That penny dreadful *ensemble* was too funny! Then he had another look at

France's letter—and frowned. The curious thing was that France himself seemed to have taken them perfectly seriously. Then he read the three again and this time with concentration. The writing was what one might have expected, a clumsy compromise between script and printing. The ink was of poor quality and once the pen had spluttered badly. Crudities in punctuation and phrasing he ignored—after all those were probably deliberate. If, however, they were natural to the writer, all the more reason why France should know who that writer was—and yet he'd definitely stated that the whole thing was a mystery as far as he was concerned. As for the rest, it was pure, full-blooded melodrama of the good old type. And who exactly was Lucy? And why had France taken them so seriously as to ask for an expert opinion? And then a thought that cast a vague sort of uneasiness. France *had* known then who he was, in spite of the fact that no reference had been made to his profession. Franklin frowned again, then turned to the other enclosures—the specimens of handwriting that France's letter had mentioned.

A. Notepaper the same as that used by France himself—parchment of good quality. Evidently a list of trains. Ink good. Writing probably a man's and showing, under the glass, signs of shakiness.

King's Cross, (d) 9.15 (arr.) 11.35
(d) 10.00 (arr.) 12.30
(d) 1.20 (arr.) 2.53

B. A piece of foolscap with the unwritten portion cut off. Ink good. Writing that of an educated person. Hand steady. Probably rough draft of something.

wing of course a very unusual way of looking at things and not what one might have expected. They intended apparently to ignore the agreement and use the opportunity to mark time till the chance came to wash it out altogether....

C. A crumpled half sheet of letter, discarded probably by the writer. Paper of fair quality. Ink none too good. Writing steady and with no indication of character.

things are come to a pretty low state with him if he talks like that. I will try to have a word with him before I go away, if I do go which doesn't seem...

As for the general deductions, none of the three resembled in the least degree the clumsy script of the anonymous threats. Still, that would be a matter for the expert. Had the client been of what one might call the rank and file, Franklin would have had his lunch in peace and taken his time over it. As it was, he cleared off the rest of the correspondence and, having first secured him on the phone, nipped off straight away to see Dyerson, whose name is as well known in forgery cases as those of the more gruesome experts who deal in poisons and intestines.

* * * * *

What actually happened was practically nothing, except that in Dyerson's opinion the anonymous letters had been written by a right-handed person with the left hand, and all three most certainly by the same person. As for the specimens of writing, Franklin's deductions were confirmed. Each of the styles was so remote from that of the script, that it seemed very unlikely that either of the three writers had composed the threats. Still, that would have to be gone into in detail under the microscope. Definite and immediate information was that—

A. was by an elderly man of nervous temperament.
B. was the work of a man of extreme fluency, using a fountain pen.
C. was written with practically no pauses by a man whose nerves were in excellent order.

Franklin took copies for temporary use and Dyerson promised him facsimiles by the end of the evening, and with that Franklin departed. One other thing he did know and that was that the interview of the following afternoon was certain to be a remarkably interesting one. And, of course, there was the thrill of coming into the very private centre of France's acquaintance-ship and all that that might imply.

One other thing of little importance remains to record. As he came out of the Tube Station at Charing Cross, he heard a news-boy holler, "Two-thirty winner!" and promptly bought a paper. Racing *had* been possible then at Lingfield! In the Stop Press was the news—

> LINGFIELD 2.30. Kampinbolo 1. Mutchkin 2. Par-son's Pride 3. Fourteen ran. Prices 5/2, 10/1, 11 /8 (fav.) Rogers rode winner.

But even the news that he had won a fiver didn't take from his mind the small cloud that remained annoyingly in the back-ground. The hero, to tell the truth was proving much more than human and unless the whole thing was a practical joke, it looked as if Michael France had sides to his character which he wasn't too anxious to have made public. Only what you'd expect of course. Women were bound to go flinging themselves at the head of a man like that and after all, men were men and always would be. There were plenty of things in his own life, for in-stance, that he wouldn't like the papers to print.

Then a thought. What if the whole thing were carefully or-ganised publicity? Say some elaborate stunt in view of the big fight! Then he shook his head. France, of all people, surely need-ed no more publicity than he already had. Then of course he started puzzling his brains again—then finally decided to leave it alone. After all, in twenty-four hours' time he'd know as much as anybody and a damn sight more than most.

CHAPTER V
DEATH IN THE POT

AS FRANKLIN LEFT St. John's Wood Station on the Sunday after-noon, the fog was at its thickest. On the Saturday, as Cresswold had mentioned, it had partially cleared away before lunch, and again that morning, but now even the street lamps were barely visible and then as lighted portions of fog. The darkness was so horrible as to be nerve racking—and even *terrifying*. Still, the experience of the Friday night came in handy and once he had made sure of No. 3, there was little trouble in carrying on along the pavement.

A single step led to the front door and with choice of bell or knocker he chose the knocker. But nothing happened. A glance at his watch showed the time as 2.35. Surely France hadn't expected him on the dot—and on a day like that! A second knock and still nothing happened. The third time he really hammered—and pushed the bell as an extra.

A minute's wait and it was obvious that there was nobody in the house, and that was curious to say the least of it, considering the implied urgency of France's letter. What was the best thing to be done? He looked at the fog, grimaced at the smell of it, then lighted his pipe and, huddled in his heavy coat, took a seat on the step with his back in the angle. France, he decided, had gone out and the fog had kept him. By the time that pipe was finished he'd be bound to have rolled up.

At three o'clock he was feeling chilled to the bone and uncommonly annoyed. Had his client been one with less glamour than Michael France, he'd certainly have gone away in a rage, or at the best have returned to his flat and waited for a telephone message As it was he groped his way to the gate, crossed the road and set about restoring his circulation. Ten minutes of that and he found he'd turned off to another road and by the time he'd got his bearings, it was getting on for half-past three. Even then he overshot the house and by the time he was once more mounting the step, it was exactly a quarter to four.

A minute later, knocker and bell unanswered, he definitely decided to go. Then a final forlorn hope suggested itself—trying to find a back door, what one might call the tradesmen's entrance. He groped his way along to the left and there in the wall was what he wanted—double doors leading probably to a garage, and a side door unlocked. A few further yards along the edge of a shrubbery and he was at the back entrance. Then, just as he was about to knock, there was the sound of steps and a figure loomed up out of the fog.

"Hallo! What do you reckon you're doing there?"

Franklin pulled the muffler down from his mouth and had a look at the newcomer. Footman probably, with that elongated, hatchet face, bowler and black overcoat; a servant of some sort most decidedly, if not blatantly. Still, whoever he was, he was most damnably welcome.

"I say! I'm most extraordinarily glad you've turned up. I've been trying to make somebody hear in this house for the last hour—off and on. I had an appointment with Mr. France for two-thirty."

The other put down his attaché case and flashed a look at the teller of the plausible tale; then apparently made up his mind that everything was satisfactory after all. At least he picked up the case again.

"I'm sorry to hear that, sir. But Mr. France is away, sir! He's been away all the week-end. And the house has been shut up too, sir."

"Really! By the way, who are you exactly?"

"Usher, sir. Mr. France's valet."

"Well, Usher, strictly between ourselves, I can show you a letter in my pocket definitely making the appointment. Mr. France told me he'd be alone."

The valet looked still more surprised. "That's very strange, sir! I don't mean to question what you say, sir, but I'll tell you what I mean, sir." He produced a bunch of keys and slipped a Yale into the lock. "Perhaps you wouldn't mind coming in this way, sir. I'll save time."

Now except for that first abrupt question which Usher had snapped out on his arrival, all this conversation had been below the usual pitch. That fog made a kind of vast, impressive interior; a cathedral that closed one in and made for soft speaking. Franklin's feet made no sound as he stepped on the doormat. Then he stopped—and listened. Usher, hard on his heels, began an exclamation—"Funny sort of smell!"—then listened too.

Somewhere inside the house was the sound of quick steps—then the slamming of the front door.

"That's Mr. France, sir—for a fiver! Just gone out again!"

The valet dropped his case and slipped out into the fog. Franklin found the switch, turned on the light and ran his eyes round the room.

Ludovic Travers, a collector of antiques, often felt like apologising for himself when he found his eyes instinctively roving round any room he happened to enter. Franklin's curiosity was even more natural—the habit of keeping his eyes open, wherever he was, and recording impressions. To his left, for instance, both the top of the range and the rings of the gas cooker, on which he put his fingers, were as cold as ice. On the mantelpiece an old-fashioned, marble clock showed the time as 3.55—and his own watch agreed. Then something that registered itself as unusual—the sink wet and the tap *not* running. At the same time his suggested a solution—then discarded it. It wouldn't have been France who'd been in the kitchen; really too unusual a place for him to enter. And yet, since the house had been deserted over the week-end, it wouldn't have been anybody else.

At that moment Usher came back. "Couldn't catch him, sir. The fog was too thick."

"Never mind!" said Franklin. "He'll probably be back again in a minute or two. But what was that you were saying about a funny smell?"

The other sniffed and suddenly seemed to get a whiff of it. It was rather funny really, to see him like a terrier on the trail. Then his nose approached the sink—and he smiled.

"Too much chloride of lime, sir! that's all," and he indicated the packet at the end of the draining board.

"But I thought you said nobody'd been in? Mr. France wouldn't come in here, would he?"

Usher wondered, then guessed. "It wouldn't have been him, sir. Somers! That's who it was, sir!"

"Who's he?"

"The butler, sir. He must have got in before me, sir... and he's probably gone out to post a letter... or something."

Franklin shrugged his shoulders. Usher's face resumed its normal impassivity as he took off his coat and placed it, with his hat and case, on the table.

"Come through this way, will you, sir."

Franklin followed and listened to the further explanations that suggested themselves to the valet.

"He must have gone out quickly, sir, or he'd have put the kettle on—and lighted the fires."

At the end of the short passage a door opened into a huge room, icily cold; the nearer part with its refectory table and sideboard clearly the dining-room. Half-way along it, a tall, eight-fold screen divided off the drawing room with its camouflaged electric fire, settees and easy chairs. To the left of the fireplace was a tall bookcase; to the left of that a door before which Usher stopped.

"May I take your hat and coat, sir?"

"Don't trouble, Usher, thanks. I shan't wait more than a few minutes."

"Then will you wait in the lounge, sir? It'll be more comfortable than here," and he led the way towards another door just beyond the fireplace. He opened it, felt inside and switched on the light, then drew back for Franklin to enter.

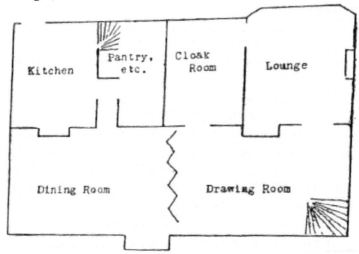

"I'll light the gas fire, sir." He moved in front again—then stopped dead with a gasp. Franklin moved forward quickly.

On the rug, head towards the door, lay a man, an oldish man; bald except for the white patches round his ears. His knees seemed half drawn-up and in front of his outstretched right hand a tumbler was lying on its side. Four feet back from the rug and parallel to the low fender was a table, with decanter and siphon on a tray. By it stood a small, blue bottle with red, poison label.

"Keep back!" snapped Franklin. "Don't go on that rug!" He leaned over and felt the man's face; it was still warm! With a quick glance at Usher, he knelt and listened for the heart, then pushed his hand down inside the waistcoat.

"Who is he?"

"Somers, sir—the butler." The valet was fumbling nervously with his fingers.

"Know anything about it?"

The other's eyes opened wide. "Why! you saw me come in—"

"I don't mean that. Do you know why he did it?"

"No, sir! I don't know anything, sir."

"Well, he's dead; dead as a doormat—and only a few minutes ago." His eyes caught the phone and he moved quickly round the table.

"Albany 0037!" He put the mouthpiece to his chest and stood with receiver at ear. "Where's Mr. France likely to be?"

"I couldn't say, sir. I thought at first that was him went out, sir."

"And Mr. Hayles?"

"I don't know, sir, but he might be—"

Franklin cut him short. "Hallo! That Albany Street?... Any of your C.I.D. men handy? . . Oh, he is! Ask him to come round as quick as blazes to twenty-three, Regent View, and bring a doctor Never mind that! There's a dead man here twenty-three, that's right... Yes, I'll be here Good-bye!"

"Now then, what were you saying about Mr. Hayles?"

"He might be at his flat, sir. His number's on the pad."

He rang Hayles's number and waited. At the other end a woman's voice spoke. Mr. Hayles wasn't in. He'd only just gone out again and hadn't said where he was going. Oh, yes! he only came in about ten minutes before—just got back from Suffolk. It was Mrs. Burgess, Mr. Hayles's housekeeper, speaking. Certainly she'd tell Mr. Hayles—to see Mr. France at once.

Another brainwave. Hayles might be with the Claires and so might France too. This time the call was more successful and in a moment or two he was speaking to Claire himself.

"Hallo! That you, Mr. Claire? Franklin speaking... Something queer has happened at Mr. France's house... Yes, number twenty-three. We've just found Somers—he's poisoned himself!... Oh! France asked me to call this afternoon and Usher let me in... I *have* told the police... You haven't seen either? Well, don't you bother... That's right! Let them know... Yes, of course I will... Ask him to ring you up... Right-ho!... Good-bye!"

The valet as he stood there, eyes on the dead man, was a tragic looking figure. Against his black overcoat his face seemed white as paper but there was no sign of hysteria; the hands he now held clasped in front of him were perfectly steady.

"We seem to be having bad luck, Usher," said Franklin. "Nobody knows where either Mr. France or Mr. Hayles has got to."

The valet looked up with a start and, as he did so, the other knew what had been puzzling him ever since he clapped eyes on his face.

"Haven't I seen you somewhere before?"

The valet's eyes fell for a second, then he looked straight at Franklin. "Very probably, sir—if you're a friend of Mr. France."

Franklin shook his head. "No, I thought it was somewhere else. Probably a mistake of mine." He leaned over and sniffed at the little bottle, then crossed over to the rug and tried the tumbler and the wet patch. When he got to his feet he was nodding with satisfaction.

"Now then, Usher; would you mind telling me what's been happening this week-end. Where've you been, for instance?"

"To Felixstowe, sir—or Martlesham rather. We've all been there; Mr. Hayles, Somers and myself."

"What for?"

"Seeing to the training quarters, sir. Mr. France is moving down there to-morrow."

"You mean he's going to do his training there and not in America?"

Usher looked round quickly as if afraid of being overheard. "That's right, sir. They say Mr. France has his own ideas about training, sir. At any rate, sir, he's always used the Low Farm at Martlesham, so we had to go down there on Saturday afternoon with the heavy luggage and so on, sir. Mr. Hayles drove his own car down later, sir. We went by train."

"When did you all come back?"

"I don't know when Mr. Hayles came back, sir, but he left the farm well before lunch and he said he was going straight to town. Mr. Somers went early, sir; called to see his sister at Ipswich and then came on by train. I came by bus, sir; changing at Ipswich—and got here... when you saw me."

The man was an excellent witness and obviously speaking the truth. His quiet, unperturbed manner gave him a certain dignity that was decidedly impressive. Franklin nodded more kindly, then, "Was there any definite time for getting back here?"

"There was, sir. Mr. Hayles had gone but the master spoke to Somers and myself, sir. I shall be away most likely till Sunday night,' he says, sir, 'or it may be Monday morning, but I want you back by four on Sunday.'"

"Then Somers got back only just before you did!"

There was a deep regret in the valet's voice. "I expect he did, sir—and I wish to God he hadn't!"

"I expect you do, Usher... and so do I. He was a good sort?"

"One of the very best, sir," and he shook his head.

"Where are his things, by the way—hat and so on?"

"I expect he took them up to his room, sir. They were his best ones."

Franklin nodded again and looked at his watch. "I wish to heaven Mr. France or somebody'd come! What about a cup of tea? You'd probably like one yourself."

"Certainly, sir! And would you mind if I took my things up-stairs, sir, and I could verify Mr. Somers's things at the same time."

"Do, please! Only, don't stir out of the house till the police get here."

As the valet shut the door of the lounge behind him, the blind of the far window seemed to flop curiously. Franklin stood looking at it for a moment, then went over. As he released the spring and let the blind flap up, he gave a grunt. Cut clean out of the window, immediately above the catch, was a six-inch cir-cle of glass. His eyes fell to the window sill—its paint disfigured with parallel scratches as if a foot had slipped. He felt the cut edges of the glass, then wiped his fingers.

For a good five minutes he stood there thinking it all out. During the week-end there had apparently been a burglary and yet the room where he stood was undisturbed. The rugs were in place on the parquet flooring, the drawers of tables and side-board were shut and the room had a general air of tidiness. Then,*had* there been a burglary? Had there been after all, some-thing in those anonymous letters? and had the entry been made with the idea of carrying out the threats? If so, what had the suicide of Somers to do with it? And why had the butler chosen the lounge to die in, rather than his own room or the kitchen? And if he couldn't take his poison neat, why not in water or a cup of tea?

Usher came in with the tray. "Your tea, sir. And you might like to know, sir, that... his clothes are upstairs, sir—on the bed in his room."

"Thank you, Usher," began Franklin—then the front door knocker sounded, and there was a ringing at the bell.

"You stay here!" said Franklin and nipped out. At the door was Inspector Cotter with the divisional surgeon and a plain-clothes man.

"Good Lord, Franklin!" began Cotter.

"That's all right!" smiled Franklin. "I'll tell you all about it in a minute. Evenin' doc! Your man's in there. Got any men, inspector?"

"Couple just coming in."

"Good! I'd leave 'em here for a bit if I were you. This way, doc!"

Menzies, a grizzled old veteran with as much respect for death as an undertaker's hack, set about his examination. Franklin left the tea to cool and whispered to Cotter the lie of the land—with nothing said however about the *reason* for the visit but in its place a subtle accentuation of the terms of friendship. Cotter, perfectly amazed to hear in whose house he was, saw one interesting side to the tragedy.

"Damn good publicity!" he whispered to Franklin. "The papers'll be full of it. Won't do me any harm—or you either."

Franklin winced. Menzies got up and blinked round at them. "When exactly did you first see him?"

"Four o'clock—or just short."

Menzies raised his eyebrows. "Then he was only just dead!" and he grunted.

"What was it?" asked Cotter.

He fumbled for his pipe. "Cyanide. Smell it a mile off. What about putting him on that settee?"

Cotter motioned to the plain-clothes man and between them they got the body round. Usher's voice broke in quickly. "Excuse me, sir, but there's something on the floor!"

Franklin caught sight of it at the same time—a sheet of greyish notepaper, lying flat where the dead man must have fallen on it. Cotter picked it up, gave a chuckle and passed it over to Franklin.

"The confession! They all do it." He chuckled again. "Wondered where it was!"

> *This is really the end of everything. I can't go*
> *on any longer with things as they are. And*
> *they say life is worth living! Good-bye.*

"Cynical old devil!" went on Cotter, having another squint at it over Franklin's shoulder. Franklin nodded mechanically with something else going through his mind. The paper was the same as that marked "A" of the specimens France had sent him—but the writing was different. This was full of character, carelessly as it appeared to have been dashed off.

"Excuse me, sir!" came Usher's voice again. "Would you allow me to have a look at that paper, sir?"

Cotter glanced at Franklin who nodded and passed it over. One look and the valet's face altered.

"This isn't Somers's writing, sir!"

"What!"

Usher shook his head confidently. "It isn't his writing, sir. It's the master's—Mr. France's, sir!" "But—good God!" exploded Cotter. "It can't be! How the hell could *he* have written it?"

"That I don't know, sir—but it's his writing, sir."

Cotter's eyes opened wide, then he began to panic a bit. "Harris! Go through his pockets and make an inventory. And mind how you handle things! Doc! would you mind getting out a report? And what about writing down those times, Jack, before you forget them?"

"They're all right," said Franklin. "I know 'em off by heart. If you don't mind my saying so, wouldn't it be as well to have a look at that window?"

They went over and Cotter felt the edges of the cut and wiped his fingers. "Some sort of sticky paper! When was it done? Last night?"

"Lord knows!" said Franklin hoping to heaven France or somebody'd turn up before those anonymous letters had to be mentioned.

"Looks probable," said Cotter. "That chap"—nodding towards the settee—"didn't suspect anything or he'd have turned up the blind. By the way, Mr. Usher, why were the blinds turned down?"

"It was dark on Saturday morning, sir, and the lights had to be lit."

"Hm!" said Cotter, then scowled. "Suppose that burglary couldn't have had anything to do with his doing himself in?"

"Too deep for me!" said Franklin.

Cotter nodded ponderously, then took a squint out of the window. "The fog's going. And it's raining. Harris! when you've finished there, go outside and scout round for that piece of glass. You *have* finished? Right-ho then! Doc! would you mind bringing that report outside and I'll close this place up."

The party moved out to the drawing-room and a man was put on duty by the door. "Now about this burglary, Mr. Usher. Anything missing from here?"

The valet ran his eyes round the room and reported everything normal.

"What's that room there?"

"The cloak-room, sir."

"Right! We'll have a look inside."

The three passed into a room whose flooring of black and white tiles struck icily cold. Cotter looked inside each of the lavatories, turned on the water in the basins and poked about among the coats and hats and all the accumulated garments that cumber the average cloakroom—and found nothing at all unusual.

"Hm! Let's have a look in the next room."

In the dining-room, everything appeared to be normal. A pair of valuable Sheffield candlesticks were in their place on the mantelpiece and the two silver salvers stood on the sideboard.

"Damn funny!" said Cotter. "What about upstairs? Anything valuable there? And what about going through that chap's belongings in his bedroom?"

"Mr. Somers's bedroom is this way, sir," said Usher quietly and showed through to the kitchen. Just inside, he seemed to hesitate for a moment, then made up his mind. "It sounds rather silly to report such a thing, sir, but one of the tea towels is missing. It should have been on that dryer," and he pointed to the swivel arm above the draining board.

Cotter laughed. "Damn funny! You mean the burglar broke in to pinch a towel!"

"You quite sure it was there?" asked Franklin earnestly.

"Dead sure, sir. I was the last one out of the kitchen Saturday, sir, and I put two towels out specially, sort of finished the place off, sir."

"Exactly! And, let me see, the only one who could have been using this room was Somers, as soon as he me in. The sink was wet, wasn't it?"

"It was, sir."

"Then what did Somers wet it for? The kettle wasn't filled, was it?"

"No, sir."

"Then he might have been having a drink of water. Look round and see if you can find a wet tumbler or anything."

As Usher began his examination, Franklin stood rubbing his hands and frowning away into space, Cotter came over and had a good look at the sink. But when Usher reported no sign of anything that had been used, Franklin whispered something and then gave the valet his orders.

"You slip off upstairs, Usher, will you, and see if anything has been disturbed anywhere. Also have a look in Somers's room in case that towel's there. If there's any sign of burglary, let us know at once."

"We didn't want him here seeing everything there is to see," explained Franklin quietly. "Now then, what about it? Did you get that stench of chloride of lime? What was that poured down for if it wasn't to disguise the smell of something else? And whatever that something else was, it was contained in something that had to be washed out and then wiped dry... and then the towel had to be taken away. It may be far-fetched but it's worth trying—don't you think so?"

Cotter agreed. "You find me a glass and I'll get a spanner out of the car."

In less than a minute he was back and then Franklin saw the reason for the spanner. Cotter unscrewed the bottom of the U-trap under the sink and while Franklin held the glass, drained off carefully every drop of water. Cotter held it lovingly to the light.

"There we are. If anything *was* poured down, there ought to be a trace or two inside this. Find a bottle, will you, and we'll get it ready for the Yard."

Franklin groped about in the dresser cupboard while *Cotter* replaced the trap and then just as Cotter was putting the corked bottle in his pocket, Usher's steps were heard at the top of the stairs—then he came down with a scurry. It was not the bursting open of the door that made the other two turn round quickly—it was the queer sort of noise he was making, as if he were trying to find words that wouldn't come. Then he did manage to speak.

"Mr. France, sir!... upstairs, sir!... he's dead!"

CHAPTER VI
AS A FOOL DIETH

AS THE VALET stood there, motioning feebly with his hand towards the stairs, Cotter's eyes nearly popped out of his head. Then he darted forward.

"Don't stand there gaping like a fool!" He pushed him through the open doorway. "Show us where—and pull yourself together!"

Franklin followed on their heels to the left at the top landing, then from the servants' quarters along a corridor to a region of rugs and ornamental furniture. Usher pointed to a door, and Cotter, six foot and thirteen stone, brushed him aside like a fly. Inside the bedroom, huddled on the rose and fawn silkiness of the carpet, lay a figure on its back. Two feet from the fingers of the outstretched left arm was a tiny revolver. On the forehead was a blackish stain and on the white front of the shirt, a small, red smear.

Cotter stopped short and looked round at Franklin.

"Is it him?" The voice sounded incredulous.

Franklin's voice sounded to himself as though it came from some remote corner of the room.

"It's France all right... and he's dead... by the look of him."

"Christ!" said Cotter. "Christ Almighty!" and stared.

Franklin felt himself move forward and feel the cheek—cold as ice and the limbs set as if in plaster. Then he pulled himself together.

"Been dead for hours." He shook his head. "It's a hellion! A regular hellion!" What he was thinking was hard to say; perhaps of the Friday night; perhaps of the contrast—the man gloriously alive and the figure sprawled foolishly on the carpet.

"What the hell'd he want to do it for?" asked Cotter angrily, as if putting a personal grievance to the world in general. "First world beater we've had for years and he blows his bloody brains out!" Then he stopped—the situation beyond him.

"Better get up Menzies," suggested Franklin. "Shall I give him a holler?" and he went to the top of the stairs that led to the drawing-room. In half a minute Menzies was up, blinking away through his glasses.

"This way, Doc!" said Franklin quietly. But Menzies refused to be hurried. He actually had to knock out his pipe on the landing and inside the room, merely clicked his tongue.

"Another of 'em! Wish to God they d send me a postcard!"

As he knelt over the dead man, his body masked his hands and little could be seen of what he was doing or what he was looking for.

"Fine figure of a man!"

"So he ought to be!" snapped Cotter. "He's Michael France—the boxer!"

"Is he really now!" said Menzies with tantalising inconsequence. "France the boxer! Well, he's a damn bad shot!"

"Bloody old fool!" whispered Cotter angrily. Franklin nodded and went on watching. Menzies' hands were now visible; he was feeling at the base of the skull. Then he examined it closely and moved back the hair with his fingers. Then he had a good look at the table by which the body was lying and when he did get to his feet he took out his pipe and stoked it up with a deliberation that was certainly as provoking as he intended.

"How long's he been dead?" asked Cotter.

"What I should call a devil of a long while... in a world of sudden changes. Say since well before midnight."

"Then he didn't go away for the week-end as—"

"And what's more," went on Menzies, "I want a consultation, so you'd better get on to headquarters, and take my tip, you'll get the General and the whole of the circus."

"What's the idea? Didn't he shoot himself?"

"Don't you worry about that. Haven't I told you I want a consultation?" He peered across to the corner. "Is that his hat and coat on that chair?" and without waiting for an answer, "Well, I'll wait downstairs. I've had no tea and it's damn little supper I'll get by the look of it."

Franklin suddenly missed Usher. "You seen him, Cotter? Expect he's in the kitchen. Get him to make you a cup of tea, Doc."

When he'd gone, Cotter fairly exploded. "Did you ever see such an irritable old swine to work with? Do you know, he makes me that damn wild—" and he raised his hands to heaven. "What'd we better do? Get hold of the General?"

"I most decidedly should. If it's a mare's nest, the Doc'll have to stand the racket. Oh, by the way, don't tell him I'm here."

Left to himself, Franklin ran his eye round the room. Behind him by the shorter wall was a walnut tallboy, flanked by two walnut chairs, on one of which, furthest from the door, were the dead man's hat and coat. In the centre of the longer wall, on his left, was the marble fireplace with electric fire, and in its left-hand recess was a writing table and in its right, a dressing table with glass top and elaborate mirror. Facing him at the far end was a bed of gorgeously figured walnut whose rose and fawn eiderdown blended with the old rose of the window curtains that reached from ceiling to floor. On one side of the bed was a stand-cupboard on which was a reading lamp. By the right hand wall was a cushioned settee between two easy chairs in tapestry.

The room as a whole was one that clamoured for attention. Whoever was responsible for its decoration knew the value of mirrors for the repetition of colour. There were four of them on the walls; one a huge concave circle that showed the room as if it were a Dutch interior. The pictures, too, seemed a trifle flaunting for a bedroom and the whole thing was somehow unmanly—not necessarily effeminate but inclined to the sybaritic and indefensibly opulent. And there was one garish note that set one's teeth on edge; not the large bowl of blood-red roses so much as the table on which they stood—a gilt, Empire, tawdry thing whose legs ran parallel to the dead man's body and touched his drawn-up arm.

Indeed, as Franklin's eyes fell again to the rigid figure on the carpet, he felt the whole thing to be strangely impossible. It was incredible! Why should France want to die? with the ball at his feet and the world for an audience. If Menzies was hinting at something different from suicide, Franklin felt himself with him. Who then killed France and staged the suicide? The writer of the anonymous letters? The man who'd made the burglarious entry through the lounge? And if so, France knew him, or how could he have approached so close as to shoot point blank? But if France knew him, why had he been forced to enter through the window? Franklin shook his head. Everything was contradictory—unless Menzies was wrong after all and France had committed suicide. And then to complete the circle, why in the name of common-sense should he want to commit suicide?

Then a quaint thought to end it all; a thought springing out of nowhere and summing it all up—"Died Abner as a fool dieth." What Menzies hinted must be right. If that man killed himself, then he killed himself like a fool. And even the manner of the killing would have been foolish—that tiny pistol, like a toy; surely the last thing a man like Michael France would choose. In those few moments that he spent there, that was all Franklin could see—the incredibility, the absurdity of everything. There was scarcely even a sense of personal loss—it was all too preposterous for that, and it was not till he got out of that boudoir sort of room with its crimson roses that he began to recall the dead man as he knew him and to feel a vague sort of pathos.

On the stairs he met Cotter with a man for duty outside the bedroom door. In the dining-room Menzies was writing his notes and sucking away at a cold pipe.

"Hallo, Doc!" said Franklin. "Ordered your tea?"

Menzies peered over his spectacles. "Couldn't find the damn fellow anywhere. Wasn't he upstairs with you?"

"No! He's probably in the kitchen. You've looked there? Very funny!" and off Franklin stalked. Menzies appeared to be right. The valet had gone out and the bowler hat that had been on the dresser when the three of them were last there, had gone too.

Franklin swore to himself as he reviewed the suspicions that came tumbling back to his mind. Extraordinarily cool customer he'd been as a witness; positively judicial as a matter of fact. Somewhere, too, he'd seen him before, though he couldn't place him at the moment. Surely he couldn't have bolted! That'd be a disaster the General wouldn't be likely to overlook. With a sudden tremor of apprehension Franklin was about to slip up the back stairs to make a quick examination of the bedroom, when outside there was a sound of a step. He stepped back quickly into the passage with the door just ajar. And only in time.

The handle of the outside door was turned furtively as the valet peeped into the room. A second and he slipped inside and closed the door quietly. Back on the dresser went the hat; the fawn raincoat was pushed hurriedly into the dresser cupboard; then he mopped his forehead with his handkerchief. Next came a rapid adjustment of his hair. A good rubbing of the wet boots with a duster, a flick or two of the black coat, then his expression changed from the anxious to the deferential. Usher was ready to report in the drawing-room and in that half-minute two distinct personalities had been on view.

Franklin moved quietly back to the dining-room, then made a fairly obvious approach to the kitchen. As he entered, Usher made play with the kettle. Franklin picked up the bowler hat, shook the wet off on the floor, then replaced the hat with elaborate care.

"Still raining outside then, Usher?"

"Yes, sir." A limpness became apparent.

"By the way, weren't you told on no account to leave the house?"

"I don't remember it, sir."

Franklin's eyes opened at the blatancy of the denial. "I see. You don't remember. Well, you remember it now! And keep that kettle on the boil. Dr. Menzies wants some tea at once—and make it for three while you're about it!"

Usher's "Very good, sir!" showed no trace of rancour or irony.

"And what exactly *were* you doing out of the house?"

The limpness became more apparent. "I'm afraid I wasn't feeling any too well, sir... so I thought I'd try a breath of fresh air. It's—er—been a great shock to me, sir."

"You'll get a bigger one if you stir an inch from this house again," said Franklin and he made an exit that was hardly as dignified as he intended. A cool customer that! Wharton'd twist the innards clean out of him when he got him alone. No use tackling him now about where he'd been; he'd be bound to have a plausible tale ready.

Over the tea, Menzies appeared far more reconciled to an evening's duty and things seemed much easier altogether as the three of them sat waiting for the arrival of Wharton and the Yard experts—the circus as Menzies had called them. If his mind had not been turned topsy-turvy with the suddenness and the personal nature of the terrible discoveries, Franklin might have regarded that prospect with something approaching complacency. Before that nervous breakdown that had led to his leaving the Yard, he had worked for a couple of years under the old General, as everybody called him. Since then they'd worked together more than once and altogether, Wharton had acquired a status that was avuncular generally and occasionally paternal. And as for the business in hand, Franklin couldn't for the life of him see how he was to be kept out of the inner circle of official inquiry. After all, before that damnable affair had happened, he'd been retained, as it were, to inquire into certain happenings that France considered suspicious. The fact that France was dead—and exactly how remained to be proved—was surely no release from that retainer. In any case he held in his hand, as he realised, if not all the aces at least enough cards to make the game difficult for a newcomer.

Cotter also was less on the jump than he had been and as he poured out the doctor's second cup of tea, he apparently thought the moment favourable for the preparation of defences against the big man's arrival.

"I don't see, you know. Doc, how they can blame you for removing that body. Everything was all right, on the face of it."

"I don't give a damn what they think" said Menzies. "We moved him and there's an end of it. If he wants photographs, we can shove him back again. And the prints are all there."

"What's your own idea. Doc?" asked Franklin deferentially. "Do you think Somers did himself in?"

"Why not? The only suspicious thing is that confession, and that's your job of work to find how it got to the wrong man."

"That's right!" said Cotter. "But absolutely in confidence, Doc; what made you want another opinion about... him upstairs?"

Menzies pursed his lips and frowned. "Well, keep it to yourselves. Not a word, mind you, till I've seen the General! Was France left-handed?"

"No!" said Franklin promptly.

"Well, he shot himself on the left side of the head. Talking without technicalities, the bullet entered his forehead plumb between the eyebrow and his hair—then travelled towards the left ear. That's a devilish awkward position to get your hand into! You try it and see."

Both tried it—and agreed.

"The bullet might have missed the brain altogether, the angle it was. You might have thought he was trying to *wound* himself—not *kill* himself. If he wanted to blow his brains out, there was only one thing to do—to put the muzzle into his mouth or against the temple and make a clean job of it. The way that chap up there did the job was what you might expect from a contortionist... when he was tight!"

"Pretty point blank, wasn't it?" asked Franklin.

Menzies shrugged his shoulders. "Further off than usual. Say six to eight inches. Also, there was something else that was unusual. There's a contusion at the base of the skull—a very slight one; where he fell presumably. But the thing is, could he have got any sort of a contusion at all, falling on that carpet. It's like a cushion!"

"He hit the table."

"Did he? Then why didn't he knock it endways? And why did he fall so mathematically parallel to it? And another thing. That chap Somers had been in the room!"

"Good God!" exclaimed Franklin. "How'd you know that?"

"There's a smear—a tiny one—on the shirt front. Most of the bleeding was internal—cerebral haemorrhage. Only a very small amount seeped out to the cheek. Supposing there had been a tiny drop that fell on the shirt front, it'd still have been a *drop,* even if it were touched. But this is a *smear.* You see the difference don't you. Somebody—and it could only have been Somers— found the body, touched the wound and without knowing his fingers had any blood on 'em, put a hand on the shirt front to feel the heart. I shouldn't say the smear's sufficiently defined enough to be printable, by the way."

"Just a minute, Doc," said Franklin. "As I see it—assuming that France didn't therefore kill himself—it needn't have been Somers after all. It might have been one of two other people; either the person whom Usher and I heard in the house when we came in, or else the man who actually did the killing and the faking of the suicide."

That information about a man heard in the house was news to Menzies, but before he could put the question, Cotter had a theory. "Between ourselves," he said, "what about this for a solution? France shot himself—or was shot; it doesn't matter which for a—"

"Oh yes it does!" put in Franklin. "If he was shot, why did he leave a confession?"

"There might have been a suicide pact for all we know" went on Cotter. "France might have carried out his part of the contract first and then the other party might have balked. However, assume he did commit suicide—just as a start-and that he left the confession. Somers came in this afternoon and went upstairs with his things. He tapped on France's door to see if he was in, then had a look inside and saw the body and the confession. He was terribly upset and felt a bit queer, so he came down to the lounge to get a drink, bringing the confession with him. Then he got so overwrought that he did himself in. I'll bet he was an old servant—been with France for years." Full of the idea, he gave Usher a holler. "Will you tell us how long Somers had been with Mr. France?"

"A long while, sir. I believe he was with Mr. France's father, then with his uncle; and when Mr. France took this house, sir, he got Somers to come here with him."

"How along ago was that?"

"About two years, sir."

"And how long have you been with him?"

"A fortnight, sir."

Franklin looked up quickly, then turned his head away.

"Only a fortnight! Who were you with before that?"

"Colonel Welling, sir—of Stanhope Street."

"I see. And Somers—he was very fond of Mr. France?"

"Very, sir... and proud of him... as we all were."

"Right! Thank you, Mr. Usher." Cotter gave a series of satisfied nods at the valet's back. "It mayn't be much of a theory, but it ain't so bad for a start. Hallo! That's them!"

Menzies wiped his mouth, groped for his pipe, then put it back again. Franklin got his back to the fire and waited for things to happen.

Wharton came in blinking and wiping the moisture from his heavy moustache and looking more like a steady-going old paterfamilias than ever. On his heels came Norris of headquarters and a regular platoon of lesser troops—photographers, finger-print and plain-clothes men. There was a staccato outburst of greetings, then Menzies and his colleague moved off upstairs. Then Wharton appeared to notice Franklin for the first time.

"Hallo, John! What are you doing here?"

Franklin gave him a half-minute outline.

"Good! I'll be with you as soon as I can, then we'll talk things over."

But that turned out to be well over an hour later. As Franklin sat by the drawing-room fire, feeling rather out of it, the house resembled a furtive beehive. People would come and go; in and out of the rooms and up and down the stairs. Most of the traffic seemed to be to the dining-room where the refectory table became a temporary museum. All the time there was telephoning and the whirr of the bell. There was a murmur of voices from minor conferences. Usher was summoned twice from the kitchen. Then, finally, after one of his trips upstairs, Wharton came over for a word.

"Sorry to keep you so long, John. We're just getting the decks cleared so that we know just where we stand. Would you mind having a look at these times of yours Cotter gave me, so as to see if they're all right?"

After that another half-hour. The ambulance drew up and Menzies and his colleague left with their double load. Then the photographers left, and Cotter and Harris, and the house became reasonably settled. A last sound of telephoning and Wharton came in, stoking up his pipe.

"Do you know a Kenneth Hayles? Writes detective stories, doesn't he?"

"Yes—I know him pretty well, but I haven't read his books."

"He's coming along soon and I'd rather like you to be here at the time. I'm expecting him to clear things up a bit." He took the easy chair opposite Franklin's. "Would you mind telling me *all* about how you got mixed up in this?"

"Hasn't Cotter told you?" Franklin asked sarcastically.

"Never mind about that. I want to hear what *you've* got to say."

Franklin plunged in. This time nothing was left out, from a sketch of the Friday evening to the happenings of the afternoon, and even his own deductions.

"You got those facsimiles with you?" Wharton asked.

Franklin pulled them out and spread them on the occasional table. As Wharton took out his glasses, there was the sound of a step on the gravel.

"He's coming! Put them away—here, in the drawer! You do the introductions."

"What's he know?" whispered Franklin.

"Nothing... as far as we know. Only what you told Claire."

The key was heard in the outside lock and Franklin moved away from the fireplace, leaving Wharton in the background. Hayles, in felt hat and grey overcoat, peeped round the screen and looked perfectly staggered to see Franklin.

"Hallo! What on earth are *you* doing here?"

Franklin smiled and held out his hand. "Just happened to come along to see France."

"Yes, but what's all the row about? Claire was telling me over the phone that something had happened to Somers. He didn't..." He caught sight of Wharton.

"Come along over!" said Franklin cheerily. "George, this is Mr. Hayles... Superintendent Wharton... of the Big Four... Scotland Yard."

Hayles put out his hand mechanically. Wharton grasped it, though Franklin would have sworn he was feeling his pulse!

"How'd you do, Mr. Hayles. It's a godsend, your coming round. Take a seat, will you?" and he drew up a chair.

Hayles looked as if he'd blundered by accident into the Zoo. "I'm afraid I don't quite—er—"

"That's all right!" said Wharton reassuringly. "We just want you to help us. You see, since you were here last, things have been happening... here... in this house. Mr. France is dead!"

"Dead... How?"

"Shot himself... in his bedroom."

Hayles drew in his breath and his eyes opened wide. He made as if to speak, then moistened his lips.

"And that's not all. Somers is dead too... He poisoned himself... in the lounge!" Wharton paused for several seconds, with his eyes full on Hayles's face, then he went on deliberately. *"That's why we want to see you!"*

Franklin leaped forward but he was too late. Hayles gave a sort of moan and lurched sideways in the chair; then slithered to the floor in a dead faint.

* * * * *

A few seconds later, with Norris looking after the white-faced Hayles and Usher searching frantically for brandy, Franklin drew Wharton over to a corner.

"I say, George; that was a damn silly thing to do, talking to a man like that! You were virtually accusing him of doing... something."

Wharton raised his eyebrows. "I was! Nothing of the sort! All I meant was, we wanted him here to lend us a hand."

Franklin was not deceived by the air of injured innocence.

"Then you made a damn clumsy hand of it!" was his comment. "If you don't get another word out of him, don't blame me!"

CHAPTER VII
HAYLES GETS RATTLED

IT WAS half an hour later before Hayles, after a stiff brandy, a cold sponging and the gradual reception of the details of the extraordinary tragedy, announced that he was all right, that he was sorry he'd made such an ass of himself, and that he was ready to give all the information he could. Wharton seemed to understand. Perhaps the announcements that greeted Hayles on his arrival had been a bit too sudden, especially as he and France were on such intimate terms, and old Somers a sort of ever-present feudal retainer.

The setting in the dining-room was calculated to put him at his ease. Wharton sat at the refectory table—the exhibits not too conspicuous—and Hayles in a vast easy chair in which he was almost lost. On one side of the fire sat Norris, back to the light and ready for a shorthand transcript; on the other, Franklin with elbow on the arm of his chair, sat looking into the fire. As the light was arranged, Wharton and Hayles occupied the illuminated foreground; the others were away in the shadowed distance.

Wharton began in his best consolatory voice. "Of course you understand, Mr. Hayles, we don't want you to be worried. If you don't feel like going on, stop me at once. You're our principal hope now—so to speak—and we want you to be in a fit condition to help us."

Hayles murmured indistinctly something about understanding and all that.

"That's capital!" said Wharton, nodding vigorously. "We're going to be very grateful to you before this case is over. And now, Mr. Hayles, these are the times Usher gave as those of you and he and Somers leaving Martlesham. Are they perfectly correct?"

Hayles looked the paper over. "There's one mistake. Usher and Somers may be correct as far as I know, but I was at Ipswich at 12.15, not before."

"That's all right," said Wharton, reaching for the paper. "The point, as a matter of fact, is this. Usher said you were very annoyed at not being able to get away from Martlesham earlier, this morning. We hoped—it sounds preposterous, I know—that if the reason you were anxious to get away was that you were fearing something had happened to Mr. France, then of course you'd be able to tell us—well, what that something was that you were worrying about."

"If Usher told you that, he was wrong," said Hayles curtly. "I was fed up with Martlesham—I always am. That's all."

Wharton waved his hand airily. "We're not paying two hoots of attention to that—or to you either. Even if we were, your word's good enough. But, we've got to inquire into people's movements. It's like setting a chess board out—how the pieces stood at a vital moment in the game, if you follow what I mean. And now, what time did you get to Martlesham yesterday?"

"Martlesham? I can't quite say... I had tea in Ipswich, at the Great White Horse, just about four. I should say I got to Martlesham at half-past five. I know it was hellish dark."

"The others were there?"

"Oh yes... they were there."

"And they spent the night there?"

"That's right. I sat yarning with Morse—he's Mr. France's masseur—and Forbes—the chap who runs the farm—till about eleven. Then I saw Somers and Usher about the morning's arrangements."

"Weather foggy there?"

"Oh lord no! Beautiful starry night. Bit of mist this morning but it soon cleared off."

"That reminds me. When you approached town to-day, where'd the fog start?"

"Well, I cut across country to Epping. You see, it was getting a bit thick there. Took me an awful time pushing on to Chingford... rather dangerous too, and as there happened to be a train leaving for Liverpool Street, I garaged my car right against the station and came on. I thought it'd be safer."

"Exactly! And what time'd that be? You see, we want to get a line on the others."

Hayles frowned. "Let me see. Chingford's the terminus, so the train started punctually. One-fifty, I think it was. Also we didn't seem to stop too much. I know it was just about four when I got to St. John's Wood."

"What'd you do then?"

"Oh—er—went straight to my flat; tidied up a bit and pushed off to the club. There was a man I rather wanted to see and I thought I'd probably miss him. As a matter of fact I did miss him, so I had tea and hung about. Then I felt a bit bored, so I rang up Peter Claire to see if he was in and he told me I was wanted urgently round here, about Somers. By the time I'd asked for details, he'd rung off."

"Good! And now about Somers. A reliable fellow?"

"Oh, quite!... though perhaps, now you speak of it... I mean I oughtn't to say so under the circumstances, but—er—I rather thought recently he was losing his grip."

"Really! That's exceptionally interesting! Exactly how?"

"Well—er—I often had to give him instructions and he—well, he used to forget things; used to act sort of funny; you know, sort of moon about the place."

"Unwell, do you think? Or just getting past it?"

"Oh, he wasn't so old as that. I shouldn't put him at much over sixty. I sort of put it to him one day and he said he hadn't been feeling any too fit... I think he was worrying about something."

"You don't know what?"

Hayles shook his head. "Haven't the foggiest."

"Hm! And Usher. Trustworthy?"

Hayles shrugged his shoulders. "Colourless sort of person. Adequate enough in his way. He hasn't been with us long."

"So I understand. References all right?"

"Oh quite!" The frigidity of the reply suggested that Hayles had inquired into them himself.

"Both servants on good terms with themselves and each other?"

"As far as I know."

"And with you... and Mr. France?"

"Absolutely! He was easy-going—a bit too much so—and I; well, I'm not a frightfully difficult person."

Wharton chuckled. "I'm sure you're not!" The chuckle tapered off and his voice acquired a delicate shade of regret. "Now about Mr. France. A terrible affair! Terrible!" He shook his head sadly, and Franklin, squinting between his fingers, saw Hayles lean forward, his head between his hands. Then the General's voice took on a fictitious fortitude. "You'll miss him... I shall miss him... everybody in the country will. But these things have to be faced... like men." He shook his head again, and Franklin could imagine him watching Hayles like a cat at a mousehole. "You were surprised to learn he was here last night?"

Hayles shook his head wearily. "No... I wasn't surprised. I mean, he'd probably come round here after the show... then go out again." He looked at Wharton. "Didn't I understand you to say he shot himself as soon as he got back here?"

"Well, that's what we thought. But wasn't he ending to go away?"

"If he said so—as he did—then he *was.*"

"Quite so! And do you happen to know where?"

"Not the faintest idea. He could be very secretive at times."

"He didn't tell you everything? I mean, you were more than a secretary, weren't you? More like a friend, lending a helping hand."

"I don't know." He closed his eyes wearily, as if too tired to keep them open. "Perhaps I was... in way. But nobody tells everything—not even a man to his wife."

"That's true enough!" Wharton laughed with extreme heartiness, then passed over a box which appeared from somewhere on the table. "Try one of these cigarettes, Mr. Hayles. I can recommend them."

Hayles shook his head and smiled faintly. Wharton's voice changed to the broadly confidential. "Now a rather delicate matter... between ourselves, as two men of the world. In Mr. France's bedroom was a huge—a really magnificent—bowl of roses. Were they there on the table when you left?"

Franklin squinted again between his fingers. Hayles frowned reprovingly and his tone was abrupt. "I didn't go into his room... never do! But why shouldn't he have flowers there if he wanted to?" The tone changed to the resentful, and, as it were, final. "Oh, I see what you're hinting at! And you can take it from me that you're perfectly wrong."

Wharton was unruffled. "Well, I'm glad to hear it. People of the importance of Mr. France get all sorts of mud flung at them. But he wasn't that sort."

"He wasn't!" said Hayles grimly. "Any more than I... or yourself."

"Exactly!... But the world's an unkind place.If I had my way I'd punish gossip like blackmail." He paused for a moment and looked at the other, sitting there forlornly, head between his hands. "You're dreadfully tired, Mr. Hayles. Just a couple of questions and we're through. Do you happen to know any woman—or did Mr. France know one?—by the name of... Lucy?".

He took a second or two to raise his head and his face, to Franklin, looked perfectly ghastly.

"So you've got hold of that, have you? Then why ask me?"

"I've got hold of nothing!" protested Wharton. "All I've done is to ask you an honest, bona fide question. Who was Lucy?"

"Lucy?... Well, she was a girl France got mixed up with at Cambridge.... Lucy Oliver I think the name was. Her father was a tobacconist." It was easy to detect the sneer. "Designing little bitch—fluffy hair and all that. You know the type. Cost him—or his uncle—best part of five hundred to get clear."

"He compromised her... badly?"

Hayles sneered again. "I think he made a pretty good job of it... I mean if you can compromise a woman of that sort." Franklin winced at the crudeness, then took another quick look. Wharton'd better go steady.

"And how long ago would that be?"

"Four years or so."

"Do you know her address?"

"Her then address, you mean?"

Wharton nodded.

"Just off Jesus Lane, I think. That'd find her—if she's still there. I haven't heard a word of her since... and I'm not particularly anxious to."

"You haven't heard her name mentioned?"

He looked up quickly. "Well, now you come to mention it, there *were* some ridiculous anonymous letters that came last week. I opened them of course, and passed them on."

"These anything like them?"

Hayles looked at them, then leaned back in the chair as if dead beat. "I expect so. I told him not to be a fool... to put them in the fire."

"You didn't take them seriously?"

"Good God, no! Do you?" Wharton ignored the danger signal.

"Well, perhaps I don't... except that curious things happen in our profession. And in your considered opinion, Michael France had no reason whatever for taking his own life?"

The result of that question made Franklin jump in his chair. It wasn't a shriek—it was a kind of hysterical snarl.

"Damn you, no! Stop your bloody questions! Stop them!" Then he broke down.

Wharton motioned Franklin to stay where he was and moved round to where the overwrought man was sobbing, head between his hands. It was a ghastly sound in that room and Franklin felt a surge of pity rise to his throat.

"There my boy... don't take it to heart," came Wharton's voice. "Just pull yourself together. There!... That's better now!"

He got Hayles to his feet. "You'd like to be getting home. Bed's the place for you to-night. We'll have Usher see you round."

"No... I'm all right. I'm sorry... it's... well, I'm a bit of a fool."

"No fool, Mr. Hayles. Just a man who does what most of us have to do." That cryptic utterance over, he picked up the hat and coat from the oak settle and his voice began to trail away to the outer porch.

"Let me lend you a hand.... You sure you won't have one of us?... You've been perfectly invaluable... We're most grateful . . Sure you can manage?... Good-bye, and a jolly good night's rest.... Good-bye!... Good-bye!"

Back in the room, the General changed his tone.

"Who's following him? Anybody?"

"All arranged, sir."

"Print people still upstairs?"

"As far as I know, sir."

"Right! Get back to headquarters straight away. Send Haliburton to Martlesham and another man to Chingford. Warn Lawrence for Cambridge and put a special man on from Liverpool Street onwards. Leave those notes with me... till you get back again."

"Very good, sir!" Norris set about his preparations like a man who not infrequently leaves for Brazil or Siberia at even shorter notice. Wharton pulled out his pipe.

"What's it like outside, George?"

"Raining like hell," said Wharton. "And it's half-past eight." He nodded to himself. "What do you think about your dear friend Hayles? Nice gutless sort of specimen? Either *he's* lying... or Usher is."

Franklin compromised. "You know he's had the devil of a shock."

"Shock be damned. If you came home and found your mother murdered—if you had one—what'd you do? Shriek... and throw a nice respectable faint?"

"Lord knows! But I'm not Hayles."

"Hm! Well, ask that valet to make some more tea. When he brings it in, we'll have a heart to heart talk. I'll go and see how the P.M.'s going... Don't rattle Usher, by the way. Treat him nice and gentle."

The General, pipe in full blast, ambled off to the lounge, looking like a harassed parent, going in search of his carpet slippers.

CHAPTER VIII
FAIR LADIES

WHAT FRANKLIN was wondering was how, in the absence of Norris, Wharton was to take a transcript of Usher's cross-examination. He knew the valet, as the only available evidence, had been questioned more than once that night, and he knew Wharton's uncanny memory, but even then he saw no sense in trusting to nothing but that memory. What actually took place however, was no cross-examination at all but something that explained itself.

"Thank you, Usher," said Wharton, as the valet prepared to withdraw. Then he beamed over at Franklin. "Was there anything else we wanted to ask?" And as an afterthought, "Oh, yes! Just take a seat for a minute or two, Usher, will you?"

He waved him to the easy chair and picked up Norris' notes. "Mr. Hayles has given us quite a lot of information and I don't mind telling you—as a man of discretion—very interesting information too. But I think it would be just as well if you confirmed, as it were, what Mr. Hayles has been telling us. Two witnesses are always better than one." He leaned forward impressively. "Tell me, now. Where did you—as a man of the world—expect Mr. France was spending last night?"

"I don't know, sir. He said he was... he'd be away, sir."

"Ah! He *said!* That's hardly the point. Speaking as man to man, where did *you* think he'd made up his mind to be?"

"Well, sir, I knew he wasn't going to the country because he'd given Ingham the week-end off."

"Ingham? Oh yes, the chauffeur. You mean, if he'd been going to the country, he'd have taken the car?"

"Well, he always did, sir... so Somers said."

"Then you and Somers discussed why Mr. France was staying in town!"

"No, sir. We didn't discuss it. Somers just commented on it, sir; said he couldn't understand why Mr. France had said he was going to the country, unless somebody else was giving him a lift."

"I see. Now if I remember yesterday morning correctly, this is what happened. You and Somers finished packing and Ingham came round with the car. Mr. Claire had called round and was going away and as soon as he'd gone, Mr. Hayles came down from his workroom upstairs and stood chatting with Mr. France in the dining-room. He left shortly afterwards and his last words were, 'See you on Monday.' Then you and Ingham carried out the trunks and Mr. France and Somers went into the lounge. When they came out, the car was ready and Ingham drove you and Somers to Liverpool Street where the fog was not quite so dense as it had been. Ingham told you the guvnor had given him till to-morrow morning off, so that he might go and see his people at Huntingdon and he could take the car. On the way to Ipswich, Somers said nothing to you as to why Mr. France took him into the lounge for those ten minutes, but you thought it might have been to discuss your successor, since you'd given notice that morning. That's all correct, isn't it?"

"Quite correct, sir."

"Was it absolutely essential, do you think, for Mr. Hayles to go to Martlesham? I mean, couldn't you and Somers have gone alone?"

"I don't know, sir. You see I don't know exactly what Mr. Hayles went for."

"What did he do exactly?"

"A gentleman called to see him with some papers on the Saturday—last night, and again this morning. He and Mr. Hayles went out together, sir."

"And Mr. Hayles really *was* annoyed at being kept?"

"Very, sir! He... well, he said a few things, sir, and as soon as this gentleman had gone, sir, he hopped into the car and went off like mad... without any lunch."

"I see. Now let's suppose, shall we? that Mr. Hayles needn't have gone down there. Now think it over. Mr. Hayles was—shall we say?—got out of the way. So were you and Somers. So was Ingham. The temporary day-cook left on Friday and the char-woman doesn't come till to-morrow. Doesn't it strike you that Mr. France wanted to remain here in this house... alone?"

The valet shuffled uneasily in his seat. Wharton took a good sup of the tea.

"Well, it rather looks like it, sir."

"Hm! Those flowers in the bedroom. Were they there when you left?"

"You didn't hear them ordered by any chance?"

"No, sir."

"Ever seen or heard of flowers in that bedroom before?"

"No, sir."

"Then tell me, as a man of the world, why were those flowers put there... secretly?"

Usher stammered inarticulately.

"Speak out, man! Don't be diffident! Mr. Hayles was asked much the same question."

"Then it looks as if he expected a lady, sir."

"Ah! That's just it!" Franklin thought the way he rubbed his hands was perfectly ghoulish. "Now, Usher does that surprise you? Would it be anything unusual?"

"I can't say, sir... I know they always said he was—er—a bit that way inclined, sir."

"A bit too fond of the ladies?"

"Well, yes, sir."

Wharton chuckled. "You and I may be the same... only we haven't been found out! Ladies here frequently?"

"Never, sir!"

"What! Never! You've never known a lady come here!"

"Well—er—one did come last week, sir."

"Ah! now we're coming to it! Tell me all about it."

"It was one evening last week—Tuesday night, sir—when she called and asked to see Mr. France. I told her he was not at home and she said she'd wait. I told her she couldn't do that as he mightn't be in for hours, but she said she'd wait all the same, so I reported to Somers, sir, and he came and saw her off. I told Mr. France about it, sir, when I got round to the Paliceum—"

"You were acting as his dresser?"

"That's right, sir. He'd been out all the evening and came straight there, and when I told him, he was furious, sir. Afterwards he told me and Somers she was on no account to be admitted."

"What was she like?"

"Well, sir, she wasn't... what you'd call a topnotcher, as they say. Smart and so on but... well, you know, sir."

"Quite! And any other ladies at any other time?"

"None, sir... except Mrs. Claire, and she was different."

"Naturally! More like a sister."

"Exactly, sir."

"And no other ladies?"

"No, sir."

"Somers ever tell you about any?"

"No, sir. Somers never discussed Mr. France with me, sir. In his eyes, sir, whatever Mr. France did was perfect."

"I see... Well, before I forget it, Somers hadn't been himself recently. He was losing his grip. Getting a bit childish, wasn't he?"

Usher's face answered before he spoke. "What him, sir! He was a fitter man than I was! Smart and—"

"Not an old dodderer."

"Not him, sir! Quiet now, that I grant you, sir... and a bit deliberate... but a healthy man, sir. At least, I never heard him complain."

"Exactly! I was making a mistake... as we all do at times, Usher." He opened a small envelope that lay on the table and took from it half a dozen long, silky, golden hairs. "Talking of ladies, did you ever see the head these were on?"

Usher was genuinely bewildered. "Never, sir!"

"The woman who called here last Tuesday?"

"I don't know, sir... but I'm sure her hair was dark... at least it wasn't that colour, sir."

"You did out the bedroom yourself on the Saturday morning?"

"Yes, sir."

"What did you do to the settee?"

"The settee, sir? Ran the vacuum over it, sir, and over the cushions; then shook out the cushions and put them back."

"You'd have seen these hairs if they'd been there?"

"I would, sir. And they couldn't have dodged the vacuum."

"You'd swear to that?"

"Yes, sir. Now... or anywhere, sir."

"Right! I'll take your word for it." He finished off the tea, produced a handkerchief and wiped his straggly moustache. "Well, Usher, you've helped us a good deal. And if you don't mind a more personal question, you gave in your notice yesterday because you didn't think you'd like Martlesham. Had you another post to go to?"

"Yes, sir—Colonel Welling, sir, who I was with before. His man's leaving him, sir, and I knew he'd have me back."

"I see. But you must understand this. For the present you remain here under my orders and when the end of the week comes, that'll be time to see about your new post. No hostility to you mind; just the other way about. You're the only witness we've got now Mr. Hayles is unfit. For instance, here's something you can do for us. Here are three specimens of writing you might be able to identify. This one, marked 'A' which looks like a list of trains."

"That's Somers's writing, sir."

"Sure?"

"Positive, sir. I've seen it hundreds of times."

"And this one?"

"Mr. Hayles's, sir. He used to give us written orders nearly every day. I can show you one if you like, sir."

"No it's all right. What about this one?"

Usher looked scared, then, seeing Wharton's reassuring smile, merely puzzled.

"It's mine, sir. An old letter I was writing at the Paliceum and threw away. Somebody must have picked it up, sir."

"I didn't!" explained Wharton blandly. "I just happened to run across it, that's all, and wondered what it was.... You don't want it again, I suppose?"

The valet shook his head and Wharton screwed it into a ball and tossed it over to the fire. Franklin touched a match to it and watched it burn.

"That's all then, Usher, thanks, and we're very much obliged to you.... Any chance of a scratch meal in about half an hour's time? I shall probably be here all night."

Wharton sat quietly, listening to the receding steps. Then he grunted and pulled out his pipe. "What's your idea about that fellow?"

"I thought he'd the devil of a job making up his mind just what he ought to tell you and what he didn't want to. And he did it damn well."

"Which do you believe? Him or Hayles?"

Franklin rubbed his chin. "Now you're asking. But why shouldn't both be partly lying?"

"Exactly!" He shook his grizzled old head. "You know the old song? 'A Boy's Best Friend is His Mother?' Well, the best friend for people like you and me is a liar! Prove that and you've got him! Reverse what he emphasises is right, and wash out what he tells you is wrong. Hayles says he wasn't in a hurry to get away from Martlesham—therefore he was. He says Somers was just the man to commit suicide—therefore he didn't—"

"And knowing all the time that he didn't!"

Wharton shot a look at him. "Hm! I don't think we can go as far as that... yet."

"But it's the logical conclusion!"

"That may be—but even *we* don't know that... at the moment. To come to that, we don't know whether Hayles was lying. It might have been Usher."

"I wish you'd keep to one side of the argument," said Franklin. "First you argue one way, then you right-about-face and prove yourself wrong."

"Well, there's some merit in being able to do that," said Wharton complacently.

"Yes, and the devil of a lot of muddle," retorted the other. "And that reminds me. You didn't say anything to Usher about slipping out of the house."

"I know I didn't. That was deliberate. I want to give him all the rope in the world. If he slips out again, he'll be followed. And we have an idea what he was actually doing. There's a telephone box on the other side of the road. We're trying to trace a call."

That mollified Franklin somewhat. "Personally," he said, "I think it wasn't he who was lying. Keeping something back if you like."

"What about that question of women? Whose statement are you to believe? Hayles's or Usher's?"

Franklin laughed. "You try to hot-stuff me like that! Calling Usher's a statement! All you did was to drag a half-hearted sort of admission out of him. You put the words into his mouth!"

Wharton shook his head. "Oh, no! You didn't see his face as I saw it. He *knew* why France stayed in town last night! I'm open to bet you ten to one I'm right." He gave Franklin a quick look. "For instance, I'll show you something. Let's have a look in France's bedroom again."

Upstairs in the room, the finger-print people were just finishing and, according to Wharton, their next objective was the bathroom. Just inside the door he held Franklin back and waved his arm contemptuously.

"Well, what do you think of it all?"

Franklin made a face. "To tell the truth, I don't know. It's rather showy." Then some sense of loyalty to the dead man produced an addendum. "But it's a damn fine room all the same!"

Wharton snorted. "Fine room! Shall I tell you my idea of it? It's the show room of a super-brothel—"

"Hi! Steady on, George! Don't be crude!"

"Crude be damned. And crudity's better than humbug. I tell you this room has something rotten about it. And you know it… only your idea of what France *ought* to have been is making you a damn bad detective!"

Franklin said nothing for a moment or two, then, "Perhaps you're right. Mind you, I admitted from the first that I didn't like that gilt table—"

"Quite so!" interrupted Wharton. "It looked out of place. And you might be interested to know that it came from the drawing-room and was there when Usher left yesterday morning. France, so the prints tell us, took it upstairs himself. That bowl there, came from the dining-room. France must have filled it with water and brought it up here for the roses. Now come over here!"

He moved over to the bedside table-cupboard and opened the door. Then, like a conjuror producing things from a hat, he took out one article after another.

"Electric kettle—all ready filled. Teapot—with the tea already in it. Milk. Bowl of sugar. Tin of biscuits. Look at 'em! And the maker's name! Cost half a quid if they cost a penny." He put them all back again. "Now you know what Usher knew—why France wanted to have this house to himself."

Franklin nodded but said nothing. Wharton turned half right.

"Something else. Those cushions on the settee had been disarranged as if somebody'd sat on 'em. That's where we found those hairs I showed Usher."

Without waiting for comment, he moved out of the door and down the stairs. When they'd got to their chairs again, Franklin was the first to speak.

"Damned if I know what to make of it! The pistol.... Are the woman's prints on it?"

"France's only... and blurred ones."

"Pistol and bullet agree?"

"Looks like it. They're on that now... at headquarters."

Wharton sat sucking away at his cold pipe. Franklin, after a minute's scowling away at the fire, suddenly looked up.

"I can't make head or tail out of the woman business but I can see what's in those samples of writing. France believed one of the men in his house was responsible for the anonymous threats and thought the writing would show me which one. That's obvious, I admit."

"Well, it's true... that's the main point. By the way, we'd better take over all that inquiry for you as part of our routine. Suppose you don't mind?"

"Not in the least. And talking of writing, where was that note written that was found under Somers's body? At the writing table in France's bedroom?"

"One minute, young fellow!" said Wharton. "What are you assuming? That Somers wrote it? Or France? Or neither?"

"That France wrote it—as Usher said."

"I see. And what exactly were you going to deduce?"

"Well—er—" Then he laughed. "To tell the truth, I don't precisely know—except possibly this. Where France wrote it, there he died. He wouldn't go running all over the house with a thing like that in his hand. Just after he wrote it, he'd shoot himself—if he did shoot himself. If he wrote it in his bedroom, then I should say he committed suicide—and, of course, there."

"Funny you should say that," said Wharton. "Come into the drawing-room and I'll show you something else."

He halted by the cloak-room door.

"See that bookcase? It's a secretaire bookcase. This top drawer pulls down... like this... to form a writing desk. Here's the pen the confession was presumably written with. The ink's gone to the Yard. This leather blotter case had in it practically a new sheet of blotting paper; on it, in reverse, the last letters of the confession. That's gone to the Yard too. The note was almost certainly written here. How it got into Somers's hands, we don't know."

"Would it be too amazing a coincidence to assume that France wrote the note here—intending to commit suicide—but was killed before he could do it?"

"Can't say. Personally I believe life's nothing but coincidences all through. What we do know is that his prints were on it... and the blotting paper... both sets blurred."

He closed the drawer and stood back. Franklin looked at the bookcase, then at the lounge door. "Damned if I can see two pennorth of daylight! France wrote the note here, if he did write it, and killed himself upstairs, if he did kill himself. And how did Somers get the note? That is, if he did get the note. And why did he kill himself, if he did kill himself? And why did he go to the lounge to do it?"

"No use being impatient," was Wharton's comment. "We haven't been in the house more than five and twenty minutes and you're expecting miracles. We've got to let the sediment settle—and there's a hell of a lot of it in this house. Isn't that Usher?"

In the dining-room the valet was setting out a frugal meal—sandwiches, cake, fruit... and more tea.

"My God!" said Franklin, watching the General pouring himself out a breakfast cup. "Never saw such a chap as you are. Your innards'll be awash!"

Wharton put in half a dozen lumps of sugar. "Never mind my innards! Have a sandwich."

Franklin rose hurriedly. "Not for me! I'll slip off to the flat and have a meal. Be back in about an hour."

"No flat for you!" said Wharton bluntly. "We're only just beginning. I want to hear all about that man you and Usher heard in the house. And I want a meticulously detailed account of what happened the other night—you know, that party you went to with Hayles; the one you were showing off about!"

Franklin's glare missed fire as the General leaned across to the plate. Then he made the best of it.

"Right-ho, then! And pass those damn sandwiches before they're all gone!"

CHAPTER IX
PRIVATE ENTERPRISE

FRANKLIN WOKE the following morning with a curious sense of elation. For one thing, Wharton had admitted that he occupied a unique position for prowling round and acquiring information among the inner circle of France's acquaintances, and although his name was not being mentioned publicly, he was, in a way, retained for special investigatory duties by the Yard—always, of course, in consultation with Wharton himself. And not only that. He saw no reason, for instance, why, if the opportunity arose, he should not do a certain amount of investigating on his own account. If nothing came of it, then nobody need be any the wiser. If anything good turned up, then the Yard could have it. And all that would be bread on the waters. A man to whom the Yard owed something could thereafter make use of their organisation and expert advice—provided of course it wasn't overdone.

As far as those extras were concerned, Usher looked like providing a promising start. Somewhere in the bottom of his mind he was positive he'd seen the man before. Then there had been something else unusual—that remark of his about going back to work for the Colonel Welling, for whom he'd worked before. Surely a curious sort of arrangement that—a valet leaving a master for another and then going back when the fit took him!

First of all came his own work, and at the office a letter from Peter Claire, dated the previous night.

Dear Franklin,—

Hayles just rang me up and told me all about that awful business of poor Michael. We are naturally very upset and should be very grateful if you would call round some time to-day and let us have what news there is, other than what might be called official. I am hoping to go round first thing in the morning to see if I can lend a hand. Perhaps I shall see you there.

Yours sincerely,

Peter Claire.

Franklin promptly rang up Wharton and gave him the tip.

"Thanks very much," said Wharton. "If he mentions you, I'll give him the definite impression that you were merely a casual caller and not connected with the inquiry. When are you going to see him?"

"I'll ring up and suggest four-thirty—if your conference will be over by then."

"Four-thirty'll do."

"And if you don't mind my suggesting it," added Franklin, "I wonder if you'd mind judiciously pumping him as to what Hayles's exact status is. I don't know if you've got a very clear idea, but I certainly haven't."

And so to Usher. Colonel Welling seemed the best line of approach and there Franklin found himself up against a brick wall. No information whatever was available, except the name of his former regiment. The only thing to do, therefore, seemed to be to send along a man to make tactful inquiries at Stanhope Street, and that was not only circuitous but far more difficult than it looked. Then he rang up Ludovic Travers. Did he know anything about a Colonel Welling? Travers didn't, but he did the next best thing—suggested approaching Sir Francis Weston direct.

Luckily for Franklin, the man who to all intents and purposes *was* Durangos Limited, had a very weak spot for the detective bureau—the child of his old age and his legitimate creating. As Franklin was ushered in, he gave him a friendly nod.

"Morning, Franklin! What's your trouble?"

"No trouble, Sir Francis. All I wondered was if you could tell me anything about a Colonel Welling—of Stanhope Street. We don't seem to have any data."

"Colonel Welling? What's he been up to?"

Franklin explained at some length. The other seemed interested and even gratified.

"I do know a Colonel Welling," he said. "He may be your man and he mayn't. Claude, I think his name is. You can check that by the directories. Also he's the man behind Hanson and Maude."

Then Franklin saw it, or thought he did, and cursed himself for a double-dyed fool. The case files were hunted through laboriously till on the general news' page of one of the sensational Sunday papers he found what he wanted—the face of Usher; seen all those months before and registered unconsciously.

WHAT THE FOOTMAN SAW

HIGH LIFE BELOW STAIRS

BUTLER GETS TWO YEARS

The story itself was one of systematic and highly organised graft; a butler with an itching palm and tradesmen who were not averse from sharing in the distribution; then the aroused suspicions and the footman planted in the hall to find out what was happening. How that latter part had been managed was reasonably obvious. Hanson and Maude, that old-established firm of inquiry agents, had been approached and had supplied Usher for the job. For any such posts where the suspicions of an employer were not to be aroused, Colonel Welling was the cloak, the perpetual employer when necessary, and the convenient supplier of references.

The thing to do, of course, was to find out by hook or crook if Hanson and Maude had planted Usher at 23, Regent View. If they had, it appeared certain that it had been at France's request; and if so, he must have had other warnings than those anonymous letters, since Usher had been in the house for a fortnight. Franklin was pleased about that bit of deduction, though just a trifle annoyed that France should have approached him while actually a client of Hanson and Maude, yet even about that there was a certain satisfaction. France must have been dissatisfied with the results that Hanson and Maude were producing or he'd never have changed his firm. However, all that didn't matter very much. The great thing would be to discover just what Usher knew. His reticences and apparent contradictions would be explained and, what was more, when Wharton knew the *truth* from Usher, he could then be certain—in cases where Hayles and Usher disagreed—not only of the lies Hayles was telling, but also of their import.

As for Hanson and Maude, he knew them quite well by repute. Their reputation was that of a conservative firm, dealing with the usual routine work, and responsible in their time for some really good efforts. A certain amount of sartorial modification and a touch or two to his face, and he set off for the Haymarket. In the inquiry room of the modest looking offices, his manner became aggressive and distinctly impatient.

"Can I see somebody important? One of the directors?".

"I'll see, sir. May I have your card, sir?"

"Card! Isn't this supposed to be a confidential firm?"

"May I have your name then, sir?"

"Certainly not! Preposterous!"

The clerk looked at a loss. "If you wait a moment, sir, I'll see if Mr. Hanson is disengaged."

Two minutes later Franklin was shown into an office that breathed secrecy. The deed boxes looked securely locked; the safe was certainly so, and the walls were austerely bare. As for the gentleman who rose at his entry, he looked the grand depository of the world's secrets.

"How do you do—er—"

"Forrest! Major Forrest!"

"Ah! Glad to see you, major. Take a seat. Any connection of the Dorsetshire Forrests by any chance?"

The major thought not, then went straight to the matter in hand. His household was worrying him—biggish sort of place up in Yorkshire, where a large staff had to be kept. All sorts of petty pilfering seemed to be going on and he was sure the housekeeper, cook and butler were in league with the local tradesmen. Could Hanson and Maude tackle the job? Money—in reason— was no object. What the major really objected to was being made a fool of. Could a dummy footman or valet be put in, secrecy being, of course, essential? Valet would perhaps be better as the major's man was going at the end of the week. The chap'd have to be tactful, and detection proof.

Hanson looked profound and thought he could satisfy the major on that point. How soon was the man wanted? Oh, yes, of course; at the end of the week to take the place of the man who was going. Hanson's face lit up.

"That's all right, major. We've got the very man. He's definitely free on Saturday, if not before. I doubt if there's another in London who's his equal."

"Could I see him?"

"Naturally! We should arrange that."

"Then let me see. I'm due at Brighton for a day or two," here came an arch look which Hanson greeted with a smile that was discretion itself. "Then on Thursday I shall be at the Byronic Hotel. At—er—noon? That suit you—and your man?"

"Suit us very well, sir, but I'll ring you up first thing on Thursday."

The major rose, then sat down again. "Er—about this man. You got a photo or anything handy? I'm most particular. And it seems rather a pity to bring him round and all that, if he's not likely to suit."

Hanson went over to the filing cabinets. "We have a photo, sir, but not as he really is. We never let our men be seen as they are. This is the man, sir. He's handled two of our recent cases with extraordinary tact... details of course I mustn't give you."

The major adjusted his pince-nez. "Hm! Looks a capable sort of chap!... And this is a sort of disguise!"

"That's right, major. That's how he'll probably come to you."

"Wonderful! Perfectly wonderful!" The major got up. "We can leave it like that then. And what do I pay you now?"

Hanson waved aside the suggestion. "Nothing at all, major! Quite unnecessary in your case. A tentative agreement perhaps on Thursday."

One or two details and Franklin was out in the Haymarket again, and until he got back to his office and the 'phone, kept chuckling away to himself like a boy who's just pulled off a super-practical joke on a gang of super-jokers. But when he rang up Wharton and gave him the news, he wished he hadn't. The General's voice sounded not in the least surprised and that was a pretty poor return for a morning's hard work. Then Franklin consoled himself as usual. Wait till he heard the details at that three o'clock meeting! That'd make the old boy sit up and take notice!

* * * * *

With that failure to impress Wharton as a vague and very minor disturbance somewhere at the back of his mind, he went in later to see Travers and found him with a batch of midday editions.

"The very man I wanted," said Travers, shoving the splash headlines under his nose. "Have you seen all this? But of course you have."

Franklin had a good look, and his comment was oddly personal. "I see they're keeping my name out of it."

"Your name!"

Franklin spun him the yarn. His final comment might have been: "A week ago you wouldn't have cared if all the boxers in England had blown their brains out and now you're sitting there looking as if the world had come to an end." What he actually did say was: "I suppose you haven't had a chance to go round?"

Travers shook his head. "Far too busy. Mason's just come in and he tells me there's half London round the house—and the whole of the police. Come and tell me some more... and let me stand you some lunch."

But when Travers had heard it all again and had asked every question he could think of, neither he nor Franklin was any nearer common sense. That suicide confession, for instance, seemed absolutely unplaceable.

"What's your idea about it?" he asked.

"Very sketchily this," said Franklin. "While France was at the evening show on Saturday, somebody broke into the house by the lounge and hid himself in the drawing-room. When France came in, this somebody shot him and carried his body upstairs and left a confession of suicide, ostensibly in France's writing. The best is Cotter's theory, except that Somers took the note to the lounge after he'd made the discovery, because he wanted to telephone to the police. The rest we don't know till the analysis comes in of that stuff we got from the kitchen sink, but he might have had a brain storm and poisoned himself."

"Carried the poison round all ready!"

"Don't be funny, Ludo! I know that theory's full of gaps. The golden-haired lady, for instance—and the man we heard in the house."

"I suppose that couldn't have been Somers? You heard the door slam, but that doesn't prove he went out. He might have slammed it deliberately and gone back to the lounge. You said he was only just dead."

"Possible—but why should he slam it?"

"Lord knows!" said Travers. "I was only trying to be helpful." He frowned slightly, then took out his silk handkerchief. "Any chance of a look in, do you think?"

"I was just wondering. Wharton's keeping me well in the background at the moment. But why not try through Claire?"

"Excellent! And didn't you say you were going round there this afternoon?"

"Yes—four-thirty."

"Then I think I'll take your advice—pop in about four." He started polishing his glasses. "There's something I'd rather like to put up to you... something I'd been thinking about before all this happened. The trouble is... well, I don't think you'll thank me for saying it!"

Franklin was immediately interested—and curious. Whatever Travers had to say would moreover be so utterly remote from the set, official mind, that it would be bound to be provocative, even if it got nobody any forrader. "Spit it out!"

Travers fumbled with the glasses. "Do you know, it's rather difficult." Then he gave his very best smile. "You're not going to be annoyed with me?"

"I shall be if you don't hurry up and get it off your chest."

Travers sighed. "Then don't blame me. The—er—thing is this. When you told me about Hayles coming to see you on that detective-novel, local colour business, it didn't somehow ring true—I mean Hayles's story didn't. It sounded more like an excuse. Not that he could have come to a better man—if he'd been genuine—because he couldn't. Don't mistake me about that. And then, after that, he fell in very readily, so it seemed to me, with your casually expressed wish—in common with several million Englishmen, myself included—to meet France personally. He even rang you up and suggested taking you to dinner. And where? Not with France. With the Claires!"

"Just a moment!" interrupted Franklin. "Didn't I impress upon you the fact that those three were really one? Didn't I call them the Three Musketeers?"

"My dear old chap, I know you did! But that's hardly the point. Hayles could have taken you to France's dressing-room, or to his house. Once more don't misunderstand me. I'm not suggesting for the world that you are an unusual person to take to a ménage like the Claires', because you're not. You're not the accepted type of professional detective. You're a man of the world; you can move in any company—except perhaps that of the Bright Young People—and you're obviously what the world calls a gentleman. Oh, no! I'm not flattering you at all. The truth is simply this. I thought it at the time a most unusual thing that Hayles should have asked you to the Claires, especially as France himself wasn't dining there. The point then becomes, would you like my opinion as to why you were there, in view of what's happened?"

"Carry on!"

"Well, France got the second anonymous letter on the Thursday. He probably thought it a lot of rot and so on, and then he began to think a bit. After all, why take risks? Why not at least take advice—"

"Hold hard a moment!" said Franklin, and told him about Usher. "He *was* having advice—and he'd got a bodyguard!"

"Don't be too sure. You're not certain as to what Usher was there for. Still, to go on. As soon as he thought of that taking of advice—perhaps he wasn't satisfied with Hanson and Maude, and that again may be why *he* gave Usher notice—at any rate, as soon as he thought of it, you came into his mind as a first-class man who'd been in the public eye. So he said to Hayles, 'There's a chap named Franklin,' and so on. 'Run your eye over him and see what he's like.' Hayles'd say, 'But how?' whereupon France'd retort, 'That's your pigeon!' Hence the milk in the cokernut.... After that, Hayles would report that you were an unusual and interesting sort of chap. 'Right-ho then!' France would say. 'Bring him along!' 'Can't be done!' Hayles'd say. 'You're full up with engagements.' 'Right-ho then!' France'd say. 'Scheme it out to bring him along to Peter Claire's to-morrow.'".

Travers looked up rather anxiously. "Do you know," said Franklin, "but I think you're right!"

The other looked immensely relieved. "I wondered how it'd strike you. And of course you realise that that was why your profession wasn't mentioned. France'd tell Hayles he wasn't to say a word. That was probably why Hayles kept up that chatter with Dorothy Claire—to keep her off you."

"You sure it wasn't a conspiracy to put me at my ease?"

"Ease! My dear chap, you're the very kind of person people love to talk to. Wouldn't Mrs. Claire—to use what would probably have been her own words—have been most frightfully thrilled?" He paused for a moment, then went on with a quiet note of intensity. "Let me put it all to you. You said there was occasionally a tension in the air; that Mrs. Claire kept putting down the soft pedal; that Claire was off-hand or gnomic, and that Hayles was inane or volatile. When France came in, it was like a climax. He sort of took possession and after that—Claire dropping out—everything went with a swing.... Was there a secret between Claire and his wife and did Hayles know it?"

"You mean, was there in that room the germ of the weekend's happenings?" He thought for a moment, then laughed. "My dear fellow, you're sitting there spinning all sorts of delicate and intricate webs... but it's the design you're interested in—not killing flies!"

Travers didn't disagree. "That may be so. As you say, spiders spin. The flies do the rest!"

Franklin laughed again, then caught sight of the clock. "I say! I shall have to hare off like blazes. I'll let you know what happens."

"Do!" said Travers. "And give Wharton my love. It might help."

"You bet I will," Franklin assured him. "And I'll tell him that bit about the flies. After being up most of the night, he'll probably be amused!"

CHAPTER X
ABOUT IT AND ABOUT

WHEN FRANKLIN ARRIVED outside the house, the crowd was still pretty dense and a couple of mounted policemen were keeping the roadway clear. The constable at the main gate evidently had his orders and as he passed Franklin through, the crowd stared excitedly.

That was the first time Franklin had seen the house properly—a two-storeyed building much like a country vicarage and evidently a Georgian survival. Curiously enough, its private road was different from the usual half-moon. On entering the gate you kept parallel to the main thoroughfare, then cut back sharply towards the house; in other words, the shrubbery was in the shape of the metal knob of a malacca cane. Moreover, whoever had planted it must have had his own ideas as to privacy. From the main road, except for its upper windows, the house was invisible since even then its laurels, hollies and privet made a screen which the eye could hardly penetrate.

As Franklin entered the dining-room and Usher closed the door behind him, Wharton emerged from the lounge with a man whom Franklin knew he had seen somewhere before. As soon as Wharton mentioned the name, he knew where—in the picture pages of the press and on the news bulletins of the screen.

"Fred! here's somebody I'd like you to meet. Mr. Franklin... Fred Dunally."

Franklin smiled. "Glad to see you, Mr. Dunally. I've seen your photo often enough."

Dunally's weatherbeaten face sort of crinkled to a smile.

"We can't help that, sir."

"Fred came along to help us," explained Wharton. "We picked him up at Ipswich this morning. He's just off to the National Sporting Club."

"Got to meet Lord Weatherlie and the Committee, sir. I hear they want eight of us as bearers at the funeral... and I suppose I'll be one."

The tone was genuinely regretful that Franklin's question was almost instinctive. "He was a good sort?"

"He was that. A real sport, sir. When he beat me, sir, he had me mesmerised from the start; I knew I was beat before I left my corner." He shook his head. "We shan't see another like him. A regular gentleman, sir, and one of the old sort like what you read about. A regular toff, sir, that's what he was—and no more swank about him than there is about you and me."

They saw him off at the door, then Wharton nodded his head reflectively. "He's a good chap—Fred. I've known him for years, when his ears were as smooth as yours. Where d'you think he's off to now?"

"National Sporting Club, you said."

"Yes, but first of all he's going to have another look at France. Curious sentimental sort of morbidity those people have!... still, it does him credit."

"Do you know what I thought as I watched him go down the path?" asked Franklin. "I thought to myself. There goes what might have been a very pretty solution to a mystery. Ex-heavy-weight champion kills rival, and so on.' Only he strikes me as the last person in the world to kill anybody."

"He wouldn't kill a kitten!" said Wharton. "But come along in. We'll have a pow-wow with Norris."

Inside the lounge, the fire looked cheerful. Outside there was a raw drizzle and the brown paper over the hole in the far window gave the room a cockeyed sort of look.

"Where's that pussy-footed valet?" asked Wharton.

"In the kitchen all right, sir!" said Norris, and conveyed a wink to Franklin. "He won't poke his nose out of there."

"Hm! Well, as I was telling Norris, things aren't breaking any too well. France and Somers were complementary, so to speak. If either had been alive, we'd have had quite a lot of information about the other. As it is we've merely got Usher. Hayles is in bed with a breakdown."

"Really! As bad as that!"

"Well, the doctor says he's to be kept quiet and the last thing to do is to remind him about this case. His housekeeper's there, and his mother's due this afternoon. Claire's taking away the correspondence and getting a man to see to what's urgent. Of course we've got Hayles's key to his room! that's something."

"Claire did come round then?"

"Oh, yes! spent best part of an hour here. Fine looking fellow!"

"Isn't he? Regular guards' officer type. They say he's the best driver in England at the moment."

Wharton gave his usual grunt. "He's welcome.... He won't break *my* neck. By the way I asked him very tactfully about Hayles. He laughed!" Wharton looked quite indignant. "He seemed to insinuate that France did all what you'd call the managerial work himself. Hayles seems to have been sort of found a job— had to make himself generally useful."

Franklin was reminded of something. "Isn't that in the book?—about France having his own original ideas about fixing up contracts and so on?"

"What book's that?"

"Two Years in the Ring. France and Hayles collaborated in it. You mean to say you haven't read it!"

Wharton snorted, then changed the subject. This time it was Franklin who winked at Norris.

"What's all this about our friend in the kitchen?"

Franklin told him in detail. "Good work!" was Wharton's only comment. Franklin failed to catch Norris's eye, then made his question as casual as possible.

"What did Usher have to say for himself?"

"Haven't asked him! Unless Hanson releases him, he'll only tell a pack of lies.... Also we're expecting the result of an inquiry to come through. What name was that you gave?"

"Forrest. Major Forrest."

"Norris, ring up Hanson and Maude and say Major Forrest wishes to see Mr. Hanson most urgently at four thirty. Make sure he'll be there—then ring off."

"Something else you might like to know," he told Franklin when the receiver was hung up again, "and that's how we stand. First about France. His turn at the Paliceum was over at 9.15 and he left the building at 9.45. Nothing seems to have happened while he was there except that he received a telephone call just before 8.00. As soon as he left the building, he stepped into the fog and how he got to this house we haven't been able to trace. He didn't call at the Claire's because he knew they'd be away, as Claire told us this morning. Also if he came straight here, it fits in with the time Menzies gave."

"Exactly!" said Franklin. "But do you know, I've been wondering a lot about that man we heard in the house and I've thought of something else since last night. Usher and I both took it for granted it was France. Just come here a second, will you, and have a look through this window."

He manipulated the General to the left-hand side window.

"Now then, look out there! You can see the kitchen light. I know you couldn't do that last night, but the point is this. Yesterday afternoon this window couldn't be said to overlook anything, because of the fog; all the same it might be said to *overhear* the kitchen door. And remember that except when Usher spoke to me first, we spoke, as I told you, very quietly. Very well then. Take the events as they occurred. Somebody who'd no right to be in the house heard me knock at the front door. He therefore prepared to bolt out the back way—"

"Why?"

"Because he knew that at any moment servants or the owner might arrive. However, to go on. He got ready to bolt out of the window—the way he'd come in. Then he heard Usher call out to me, and thinking it was himself that was being spoken to, bolted like a rabbit for the other way out—the front."

"And he had time to shut the lounge door after him?" asked Norris.

"Why not? It's instinctive. You try it and see."

"And the blind was still down as Usher left it on the Saturday?"

"Why not? He hadn't got so far as getting out of the window. He was *at* the window."

Norris looked at Wharton. The General took up the argument. "You're assuming that the marks we found on the window were footmarks."

Franklin looked surprised. "Naturally!"

"But they weren't! They weren't made with a boot at all. All we can say is that they're scratches. We daren't go so far as to rely implicitly on their having been made to imitate a boot mark—though that's almost certain."

"In other words there's no proof that anybody actually did come through that window!"

"That's right."

"Then why make the cut to get at the fastener, if the window wasn't opened?"

Wharton shook his head. "We don't know if the window was opened or not. All we know is what I told you. If anybody did get in, he made no mark. On the other hand, this mark is here— looking as if it might be a footmark... only it isn't."

"If I might suggest something," said Norris. "Mr. Franklin hinted at two things. First, that whoever was in the house, or shall we say whoever got into the house while he was temporarily away, knew he'd be alone. Now, how could he know that unless he were Hayles? Who else'd know the servants weren't due back till four o'clock?"

"Anybody might!" put in Wharton quietly. "France might have told half London for all we know."

"Well, I suppose that is so, sir.... And then, secondly, Mr. Franklin said whoever was in the house would want to bolt because at any moment somebody might be coming in. Now if you substitute the words 'at four o'clock' for 'at any moment,' things look different."

"Hm!" went Wharton. "Why don't you say 'Hayles' direct, instead of being mysterious? You see," he explained to Franklin, "we followed up Hayles from the time of boarding the train at Chingford. If he left the train en route, he couldn't have got here so soon, because the train travelled faster than anything else. The line was clear for one thing. And as he kept on the train to Liverpool Street, he could have got to St. John's Wood at 3.30, because we've tested it both ways and seen the actual times done yesterday. He could have been in this house before 3.35. What did his housekeeper say exactly?"

Franklin pulled out his notebook.

"At about 4.10 she said he'd come in about ten minutes before. That might mean anything... but it gives us twenty minutes when Hayles *might* have been in here."

"A job for you," said Wharton. "We'll have to pin her down closer than that."

Franklin smiled. "I know it's no affair of mine, but why go to all that trouble? If there was any killing done, Hayles couldn't have done it."

"Possibly not—but he might have been in partnership with the one who did."

"I suppose you haven't anything new about that woman—the golden haired one?"

"Not at the moment. We're on that Lucy business now, and the woman who called here on the Tuesday night—unless that was one of Usher's red herrings. All the same, I doubt if a woman cut that hole."

"You found the paper?"

"In the park... thrown over from the road. Usual brown paper and seccotine." He caught the further question in Franklin's eye. "Nearer St. John's Wood Station than this... in the direction of Hayles's flat. And there isn't a single print in the house that we can't account for. Whoever broke in—if he did break in—had gloves on."

"And there were no burglaries in the immediate district," added Norris.

"Any point in arguing out what he was in the house for?"

"I don't think so," said Wharton emphatically. "There are too many things to be taken into account. Time enough for that when we've found out if France did kill himself and if Somers did commit suicide. That might be out to-night."

"One unusual thing did strike me as I came in. You might imagine that all this business depended on the fog. Don't you think, considering the way the house is shielded from observation, that the fog had nothing to do with it?"

"Hm! And what's the application?"

"There isn't any—it just struck me, that's all. And what about the back way?"

"The fog wouldn't make any difference to that. You could slip round to the back of the house without risk."

"Just a second, sir, before I forget it," broke in Norris. "We were rather taking Mr. Hayles for granted. But now I come to think it over, he couldn't have been the one in the house!"

"Why not?"

"For this reason, sir. He daren't have been in the house when he was heard—and that was about four o'clock—because he was the one person who *knew* the servants were due back then."

Wharton's smile was an exasperating one. "Couldn't he have been here? He's the very fellow *who had a right to be here!* If anybody had come back he could have rushed to the door and claimed to have made the discovery of the bodies!"

But Cotter still had a shrewd thrust. "Then why did he bolt?"

"Because... well, I'll give you some reasons. He may have thought an alibi was safer. Or he may have lost his nerve. *But*, this is what I think. It was the voice that scared him and made him bolt. It was the unexpected voice. Franklin's voice!"

"Just a minute, sir. Mr. Franklin just said he and Usher were talking sort of quiet. Then how did Hayles hear *him*?"

"That's where I venture to differ from both of you," said Wharton. "You both have the idea that fog deadens sound. Quite the other way about—the more water vapour in the air, the easier to hear. We can't test it at the moment, but I'm sure I'm right. I think it was Hayles in the house. I think he heard Usher's voice as he stood at this window. He didn't worry about that because what he next expected to hear was probably the voice of a stranger. But the voice he did hear—Franklin's—was quite different. He was a detective, as Hayles knew. That brought the panic. But remember there was a delay before he bolted. That was because he had some job to finish. Then as Franklin stepped into the kitchen, the job was done—or undone—and he was out of the house like a madman."

Each was putting to himself the same question—what was the job that had to be finished? Then, "What about the Saturday night?" asked Franklin. "Alibis correct?"

"Absolutely! Usher, Somers, Hayles—everybody. Not a flaw anywhere." He made himself a spill and lighted his pipe. "Still, that's nothing—merely the first casting of the net."

"And yet France had suspicions of each of the three you mentioned, or else why did he send me the specimens of their writing?"

Wharton shook his head.

"Perhaps Usher may have some idea," went on Franklin.

Wharton shrugged his shoulders. "Usher's was included. He was suspected... with the others."

"Surely not! That must have been all bluff. How could he have suspected the man he put in the house?"

The General shook his head and left it at that and if Franklin had found leisure to think it out, he'd have known that far more was known about Usher than he d given the others credit for. However, the argument went on, about it and about, till finally Wharton looked at his watch.

"Quarter past four. Norris, tell that flat-footed sleuth to bring in some tea... for three."

"Not for me!" said Franklin quickly. "I'm going out."

"What's the hurry? You're not seeing Claire yet." He laughed. "I see. Want to enjoy a free meal! And where'll you be when you leave Claire?"

"Home probably. Want anything?"

"Hm! May do... about the inquest. Cotter'll be in charge. We'll simply have an adjournment for a fortnight."

"But won't that spill the beans? I mean, won't everybody wonder why?"

"Let 'em!" said Wharton laconically. "We'll fill this case so full of technicalities that they won't know what the devil we do want."

"My God!" said Franklin. "And they call it an inquest!"

Norris came back. "He's bringing it, sir. Had it all ready." And as an afterthought, "He's a wily bird that!"

"Then he's a lesson to us all," said Wharton sententiously. "And mind you keep an eye on him while I'm out. If anybody asks for him—at the door or on the 'phone—say he's out. When I ring up for him, have him here at the double. See you later, John!"

"Right-ho!" said Franklin. Then at the door he hesitated. "Oh, that reminds me. Any chance of Mr. Travers having a look round?"

Wharton glared. "Not the least... at present?"

"Right-ho!" said Franklin casually. "You're probably right. It might have been a bit awkward." And he drew back to let Usher pass with the tray.

CHAPTER XI
WHAT THE FOOTMAN SAW

As HANSON LOOKED up from his desk with a 'Good-evening, major,' on the tip of his tongue, his expression became so startled as to be really funny.

"Sorry, Mr. Hanson!" said Wharton. "Don't blame your clerk—it's all my fault. I'm representing Major Forrest."

Hanson frowned. "I don't quite see.... Who are you exactly, sir?"

Wharton helped himself to a seat. "Superintendent Wharton—of Scotland Yard. I've come to see you myself because there's a little matter which you and I, as two reasonable people, can settle in a couple of minutes. Let me come to the point. You've heard all about this France suicide affair. Seen it in the papers perhaps."

"Oh, yes."

"You have a man under the name of James Usher planted in the house on behalf of a client of yours."

Hanson shook his head. "I'm afraid I can't discuss that."

"Now isn't that too bad!" said Wharton plaintively. "And me so friendly... and coming all this way! Then you won't say whether you have a man or not?"

"Even if we had a man—which I don't for a moment admit—"

"You don't admit it!" Wharton laughed. "Somebody engaged in that house mentioned to me last night that he was sure he'd seen Usher before. During a special pose we got his picture and this morning it was circulated among those likely to know. He was identified before noon to-day."

Hanson fidgeted in his chair. "That may be so, but even then I have my duty to my client."

"I see. You claim the privilege of a doctor or priest." He got to his feet. "Very well, Mr. Hanson. I'm too busy a man to waste time on you. To-morrow you'll be in a coroner's court, and Usher with you, answering such questions as we care to put—and they'll be uncommonly awkward ones. What about your client then?"

Hanson looked decidedly uncomfortable.

"I repeat; what is the name of your client?"

The other looked more uncomfortable still. "Really, Superintendent! I can't divulge that. I must communicate with the client and get his sanction before—."

"Now wait a minute! You know what I stand for, and why I came here to speak as man to man in confidence. I'm asking you to notify your client that you are abandoning the contract unconditionally and calling your man off—and without assigning reasons. That lets you out. For the last time—what is your client's name?"

Hanson waved his hands excitedly. "I can't do it, sir! I can't do it!"

"Sit down, Mr. Hanson, please!" Strange to say, Wharton was perfectly satisfied with the way things were going. The last thing he wanted was a favour, with its subsequent admission of indebtedness. "I take this sheet of paper... I write on it your client's name... I fold it and put it here, under the inkwell. Now will you tell me?"

The other fidgeted and said nothing.

"Very well then. Let me tell you some more. Last night your man Usher slipped out of the house—23, Regent View—and rang your client up—the only call all day from that box. This morning I deliberately allowed him to go to the door for the post. He did what was expected. Gave the postman a letter—

for you—and a tip. That letter made a report and asked for instructions, didn't it?"

"You opened it!"

"My dear sir! As if we should do a thing like that! Then later on, Major Forrest—nothing to do with the Yard, by the way—came here and saw Usher's photo. And now what about that name?... Don't feel like it?... Very well. I shall see you both to-morrow."

Half-way to the door Hanson stopped him.

"You'll keep it strictly confidential?"

"Perhaps."

"Er—it was a Mr. Claire."

Wharton came back and tossed the folded paper on the desk. "Have a look at that!" Then he leaned forward with his jaw thrust out and his voice almost a snarl. "The next time Scotland Yard takes the trouble to come here, Mr. Hanson, to make you a proposition—a civil and necessary proposition—be very careful what you do. Don't start prating about your clients and professional privileges and all that flummery! You've been telling me what you *ought* to do. Now I'll tell you what you've *got* to do!"

* * * * *

When Wharton returned hot-foot to No. 23, Usher also noticed a change in his attitude—a change as remarkable as that witnessed by Hanson. Summoned to the lounge, he found a man who was apparently disposed to treat him as an equal and who actually began his interrogation with a few commendatory words.

"Now, Mr. Usher, I'm not blaming you for the methods you've had to employ during the last twenty-four hours. As a matter of fact, I think under the circumstances you did your duty to your employers extraordinarily well. However, you have heard Mr. Hanson's instructions over the 'phone. I now add my own.... What is it exactly you know?"

"Where shall I begin, sir?"

"Plumb at the beginning. Anything which deals with private matters outside the scope of this inquiry will be treated with the most implicit confidence."

"Well, sir, I received my instructions from Mr. Hanson direct, not from Mr. Claire. I was to keep an eye on Mr. France and Mrs. Claire. Mr. France's man Matterson was actually taken ill at the time—appendicitis, sir—and Mr. Claire approached our firm, and then told Mr. France he knew of a good man who'd take Matterson's place till he was fit. Colonel Welling gave me the reference and Mr. Hayles checked it."

Wharton nodded.

"So I reported to Mr. France and was told I should have to valet him and put in any spare time under Somers as footman. He didn't see anything suspicious, I'm sure of that, sir; nor did Mr. Hayles until about a week ago, and then I noticed a change which I... well, I couldn't put it into words. It was the way he looked and the way he spoke—"

"Mr. Hayles, that is?"

"Yes, sir. He was quite different from what he had been. I'm sorry I can't be more exact, sir, but you know what I mean. It was there, sir; I'm sure of it."

"I understand. And what had you actually learned?"

"Very little, sir—up to the Friday night. Mrs. Claire used to come round quite a lot—with Mr. Claire not very often—but usually alone or with the others."

"Mr. Claire ever come round alone?"

"Very often, sir! He had his own key. He was round on Friday and on the Saturday morning as I—"

"Quite so!"

"Well, sir, when Mrs. Claire came round, it was generally about tea-time and she and Mr. Hayles or Mr. France'd have tea together and then perhaps they'd go out; sometimes all three of them, in the car or walking. And when they were in here, sir, they always struck me as a lot of tomboys; chipping each other and laughing, especially at Mr. Hayles. Once he was rather annoyed, Mr. Hayles was, when Mr. France said something to him while I was in the room and after I'd gone out I heard him say,

'Damn it all! You might wait till the servants are out of the room! It makes for bad discipline,' or words to that effect, sir."

"What'd you think of that?"

"I thought it was silly sir. People like me aren't supposed to exist, whether we're in the room or not. Another thing, sir, was the difference in the way Mrs. Claire treated the two men. She always took Mr. France more seriously. If Mr. Hayles was talking, they'd often interrupt and start pulling his leg, just as if he was a youngster."

"Any special treatment for Mr. France—you know, as a sort of national hero?"

"Never, sir. They never mentioned boxing while she was here. Mr. France was a gentleman sir. They kept all that for when she was gone; for Mr. Hayles's upstairs room."

"Any details about this—er—chipping and so on?"

"Well, sir, they always called each other affectionate names. She was 'Dorothy dear' and 'Dorothy darling,' and she'd call them 'Midge dear' or 'Kinky darling,' and so on, sir; not that they meant anything particular, because that's what they always do—people like that."

"I know. A sort of high-class gush which becomes second nature. And what was your opinion as to the relationships between Mr. France and Mrs. Claire?"

Usher hesitated. For a moment or two he appeared to be collecting his thoughts. "Well, sir, up to the Friday, I couldn't make up my mind. First I'd report one way, then I'd report another—"

"To Mr. Claire, that is?"

"That's right, sir. You see the trouble was to know just what was innocent-like, sort of fooling about, and what wasn't. One thing I did know for a certainty, sir, and that was that Mr. France was a lot more serious than Mrs. Claire. If I had to put it bluntly, sir, I should say that he meant business!... And something else, sir. Mr. Hayles knew it!"

"Really! You think Mr. Hayles thought a lot of Mrs. Claire?"

"I should say he did, sir, only in a different way. Only he used to look at the other two sometimes as if he didn't know what to do with himself."

"I understand. And you reported all this to Mr. Claire?"

"Yes, sir. It was my job, sir. Four or five reports in all."

"Got any copies?"

"No, sir. We weren't allowed to make any, except after special instructions."

"Mr. Claire make any comment to you?"

"No, sir. When he used to come round here he used to pay no more attention to me, sir, than if I didn't exist."

"I see. He struck *me* as a person who had a proper appreciation of the awful importance of being Mr. Claire. And now... what about the Friday?"

Usher's pause this time seemed an instinctive preparation for a grand climax. Norris looked up and Wharton shuffled in his seat and bit hard on his pipe.

"The first thing was, sir, when Mr. France and Mrs. Claire came in about five-thirty. I happened to be in the drawing-room at the time, sir, so I slipped into the lounge, knowing Somers was handy. He took Mr. France's hat and coat and put them in the cloakroom and I heard Mrs. Claire say, 'No! don't trouble, Somers, thanks. I'm going at once.' Then I went through to the cloakroom myself, sir, because I could dodge from there to the lounge or back to the drawing-room, whichever they came into."

"And supposed you'd got trapped?"

"I shouldn't have done, sir. I could have slipped out of the lounge window and got round to the back door."

Norris looked up quickly and caught Wharton's eye. "That bit about the window is very interesting!" the General remarked. "Had you often used it like that?"

"Oh yes, sir! Several times—but always by the side window; never by the one that had the marks on it."

"Quite so!" The aptness of the reply had rather taken the General aback. "And what happened then?"

"The first thing I heard, sir, was Mrs. Claire. She said, 'You're sure Kinky's out?' and he said, 'Of course he is. He's got that job of work I gave him in town.' Then she kept quiet for a bit, sir, but he must have seen something on her face because he said, 'Now don't you start worrying all over again, darling! Didn't we have all that out at tea?' and she said, 'I know we did, but I'm so scared!' Then she laughed, sir, that nice little laugh she has, and then he said, 'Rubbish!' just like that, then she laughed again and said, 'I'm a silly little thing and you'll just have to put up with it, Midge dear.'"

At that moment there was a question on the tip of Wharton's tongue, and had he asked Usher what he *saw*, things might have ended differently. What stopped his asking it was the fact that the valet, in his recital, seemed to be actually visualising the scene, but a scene that was far too pregnant with moment to be interrupted.

"Then Mr. France said, 'No, but it upsets me, darling, when you keep worrying like this. How can Peter ever know anything? There won't be anybody likely to chatter. And you say you can rely on Mary?' Then she said, 'Mary will do anything for me. She'd kill herself if I asked her!' There you are then!' he said and then he must have done something—put his arm round her, I thought, sir—because she suddenly spoke out loud, much louder than what they'd been doing. 'Don't be foolish, Michael!' angrily, like that, sir. Then he whispered something I couldn't catch and then she said, 'You'll be tired of that after to-morrow night!'"

"You're sure of that?"

"Not to a word, sir, but what it means. And that was the first time I ever heard her call him Michael."

Wharton grunted.

"Then he said, 'I shan't have a chance to see you again, darling. Are you sure you know what to do?' I had to listen very close for what's coming, sir, because though they were on the chesterfield, they were talking very quiet. Then she repeated what they'd most likely been talking over.

"'If the fog keeps on, I'm to say I'm not going—'

"'Yes,' he said, 'but you've to have the bag ready.'

"'Oh, yes!' she said. 'I forgot that. I'm to have the bag ready and say I don't think I shall go unless the fog clears and then, just after nine, I shall make up my mind and say I'm going after all—by Tube to Paddington—and Archer is to carry the bag to the station and then I go—'

"'You've forgotten something!' he said.

"'Oh, yes!' she said. 'Archer is to get the ticket and see me into the train. Then I go to Baker Street and wait there a bit and take care I'm not seen and then come back here, and you'll be waiting.' And then there was some whispering I couldn't hear, sir, and then he said, 'The fog'll be absolutely priceless—if only it holds up.' And then she suddenly thought of something else, sir. She said, 'Who's this man Franklin, Kinky's bringing along to-night?' and he said, 'Just a friend of his, darling. Awfully good sort, I believe.'"

"Did you know to what they were referring?"

"No, sir, I didn't. But when she said that, I had a notion I hadn't better stay there any longer so I nipped out by the lounge window and that was lucky for me, sir, because he'd just pushed the bell for Somers and told him to send me in, so I made as if I'd been upstairs. When I reported, he told me to escort Mrs. Claire home through the fog and that was a curious thing, sir, because you'd have expected him to do that himself. It could only have meant that he didn't want to run the risk of being seen with her. At any rate, I did it, sir, and very foggy it was, and when I got to the main gate she thanked me and gave me half a crown. Then when I got back Mr. France was still there and he said, 'Usher! don't mention that Mrs. Claire was here to-night!' and I said, 'Very good, sir! Certainly not, sir!' and when I got to the kitchen I found he'd given Somers the same instructions."

"And did Mr. Hayles come in again?"

"Not till later, sir—about half-past six I should say it was. I heard him in the hall and he said he'd just called to get something. He sprinted upstairs, sir, and when he came down he said he'd a good chance of being late for dinner."

"Could Mr. Hayles enter without you hearing?"

"Quite easily, sir... if he wanted to."

"Exactly! Well, go on, Usher."

"As soon as I got back to the house, sir, I told Somers I wanted some cigarettes and slipped out to the telephone box across the road and tried to get Mr. Claire I got him first go, sir—at his house—and told him what had happened. I couldn't form any idea how he was taking it, sir, because all he said was, 'Quite!' and 'Yes!' Then at the very end he said, 'Right! Let Hanson know you've finished with the case. To-morrow morning you're to give a week's notice and if you can get his back up so that he sacks you on the spot, there'll be a tenner for you that Hanson knows nothing about. And keep your mouth dead shut!' he said, 'and there may be another tenner to that!'"

"And what happened when you gave notice?"

"I was as rude as I dare be, sir, and I told him I was fed up and it wasn't fit for a dog the life I had—and he took no notice! He just laughed, sir! taking everything easy like, as he always did. 'You're a bit liverish, Usher!' he said, like that, sir, and walked out of the room, humming to himself—the lounge it was, sir."

"And what did you tell Mr. Claire last night when you rang him up?"

Usher looked hard at Wharton before he answered that.

"Go on!" Wharton told him. "No hard thoughts, Usher. The slate's clear."

"I told him what we'd found here, sir…. Then he said I was to let Hanson and Maude know at once and he'd tell them to keep their mouths shut about me and I was to keep mine shut about him…. Only I didn't have a chance to slip out again, sir… it was risky enough as it was!"

"What'd he say when he came round this morning?"

"Not a word or sign, sir."

"Hm! And when did you first know you were all going down to Martlesham?"

"Early in the week, sir—as soon as the news arrived about the big fight."

"I see. And tell me. Isn't there a big flying camp down at Martlesham?"

"Yes, sir. About a mile away from us, sir."

"Could Mr. Hayles have induced a friend of his to have picked him up with a plane and slipped him into town on the Saturday night without you being aware of it?"

"He might, sir... but he didn't! He was sound asleep at one o'clock because I was up with toothache and passed his door and he was snoring."

"No possibility of mistake?"

"No, sir. It was Mr. Hayles all right. He occupied that room alone... and he was there, sound asleep, when I took him in a cup of tea just after seven-thirty."

"I see. Now to go back a bit. You said Mr. Claire had a key to this house. It's his house, I understand that. But isn't it unusual for a landlord to have a sort of right of entry to his tenant's house?"

"It wasn't that, if you'll excuse me, sir," said Usher hastily. "I don't think I can have expressed myself very clearly, sir. Mr. Claire only came in when he knew there was somebody in. He and Mr. Hayles always carried on as if they were relations, sir. They all did as they liked with each other's things."

"I see. Only I doubt if Mr. France or Mr. Hayles had a key to number three?"

Usher smiled. "Well, sir, that'd be different. For one thing, there'd always be servants there, whereas sometimes we weren't here and I understood from Somers that when the others were away, Mr. Claire'd pop in and arrange to send on letters and so on. Or he'd send his butler, sir."

"And all that other information you gave us was perfectly correct? Let me repeat the questions. Somers was a fit man, bodily and mentally? Mr. Hayles was most annoyed at not being able to get away from Martlesham earlier? A woman called here last Tuesday, as reported?"

Usher nodded. "Everything correct, sir—as reported."

Wharton nodded heavily once or twice, frowned, then toyed with his pipe. Then he leaned over to Usher and pointed it straight at him.

"You prepared—with Mr. Hanson's full permission—to do a job of work for me? A job that'll need tact, and a still tongue?"

"Most decidedly I am, sir."

"Right! Then first thing of all you must let Mr. Claire know, ostensibly on the quiet, that you haven't been able to get away from here, because I want you to look after us—and of course *we* pay. Tell him I said you might go when your official notice was up. If he wants to know how things are going, tell him everything's O.K., but tell me what he says. As for the other job of work, it depends on what happens to Mr. Franklin tomorrow morning."

"Very good, sir."

"Some time later this evening I shall want you to go over things again." He glanced at his watch. "Whew! Gone six-thirty! Right-ho, Usher! I'll give you a holler when I want you... and thanks very much."

The General took off his spectacles and beamed down his nose on Norris.

"Things seem to be moving!"

Norris beamed back. "Certainly looks more like business, sir.... He's a wily bird, that Usher!"

Wharton grunted, replaced the spectacles, then shuffled off to the lounge and the telephone.

CHAPTER XII
TRAVERS GETS A BACK SEAT

As THEY CAME OUT of the gate, Franklin turned to the left. Travers, who had made a step or two to the right, recovered his lost distance.

"Sorry! But isn't this the way to the station?"

"Wharton wants to see me at once," explained Franklin. "It was he who rang me up. You'd better come along and chance your arm. He can't very well kick you out once you're there."

"Do you think so? Well, I don't mind taking the risk. Claire didn't seem to take all the rather blatant hints I threw out."

"May be all the better in the long run," said Franklin mysteriously. "We'll get you a front seat—Claire or no Claire."

"Splendid!... By the way, I wonder if I know why Wharton rang you up."

"Bet you fifty cigarettes!"

106 | CHRISTOPHER BUSH

"Of course that's rather intimidating," said Travers. "However, here goes! It was to ask you to get preliminary details about Claire's alibi."

Franklin shot a look at him. "How'd you guess?"

"Well—er—it was a long shot. The footman said you were wanted on the' phone; then when you came back you hadn't been talking a couple of minutes when you suddenly asked, 'What was the fog like where you were this week-end?' And that's all there is to it."

"Good Lord! Was I as obvious as that?"

"I don't think you were, really. But I'll tell you what I did think—as an onlooker who's supposed to see most of the game. I thought Claire was overjoyed to be asked the question. He was bursting to tell you where he'd been, in spite of that bored air of his. And the details he gave you—all ready to be examined and found correct!"

Franklin laughed. "Come, come, Ludo! Show you a murder case and you're ready to suspect your aunt! Claire isn't that sort of chap."

"You're prejudiced," retorted Travers, "and that's a paralysing thing for a detective—the one man who's bound to view things dispassionately. I think Claire's quite an excellent fellow in many ways, but that doesn't prove he wouldn't commit murder."

"Prejudice be damned! Surely you'll allow me to have an elementary psychological sense?"

Travers smiled to himself. "I don't know that I do. The poet warned mankind against elementary knowledge years and years ago. In matters of true psychology, detectives have more to learn than to teach."

"You're too elusive for me," said Franklin. "By the way, what excuse did you give Claire for calling round this afternoon?"

"I got him to ask me round—just rang him up and wondered if he could give me any information about the value of a Brooklands' test of the springing of my car, in view of giving her a first-class run."

"Hm!" said Franklin. "Wish I could lie like you amateurs. However, here we are. Mind your P's and Q's."

Norris let them in and by the time they'd got their backs to the fire, Wharton made an appearance from the lounge. Travers happened to be one of the few people for whom he had an intense admiration, and that wholly unconnected with the fact that the Chief Commissioner was his uncle. One reason was that he really liked him; the other was a whimsical kind of inversion. Wharton, in short, had once bought a copy of *The Economics of a Spendthrift,* assuring himself that such highbrow stuff was bound to be above his head, and then had found to his amazement that he'd thoroughly enjoyed it. The trouble on this occasion was, however, that the General had no intention of letting personal likings get the better of his sense of duty. But he shook hands as if welcoming a very dear friend.

"Well, Mr. Travers! This is a pleasure, sir!"

Travers smiled. "It's good to see you. How're things going? Pretty well?"

Wharton looked inscrutable. "Slow! Very slow!... By the way, you can make yourself comfortable here by the fire for a minute or two. We've just got a small job to do... in the lounge." He nodded reassuringly and sidled away, with a final word at the door. "Usher'll get you a cup of tea if you ask him."

Inside the lounge, Franklin fired his shot first. "Travers happened to be calling on Claire when I got there and we came away together. You wouldn't have him go one way and me another! And what was the idea of ringing me up for Claire's alibi?"

Wharton told him, or rather, Norris read out the story as related by Usher. Franklin, every pre-formed theory gone wrong and that newly-found world of charming acquaintances dissolving into air, looked disconsolate.

"Do you know, it's incredible to me. She's the last woman in the world I'd have thought of like that." Then a flash of inspiration. "But her hair isn't golden! It's black... and she's close-cropped!"

"I know. Usher told us that.... And you don't think she's that sort?"

"I don't!" Franklin was indignant, then maybe remembered Travers' comments on prejudice. "Of course, you never know. Women can be very secretive at times."

"Protective colouring," said Wharton gently. "And what about the alibi? Get anything?"

"The whole bag of tricks. But you were lucky. We were just going when you're call came."

"Right! Norris! you'd better take it down.... Now then, let's have it!"

"Some of it you've already heard. Claire took what he calls his own car—I suppose he means not a racing car—down to Lingfield, leaving at about eleven when the fog was a bit thinner. He said it took him about an hour to get clear of London and he missed the first race. By the way, he gave me a tenner over that horse of his because he got fives on the course before the price shortened. His course bookie is Rossler, of Coventry Street. He stayed there till three-thirty, then started for town, only the fog got so bad that he garaged the car and 'phoned his butler to send the chauffeur for it in the morning. Then he came on by train to his club—the Wanderers', Pall Mall—where he met a Captain Utley whom he should have met at Lingfield, only when he got there he found a wire from this chap saying he daren't risk it on account of the fog and he'd see him in town instead. Then about seven they rang up Liverpool Street about trains and found the Company was putting on a special for Cambridge at eight, so they caught it. From Cambridge they went by car to Paddenham—a village near Royston—and spent the night at Utley's place—the Hall—"

"Excuse me a moment," said Norris. "You remember that question we agreed to ask Usher, sir, about a flying camp at Martlesham? Isn't there one at Royston?"

"Yes, there is," said Franklin. "At least it's about four miles on—Newmarket direction."

"Coincidence probably," said Wharton. "Carry on, John!"

"Then, yesterday morning, Claire inspected a couple of yearlings—racehorses—which Utley had for sale privately. All this Royston business was previously arranged. Then Utley, who had to come back to town in any case, brought Claire along. The fog had just eased up a bit before noon, you remember, and they got as far as Euston, where Claire was dropped and then came straight on to Regent View. After that he was in the house till he went to bed. That's the lot."

"And enough too. What do you think, Norris? Better do it yourself?"

"Just as you like, sir."

"Right! Wait till Mr. Franklin's gone, then get straight off—to Royston, if you can." He turned to Franklin. "I suppose you weren't lucky enough to get anything about Mrs. Claire?"

"Oh yes, I was! Claire happened to say how upset they all were, so Travers said, 'How's Mrs. Claire keeping?' Then Claire said, 'Oh! she's frightfully upset. I thought she was going to be really ill, so I sent her down to—to Mar...' Mar something."

"Marfleet?"

"That's it!"

Wharton nodded. "Marfleet Parva—Reading. That's his country place. He keeps his racing cars there and dabbles in horse breeding. Any other news?"

"Don't think so."

"Nothing bearing on the case in any way?"

"I don't know that there was. Of course we talked a lot about France. Claire said he couldn't understand it at all. He was the last man in the world who ought to have committed suicide. He seemed very upset—relatively of course. People of that kind don't gush about things." Wharton smiled ironically. "And he was sorry about poor old Somers too. He'd known him for years and his opinion was that he was temporarily deranged—sort of shock on seeing France's body—"

"You discussed theories then?"

"Certainly we did! Aren't the papers full of 'em? He said Somers thought the world of France. Oh! and France won't leave any money, so that motive's missing. His uncle gave him an annuity while he was at Cambridge and though he'd picked up some pretty hefty sums at times, his expenses were heavy. Claire financed him and he said the way France lived was excellent publicity. Also Claire reckons that if France had gone to America he'd have won easily—and scooped in best part of a quarter of a million into the bargain. He'd have made a young fortune himself."

"Did he stress that at all?"

"No, not really. It just arose in the course of ordinary conversation. He seemed to be speaking of France as a—well, as a sort of brother, not as an investment. And that reminds me. France had no relatives that Claire knows of. His mother was Russian—that is to say her mother was English and her father Russian—but France hadn't heard anything of his mother's people since the war. Claire said France spent a lot of time out there when he was young." He clicked his tongue. "I remember now. It's all in the book."

"What book? *Two Years in the Ring?*"

"That's it."

Wharton had a look at his notes. "I shall have to read that damn book before I've finished.... Did Claire hint who the executors were?"

"Himself—and the bank."

"That's all right then. We're seeing his solicitors to-morrow and we've seen the bank people... though not about that. Now I've got some real news for you. That U-trap analysis is in. Came a few minutes ago. You and Cotter were right!"

"Really!" Franklin was most excited. "They found cyanide?"

"The merest traces—but *none* in the decanter. Also Usher says the two bottles that were in the bathroom—liniment and some tonic—are still there."

"Then Somers definitely *didn't* commit suicide! I say, that complicates matters."

Wharton grunted. "Or the other way about.... The only thing that worries me is this. We'll say the whisky was poisoned in the decanter and that afterwards the contents were poured down the sink, the smell disguised with the chloride of lime, the decanter wiped and refilled, and the towel taken away. We'll assume that the man you heard in the house broke in and laid that trap for Somers. Then tell me this. How did he know Somers was going to have a drink?"

Franklin shook his head. "I don't know. It seems impossible. And why didn't Somers smell the cyanide in the decanter or in his glass when he put it to his mouth?"

"I think we can explain that. Somers, so Usher tells us, had the snorter of a cold in the head. He probably felt pretty cold when he got here and slipped into the lounge to get himself a drink—which Usher says wouldn't have been an untoward thing for him. He took a quick gulp before he smelt it, only it was too late. Then the rest spilt on the floor. Still, that doesn't explain why somebody knew he'd be having such a drink—and at that time."

"Mightn't somebody have poured him out the drink?" suggested Norris. "I mean suppose Hayles was waiting here for Somers and offered him the drink, and then did the fake suicide business after he was dead."

"How was Hayles to know that Somers was coming in without Usher—or coming in first? And why should Hayles want to kill Somers?"

Franklin suddenly hopped up. "I've got it! Or I think I have. France couldn't smell very well!"

"How'd you know?" fired the other two together.

"Dunally broke his nose for him. It's all in the book!"

"Blast the book!" said Wharton fervently. "You mean the whisky was meant for him?"

"That's it! You send for Usher and ask him. When France was in training, he cut out drink altogether. When he was what he called in semi-training, he allowed himself *one* whisky and splash *after* his show. I heard him hint at it on Friday night and later the same evening I heard him explain it. That whisky was left doped for him!"

"Then he was meant to be killed on the Saturday night—before he actually was, and by a different method?"

"That's it! And that poor devil Somers got the benefit of it."

Wharton shook his head and sat frowning away, his eyes on the other end of the room. Franklin watched to see what would happen, but the comment, when it came, was disappointing.

"It's all too complicated... at the moment. The doped whisky, the cut window, the probable murder by shooting the fake suicide, the man in the house, Somers and his tot, the second camouflage... and the suicide confession." He wagged his head with ponderous deliberation. "We'd better sleep on it. When I've seen Mrs. Claire we'll know all sorts of things... or we should do." He got to his feet. "I should push off now, Norris, if I were you."

Franklin got up too. "No more news yet?"

"Not yet—may be in to-night. They're still on that pistol business... and there's all Dyerson's stuff. That reminds me. Norris! would you mind taking along with you when you go that new batch of specimens of France's writing, and those signed autograph albums we got from Hayles's room upstairs." He turned to Franklin. "If Hayles could fake France's signature, he might have faked that letter—the confession one."

"What about the inquest?"

"We shan't want you. Usher and Cotter'll do all that's necessary—with Menzies. The Press'll start hollering but we can't help that. What are you doing to-morrow, by the way?"

"Nothing very much. Why? Do you want something done?"

"Yes... this. What we've been thinking is that you, as a friend of Hayles, might call at his place tomorrow morning, see the housekeeper and pin her down to the actual times when Hayles came in and went out. There may be other questions that occur to me and if so I'll send them round first thing in the morning. Then try and see his mother and suggest to her that as there's such a lot to do, we can spare Usher to go over during the day to lend a hand. He can get his breakfast and supper here, and sleep here. It's rather crude, but there's just the chance we might get Usher planted there. And see Hayles if you get the chance. I'd rather like your opinion on what he's really like."

"You think he's going to bolt?"

"Don't think so—I mean, the doctor says he's really ill. General purposes, that's what we want him there for, don't you think so? And you'll do all that?"

"I'll have a shot at it." He hesitated for a moment. "Why don't you make some use of Travers? He's a friend of Hayles and he'd never be suspected... and he's frightfully keen."

"Hm! May do... if the worst comes to the worst." He went off at a hasty tangent. "Come and see me about tea-time to-morrow and tell me what's happened. I'll be away all day myself—Reading and one place and another—but Norris'll be here if I'm out." He took off his glasses and rubbed his eyes. "Wish I could get a really decent murder; middle of July, down at Margate." Then he grunted and motioned to the door. "Better say good-night to Mr. Travers."

* * * * *

Just after midnight Franklin was yawning his way to the outer door of Travers's flat, with his host hovering round in final attendance.

"Well, we've had the hell of an evening, Ludo! What's the bard say? 'Supped full of horrors' or something. Well, don't go making noises in your sleep."

Travers smiled feebly. "As a matter of fact I'm not turning in just yet. I rather thought I'd have another try to think something out."

Franklin stiffed a yawn. "Got a new idea?"

Travers shook his head.

"You're a weird bird," went on the other. "Now I come to think of it, I believe you went all over that house while we were in the lounge."

"Oh, no! Not all of it!" protested Travers. "Only the rooms which looked interesting. Er—Usher was very helpful."

"You weren't in the cloak-room, were you? I thought I heard somebody there."

"Well—er—not in it exactly. Sort of had a look round."

"You'd better not tell that to Wharton or Usher'll get his tail twisted good and plenty." He yawned—a good one this time. "Well, cheerio, Ludo!"

"Good-night, old chap!"

Travers shut the door and poured himself out the tiniest of drinks. Then he opened a drawer of the bureau and took out two books in brightly coloured jackets—*The Madison Gardens Mystery* and *The Fighting Chance,* both by Kenneth Hayles.

CHAPTER XIII
THE PRETTY LADY

WHARTON'S TUESDAY plans, as given to Franklin, were carried out in rather a different way from what he expected. Reports came in which made modification necessary. Moreover, Norris was not available, and as it was part of the General's method to keep what might be called the big features of a case in the hands of himself or his immediate understudy, there was nothing left for it but to go to Harrow himself. About this new matter and the way it became available, were certain unusual features.

The trailing of Lucy Oliver began when Detective-Sergeant Lawrence arrived in Cambridge on the Sunday night, ready for an early morning start. In an old directory he located an Oliver, tobacconist, in Wychwood Street, just off Jesus Lane, but inquiries there found the shop in new hands. Oliver had died two years previously and as he was a widower, the two younger children had been taken over by an aunt, while the third—the daughter Lucy—had secured a situation in a tobacconist's shop at Felixstowe.

The time was then eleven and it was three o'clock before Lawrence reached the seaside town. His idea that the shop would probably be a stylish one, proved correct. At the second which he tried, he learned that Lucy Oliver—or Lucille as she now called herself—had been engaged there as an assistant but had left a year previously, and, so the proprietor informed him, without asking for a reference. Where she was at the moment he hadn't the least idea. Then, to counterbalance that piece of bad luck, another girl assistant knew the address of her room—76, Providence Street.

Then another check. The landlady, according to a neighbour, had gone to Dovercourt for the day and Lawrence was left to kick his heels till seven o'clock. Then he got his information. Miss Oliver was marrying a gentleman who, strangely enough, was called Oliviere, and she had left an address to which letters were to be forwarded. What was more, the landlady found it— The Malplaquet Hotel, Bloomsbury. Lawrence sprinted to the station and caught the last train for town, where he arrived too late to carry on with inquiries.

Early in the morning he was at the hotel—a boarding-house affair just off the Square. The manageress remembered Mrs. Oliviere and moreover turned up the address to which she had been requested to forward any letters—"Ivycourt," Joyland Avenue, Harrow.

Just after eight he was outside the house—a tiny detached villa in all the bravery of modern brick and timbering; quite secluded and overlooking a recreation ground. A handy milkman gave him the information he wanted. It wasn't a Mrs. Gray living there; it was a Mrs. Oliviere. Young? The milkman winked. And, he confided, he'd never seen the husband. Thereupon Lawrence hurried to the nearest 'phone and at the very moment that he was put through to Wharton, the General had finished reading a perfectly independent report and his face, as he received Lawrence's news, showed signs of extraordinary interest.

In the locked drawer of the writing table in France's room there had been found on the Sunday a cheque book for a private account at the Baker Street Branch of Barclay's Bank. On two of the counterfoils appeared payments of fifty pounds to X. For that inquiry, and only after a preliminary talk by Wharton over the 'phone, a specially tactful person—Inspector Eaton— was sent down. Further information was suggestive. France's private account had been at the St. John's Wood Branch; this one was a super-private account. The X of the counterfoils was a Mrs. Oliviere.

"Were they paid out over the counter here?" asked Eaton.

"No! At our North Harrow Branch. Mr. France asked me to arrange that. I imagined he didn't want any inquiries."

"You don't know anything about her?"

The manager shook his head.

Wharton, informed over the 'phone, made one of the few slips of his life in that he saw no connection between Mrs. Oliviere and Lucy, as he thought of her. His instructions to Eaton were that the woman must be located so that Usher could be brought along on some pretext or other to attempt an identification with the woman of the Tuesday night. That was harder than it sounded. The Harrow Branch had no information and the name wasn't in the Directories. With his only clues the name, and the probability that the house was one of those mushroom growths which the Directory had failed to catch in its panting progress, Eaton was lucky to be knocking at the door of "Ivycourt" at about nine o'clock on the Monday night. The door was opened by a smart-looking maid.

"Mrs. Cross in?"

The maid shook her head. "Mrs. Oliviere lives here."

"But this is 'Ivycourt'!"

"Yes, but Mrs. Oliviere lives here."

"That's very annoying. I was sure she was living here. Have you been here long?"

"Only a year."

"Ah! that accounts for it. By the way, I called here last Tuesday evening and couldn't make anybody hear."

"What time was that?"

"Just before seven."

"I was going to say; we were out till nine, but we were in after then."

Eaton thanked her and moved off. His report, left at the Yard, didn't reach Wharton's hands till just before Lawrence 'phoned. Ten minutes later, the General, in the wedding garment intended for the Marfleet visit, was on his way to Harrow. The story, romantic though it was, seemed perfectly credible. Those novels—wholesome and eternally triangular—which his wife read, insisted, he remembered, that a man's real sweetheart was his first. The amorous progress of Lucy Oliver, too, seemed clearly defined; even her acquisition of a married title—the escape from the odour of patchouli to the odour of sanctity—was a perfectly natural haven of shelter, if not the full matrimonial port of rest.

The maid opened the door. Wharton gave his most disarming twinkle.

"May I see Mrs. Oliviere?"

"She isn't... isn't down yet, sir. What name is it, please?"

"She'll know who I am. A very old friend. May I come in and wait?"

The maid, slightly flustered, showed him into a small sitting-room overlooking a modest garden. In a minute she was back again.

"Mrs. Oliviere isn't very well this morning, sir, and she doesn't think she'll be able to see you... and what name was it, please?"

"She'll see *me* all right," said Wharton confidently. "Tell her a friend of Mr. Oliviere's."

The maid gave a quick look. In ten minutes, however, the mistress appeared—in a brown and gold dressing-gown. Wharton looked surprised. This was a woman scarcely out of her teens; slim, petite, graceful and alluring as a first-class mannequin; with perfect rosebud mouth, glorious eyes, and hair of a rich brown colour. At the first sight of him, she looked nervous, and Wharton had to assume that paternal manner that went so well with the wrinkles at the corners of his eyes, and the straggly moustache.

"Good-morning, Mrs. Oliviere. Won't you sit down? Too bad of me worrying you as early as this." He saw the frightened look become a puzzled one as she sat on the edge of the chair, hand clutching the collar of the gown.

"I don't want you to be worried when I tell you who I am... Superintendent Wharton of Scotland Yard."

The name seemed to convey nothing to her. "Scotland Yard? Did you want to see me about something?" After the face, that voice was disappointing and colourless.

"I want you to help me," smiled Wharton, and paused. "Tell me, Mrs. Oliviere, were you a... great friend of... the late Michael France?"

The voice was now nervous. "Y-yes, in... in a way."

Wharton nodded kindly. "Please don't distress yourself about these questions. Everything you and I are going to talk about is never going to be known outside this room. Everything's in confidence, only as you realise, now Mr. France is dead, certain things have to be cleared up and that's where you can help us. Have your maid in while I talk to you, if you like."

"What was it you wanted me to do?"

"Well, in the first place, wasn't it you who called at twenty-three, Regent View, last Tuesday evening?"

Her face coloured up; then what happened was what he might have anticipated. For the next ten minutes he was consolatory and admonitory by turns and it was only when his panacea of "a good strong cup of tea" had been brought in by the maid that the conversation resumed a spasmodic course.

But in those ten minutes Wharton's views had undergone a considerable change. What he saw now was the same seductive person but devoid of background and insipid of mind; a woman with a Park Lane body and a provincial accent; easily summoned emotions that took the place of balance and poise. Add a tendency to cling, a partiality for the amorous and an appreciation of the things that make life comfortable, and there was the girl with whom France had got entangled five years before. Wharton's own attitude responded to the reaction.

"In other words, you were jealous. Mr. France hadn't been to see you for a fortnight and you thought he was carrying-on with some other woman. Any particular woman?"

"I saw something in the paper."

She found her handbag and took out a cutting from one of the picture papers; France walking with a woman in a racing paddock.

AT KEMPTON PARK

Mrs. Peter Claire, wife of the well-known owner, with
Michael France, the famous boxer.

"So that's Mrs. Claire!" thought Wharton, and had a good look at it. He passed it back. "Seen anything of the sort before?"

"Yes; I saw another in one of the papers."

"I see. And you've never been round to Mr. France's house—except last Tuesday night—ever since the day he took you there when you first came to London?"

"No!... never I haven't!"

"And he wasn't pleased about it?"

"N-no. He came round the next day and... and he didn't half give it me."

"Hm! And where did you spend this last week-end—say from Saturday evening onwards?"

"Mabel and me went to the pictures—"

"In all that fog!"

"Yes. You see we got the creeps sitting indoors, so we thought we'd go out; the Metropolis at Harrow it was. Then we had tea upstairs... and did a little shopping on the way home and then we listened in... and went to bed. Then on Sunday he promised he'd come round in the evening, and we kept waiting and waiting and Mabel said it'd be the fog—"

"Right! Thank you, Mrs. Oliviere. Now just one other matter—a perfectly private one. I want you to answer frankly. And I want you to remember that the police and myself know a lot of things people don't give them credit for." He let that sink in. "Let's go back a few years. You first met Mr. France at Cambridge, in your father's shop."

"Y-yes."

"And he got very attached to you."

"Yes... he said he'd marry me."

"And how old were you then?"

"Nearly seventeen... only I was always a big girl for my age."

"Exactly! Now tell me what happened—in so many words—between you and Mr. France."

She made no bones whatever about that. "Well, dad was away on holiday and he found out that Mi—Mr. France had been there. One of the neighbours must have let on, and he kicked up an awful row and threatened all sorts of things and got a lot of money out of him... and I didn't see him again because he left Cambridge soon after that."

"And then your father died."

She seemed to anticipate the question. "Yes, but he didn't leave anything. He used to gamble it away on horses."

"And then you went to Felixstowe. How exactly did you happen to run across Mr. France again?"

"It was ever so funny! He came in the shop one day when he was living down at Martlesham and he recognised me and we went out together once or twice on the sly and then he said would I come to London, and... and—"

"And here you are!" He gave a gesture of infinite comprehension. "Well, that's all very plain sailing. Now here's the important point. When that money was paid to your father it was paid because Mr. France was supposed to have treated you badly. Had you any brothers?"

"No."

"Any relatives or friends who thought the same thing? Who were what you might call 'furious'? Who threatened to kill him, or anything like that?"

Her eyes opened in genuine surprise. "Why! That's what Mi—Mr. France asked me when he came round and I told him there wasn't anybody... no young man or anybody! I didn't have a penny of his money! And I never said a word to a soul about it!"

"That's what I thought. You kept it a thing of the past. You knew it wouldn't do you any good if it were known."

The very vehemence of her protestations was on the point of bringing more tears and Wharton closed the subject with another benevolent gesture. "That's all right then! You're not the woman to bring up old grievances—which perhaps weren't grievances at all... to you. As a matter of fact, I suppose only your father, and his lawyer, knew anything about it."

"And my aunt... and she's an old cat!"

"They often are!... Your uncle alive?"

"No! And a good thing for him!"

"Exactly!" said Wharton, and that virtually concluded the inquiry, though he took the name and address of the aunt and made a note to have the gambling propensities of the late Alfred Oliver inquired into—both as matters of routine rather than urgency. The great thing was that her story rang true. As for the moralities, that was no business of his. And when he had questioned the maid and thought the whole matter out again, he felt really satisfied. And other considerations added to that satisfaction. France had asked her the same questions and had been convinced of the truth of her replies, otherwise he'd have taken direct action and not have written to Franklin. Further, in that letter to Franklin he had expressed himself as puzzled—and puzzled he was, because he was certain that there existed no champion who was likely to take up so melodramatic a cudgel on behalf of little Lucy. And lastly, if there were such a champion, why had he waited all those years? Not because he was waiting for France to be in a position to pay, and pay well, for the mischief he'd presumably caused—there had been no mention of money or suggestion of blackmail in any of the threatening notes!

One other thing did occur as he was going away, something that confirmed the guilelessness of her attitude and the precarious position in which the death of France placed her. She came fluttering to the door, apologetic and anxious.

"Could you tell me what is going to happen to... to Mr. France's money?"

"You mean, has he left you anything?"

"Yes... You see I don't know what to do with the house and things." Then naïvely: "Should I be allowed to keep it?"

"I expect you'll hear from Mr. France's solicitors," he assured her as he got in the car.

That seemed to be the clearing up of a loose end. So sure indeed was Wharton of the elimination of Lucy Olivere as a vital factor in the case that, occupying his mind for a good part of the next half hour, was the wonder who had been responsible for the species of practical joke that had been played on France—the threat and the prophecy that had turned out so uncannily true.

CHAPTER XIV
STILL MORE LADIES

BUT WHAT OCCUPIED Wharton's mind in the latter stages of his progress from Suburbia towards Arcadia, was the attitude he should adopt with the lady he was about to question. Beyond the fact that she was certainly young and presumably patrician, he knew little except what he had gathered from Franklin and Usher. The problem presented indeed perplexities which were not cleared entirely away as the car was gliding along the mile of private road to the Hall of Marfleet Parva. During that short journey along the smoothly gravelled drive with its trim hedges and ornamental trees, the wealth of its owner became so consistently apparent that, before he knew it, he had decided on a certain suavity of directness, and a courtesy that should hint at the omniscience and the dignity of the law which he represented.

As the car drew up at the portico of the long Georgian building, his eye took in the stretch of lawns and parkland and the general air of spacious opulence. At the door a footman took his card—a private one—and showed him into a kind of library. Almost immediately Mrs. Claire came in.

As he caught sight of her for the first time, Wharton understood Franklin's point of view. She certainly did look boyish in the tweed skirt and close-fitting jersey and with that Eton-cropped head. And there was no mistaking the natural buoyancy of her temperament as she came forward with a delightful smile.

"How d'you do?" Then a pause that might have meant anything.

Wharton bowed. "I *am* speaking to Mrs. Claire—Mrs. *Peter* Claire?"

She nodded and smiled. "Won't you sit down?"

"Thank you," said Wharton. "But first of all, Mrs. Claire, may I apologise for a little piece of deception. I'm *Superinten-*

dent Wharton, of the Criminal Investigation Department of New Scotland Yard."

The smile went—then reappeared timorously.

"Then it's—er—*Mr.* Claire you want!"

"No, ma'am; not necessarily. I came purposely to see you." He cleared his throat. "You see, it's like this. Mr. Michael France is dead, but certain things have still to be cleared up. He was a friend of your husband... and yourself, and that's why I'm here, to ask you to help us."

She looked puzzled. "But how?"

"I'll come to that in a moment, ma'am. But may I say to start with, that I preferred this morning to see you alone, that is to say, not in the presence of your husband. And I hope that whatever information you give me need never reach his ears—"

She laughed, just the least bit nervously he thought. "Aren't you being very mysterious?"

Wharton shook his head. "I don't think so... not to you. For instance, may I tell you some facts that are in my possession; facts that may have to be acknowledged by you in the full publicity of a coroner's court?"

She closed her lips and watched intently. "Well... go on with what you have to say."

Wharton went on. He repeated the events and conversation of the Friday night, with Usher, of course, entirely out of it. Once or twice she frowned, then she leaned her chin on the back of her hand and her eyes narrowed. Once her lips puckered to the demurest suggestion of a smile.

"You agree with those statements I've just given you, Mrs. Claire?"

"Well—er—suppose I do? How really—I mean, I don't see how I'm affected."

"Then I'll tell you," said Wharton patiently. "We know that Michael France died round about ten o'clock on the Saturday night and therefore when you were with him. I've told you the arrangements—elaborate and careful ones—you made, so as to be in that house at that very time. Did you see him die, Mrs. Claire?... Or was he dead when you got there?"

Her mouth opened. She made a quick breath or two, then as quickly recovered her poise.

"How could I have gone to the house? I was at Maidenhead."

"At Maidenhead? What for?"

"To see my old nurse. I spend a day or two with her every year."

"She's the Mary to whom you and Mr. France were alluding?"

"Yes... I mean her name's Mary."

"I see. Then you broke your appointment with Mr. France?"

"No. He telephoned me he couldn't come."

"Where and when did you receive the message?"

"At my house... at nine o'clock."

"You are sure of the time?"

"Perfectly sure! That was when I decided to go to Maidenhead after all."

"You sure it was Mr. France's own voice you heard?"

"Oh, quite!"

Wharton gave a dry sort of smile. "Well, Mrs. Claire, the age of miracles is not yet over. Mr. France was 'phoning to you and doing his turn on the Paliceum stage at the same time. He was there from 8.45 till 9.15."

"Do you disbelieve me."

"Oh no, ma'am. I disbelieve the evidence of my own senses!"

"Please don't be ridiculous!" She stamped her foot, then sprang up with a rare assumption of indignation. "How dare you! What do you mean by your... your beastly questions!"

Wharton sat on. He merely shook his head reprovingly. "Words like that won't get us very far, Mrs. Claire. Sit down... please! That's better. Do you want me to have to bring you in front of a coroner's court? Do you want to be forced by the law to state in public what you and I can discuss here in confidence? Do you want publicity?... crowds?... the Press?... gossip?... and scandal!"

She glared at him. "What do you mean by scandal?"

Wharton shrugged his shoulders. "Maybe men and women aren't what they used to be! Are *you* so deliberately blind as you're making out? No scandal, you say! You who will have to admit in public that you deliberately schemed, behind your husband's back and with the connivance of your nurse, to go at night to the house of another man!" He broke off exasperated. "Mrs. Claire! Answer my question! Did you go to that house or did you not?"

"I told you I did not."

"I see. You still persist that you went to Maidenhead?"

"Ask my nurse! Apparently you don't believe *me.*"

"And whose fault is that, Mrs. Claire?"

Up she jumped again, this time with an infuriated nod and a voice shaking with temper.

"You beast!"

Wharton refused to be annoyed—and for good reason. Mrs. Claire was perturbed. If her suggestions of insult had been made more quietly, they'd have carried more weight. Had she left the room without saying a word, he might have been alarmed; as it was he produced his notebook.

"The name and address of your nurse, please."

She fairly threw it at him. "Mrs. Doran, The Cottage, Long Lane, Maidenhead."

He took it down, put the notebook back with elaborate care, then prepared to rise.

"Before I go, Mrs. Claire, may I impress something on you most earnestly. You're not dealing with me, Superintendent Wharton; you're dealing with the law; with things that land people in places of public trial—"

"You threaten me!"

"Not at all! I merely advise. Though you're the wife of the man who owns all this"—he waved his hand at the window—"the law will treat you with the same courtesy and the same cold justice as it would the poorest servant in your kitchen. Remember that, Mrs. Claire; and for the last time let me ask you. You adhere to the statement that you did *not* see Michael France last Saturday night?... living or dead?"

The two looked at each other; Wharton calm, magisterial, and with something earnest, almost pleading in his voice; she with eyes looking daggers and lips moving convulsively. Then she shook her head fiercely.

"Will you leave this house!"

Wharton shook his head. "I *shall* leave your house, Mrs. Claire, but not because you order me. I shall go because I see no further reason for staying." He shook his head again, with genuine regret. "You insist on publicity and scandal? Very well, you must have them. I shall see your husband—and your nurse—at once. Tomorrow, if not before, I must question your servants... unless, of course, you've changed your mind." He rose. "Is your maid here?"

A defiant, "She is!"

"I wish to see her at once; here in this room. If you choose to remain, please do so."

If looks could have finished him off, that would have been the end of Wharton. She flounced out of the room with a slam of the door. Wharton sat down and mopped his forehead. Five minutes wait and the girl came in—a tallish girl of about the same age as her mistress, but so blond and natural as to be almost startling after the jet hair and dynamics of the other. And as he saw the hair of the newcomer—bobbed, fringed, silky, medieval-looking—Wharton wondered. She looked very timid as she caught the stranger's eye. Wharton smiled.

"Good morning! Has your mistress told—"

The door opened quickly and Mrs. Claire re-entered. Like a late-comer at church, she sank into the nearest seat.

"You are Mrs. Claire's maid?"

"Yes... sir."

"Well, your mistress and I have had a little argument and—to tell you the whole truth—we've had a little bet on it. What we want you to do is to be a sort of umpire and settle it. I suppose *you* have a bet sometimes?"

His manner was so jovial that she smiled. "Sometimes, sir."

"Splendid! You're the very one we want. Now then, what time did your mistress leave the house on Saturday night? You remember Saturday? The foggy night?"

"Just after nine, sir."

"Capital!" He rubbed his hands. "And Archer carried her bag to the station?"

"Yes, sir."

He chuckled again. "And when did she come back to town again?"

"I don't know, sir. I wasn't there.... But the mistress got back here on Sunday just before ten."

His face fell. "I say, that's bad!" He turned to Mrs. Claire. "Well, I suppose I'd better pay up! Thank you very much—er—"

"Warren, sir."

"Thank you, Miss Warren."

He watched her leave the room, then apparently unaware of the other woman's presence, made his way to the door. In the huge mirror canted above it, he saw, however, the quivering lip and the eyes welling to tears. A courteous, "Good morning, Mrs. Claire!" and he was out in the hall. Just over an hour later, the car drew up alongside a small, detached, creeper-covered villa on the fringe of open country a bare mile out of Maidenhead.

* * * * *

He knocked three times before the door was opened, by an elderly woman who seemed rather in a fluster. She looked motherly and dependable; grey-haired, dumpy and ample bosomed. He noted the violet-coloured dress, the tidy hair, and the cameo brooch that had been put on slightly askew.

"Am I speaking to Mrs. Doran?"

"Yes... I'm Mrs. Doran."

"I rather wanted to see you about somethmg important. May I come in?" She hesitated. "I'm here really on behalf of Mrs. Peter Claire, who told me you were her old nurse."

There was an attempt at a smile, but the attempt ended badly. If anything she looked more nervous than ever as she drew back from the door and showed him into a typical best room.

"I've come at an awkward time," said Wharton apologetically. "You were just going to have your lunch."

"Oh, no! I've had it. I always have it early." Her voice was husky and mechanical.

"And a very good plan too. You're a widow, Mrs. Doran?"

"Yes. I lost my husband in the war."

He shook his head consolingly. "A terrible business that! And you're sure I'm no trouble to you? You weren't going out?"

"No... I wasn't going out... I never hardly go out."

"That's all right then." Most difficult sort of woman, thought Wharton. About as effusive as a mute—and a damnably suspicious look in her eye. However, perhaps she'd respond to different treatment. "I'm a policeman, Mrs. Doran; what they call a detective. Now don't get alarmed. I'm the most harmless man in the world—so my wife thinks! All I want to know is something that concerns Mrs. Claire—for her good. You see it's like this. A certain gentleman who died suddenly on Saturday night, is supposed to have seen Mrs. Claire before he died. Between you and me, I know he *couldn't* have done. And why? Because she was here with you!"

She nodded eagerly. "Oh, yes! Miss Dorothy was here! She came at ten o'clock and she'd have been earlier only the fog made her late, and she was here till Sunday evening, when it cleared."

The words came pat—too pat. A woman all nerves as she was, should have mentioned nothing but what was extorted, not have added information to information. Wharton frowned as he listened to the brief account that had obviously been rehearsed.

"At ten o'clock. Hm! And how did you know the time so exactly?"

"I looked at the clock in the kitchen when I put the cat's basket out and I said to myself, 'Miss Dorothy won't be coming now,' and I was just going to bed."

"And what was she like while she was here? Happy? And what you'd call in good spirits?"

"Oh yes, sir. She was always a jolly one—Miss Dorothy was."

"Quite so! And now just one little thing, Mrs. Doran. Saturday was remarkably foggy. How did Mrs. Claire get from the station?"

"The buses—they go right past. Look! There's one now!"

"So there is!... And does Mr. Claire ever come here?"

"Oh yes, sir! He called once, with Miss Dorothy, in the car."

"You known him long?"

"I knew him as a boy."

"Really!" He appeared for a moment or two to be thinking deeply, then suddenly looked up and caught her eye. "I can't understand it. An hour ago, Mrs. Claire told me she was sure she didn't leave town till past nine. How could she have got here by ten, in that fog? She'd go by Tube to Paddington, then have to catch a train, then get a bus." He shook his head perplexedly. "Of course you'd be prepared to swear to everything you've told me, in a court of law?"

"It's all true!"

"I see." He got as far as the door. "Just one other thing. Would you mind showing me the telegram you just received from Mrs. Claire?"

The question was out of the prepared and expected and her hand went instinctively to her bosom. She moistened her lips, looked at him, then let her eyes fall.

"Mrs. Claire sent you a telegram. She had to! She telephoned it to Maidenhead. You knew I was coming. You were actually dressing when I knocked at the door. May I see that telegram?"

She looked so genuinely frightened that he didn't press the point. But distasteful as it was, the job had to be finished.

"You think you'd rather keep it. Well, perhaps it's better. And one last word, Mrs. Doran; it's a hard thing to say, but you've told me neither the truth nor the whole truth—"

"But she *was* here at ten!"

"I know! I know! That's the vital point!" He nodded heavily. "Well, you must have it your own way. There'll be the Sunday papers, with her picture in them. All the story for everybody to gloat over. People saying horrible things."

She made no sign as she stood looking quietly at him. It was almost as if she didn't understand, and yet her bosom rose and fell more quickly.

"And her husband—she's probably fond of him, and he her—I wonder what he'll think of it. More scandal probably—and a divorce case. You never know what men are going to do."

At the door he turned for a final word.

"When Mrs. Claire sent you that telegram, she didn't realise that I'd know about it... and that I should be able to get a copy, if I considered it necessary, as I most decidedly do. I wonder what she'll say when she sees that telegram in my hand? When I go to her this afternoon—"

She came to life for the first time. The voice that had answered his questions so mechanically, suddenly became human. Her face was swept by overwhelming fear and terror. As she raised her hands, Wharton thought for a moment she was going to have a stroke—or go into wild hysteria.

"Oh, you mustn't! You mustn't!"

The features relaxed; the voice became pleading.

"Please don't worry her again!... She couldn't do any harm! She's a *good* girl!... Please don't!... Oh! you don't know!"

"What don't I know?" Wharton asked gently.

Her face coloured as she sank back in the chair. Her lips quivered—a pitiful sight for a woman as old, as respectful as that. Wharton came forward, shaking his head.

"There!... Don't distress yourself, Mrs. Doran.... Just tell me. What don't I know?"

She glared at him—a change so surprising that he drew back his hand sheepishly. Her voice shook with passion.

"Don't you dare worry that poor lamb!... She's not fit to be frightened! Don't you dare!"

Wharton had a sudden glimmer of understanding.

"You mean... she's going to—er—"

That broke her down. She fumbled in her bosom and with the handkerchief out came the telegram that fell unnoticed to the floor. When she looked up she could only nod the answer.

"Hm! I see." said Wharton, rather helplessly. "And how long has she known this?"

The answers now came between the sobs. "Only a few days... for sure.... That's why she... wanted to see... me."

"Did her husband know?"

"N-no... they quarrelled about something.... She was going to tell him... after she'd seen me."

Wharton left her there, sobbing quietly to herself, and made his way out to the car. But he didn't return to the post office. If he guessed correctly in five minutes that nurse would summon up the pluck to slip out and 'phone. Either Mrs. Claire would speak for herself or confess to her husband, and whichever it wasthat came to him, the information would be voluntary. Moreover, Wharton was worried about that intimate information he'd received. There were things in it he didn't understand and when the car swung into the main road, he gave the chauffeur new instructions. At two o'clock he was in his own house, having an unexpectedly good lunch—and putting certain vital questions to his wife.

CHAPTER XV
EXIT AN INVALID

IT WAS ABOUT eleven-thirty when Franklin knocked at the door of Hayles's flat in Curtal Square, St. John's Wood, and was admitted by an elongated landlady sort of person—the housekeeper almost certainly. He had taken the preliminary precaution of 'phoning up and asking if he might call, and before she could leave the small living-room into which she had shown him he managed to get in his questions.

"I expect you're the Mrs. Burgess who was good enough to speak to me over the 'phone on Sunday night."

She said she was, and seemed rather flattered at the small attention.

"It was very lucky you happened to be in. You see we wanted Mr. Hayles so badly—he was the only one who could give us any information. He'd only just gone out as I rang you up, hadn't he?"

"Only the very minute before!"

"Really! That was bad luck.... And he came in just on the stroke of four, didn't he?"

"I think it was about then."

"And I'll bet you wanted to make him some tea!" said Franklin archly.

She smiled. "I did—only he wouldn't wait for it. I remember now; just before four it was when he came in."

"Good! And you're sure Mrs. Hayles won't mind seeing me?"

Mrs. Hayles was a woman of a vastly different type; tiny, silver-haired, fragile as a January snowdrop and obviously as delightful. The white, lace cap made her age seem greater than it was, and her voice was placid and quaintly formal.

"You came to see how Mr. Hayles was, Mr. Franklin?"

"Yes," said Franklin. "I'm a friend of his. I don't know if he's mentioned me."

"That was very kind of you." She smiled gratefully. "Won't you sit down?... I'm sorry to say he isn't quite so well as we hoped; so restless and feverish—and he hasn't any temperature!"

Franklin nodded sympathetically. "It was a terrible shock. Rest—that's what he seems to want."

"Sh!" She put her fingers to her lips. "His bedroom is just through there and the walls are not very thick.... As you were saying, it's rest he wants.... And what a terrible thing it has been!"

"Too terrible for words. And apparently inexplicable."

"You mean they—the police—have *some* idea why it all happened?"

"Well, I wouldn't say that. I believe they hope to give an explanation... of sorts... in the near future," said Franklin lamely.

"Kenneth is always asking if there's any news." She shook her head sadly. "And it's so distressing for everybody. Mr. Claire must be worried to death."

"You know him very well?"

"Oh, yes! He and Kenneth... and poor Michael were boys together. They've all stayed with us at Ripley Norton, when Mr. Hayles was alive. He was vicar there, you know."

"Indeed!"

"And Mrs. Claire of course we know. How is she keeping?"

"Very upset, I believe."

"I was afraid so. Such a sweet little thing I always think."

"Isn't she!" said Franklin. "Now I come to remember, I understood from Mr. Claire that she was so frightfully cut up that he insisted on her going down to the country."

"Marfleet Parva?"

"Yes, that was it."

She sighed heavily. "I do wish Kenneth would forget all about it. He simply won't rest. He was just the same when he was a boy. Men never grow up, Mr. Franklin."

"Not to their mothers!" smiled Franklin. "But—er—does he have to be sat up with all night?"

"The doctor said not. But what can we do? Still, we manage very nicely. Annie—Mrs. Burgess—and I are going to take turns to have the bedroom next to his, so we'll be ready if he wants anything."

Franklin nodded. "That's just what I wanted to speak to you about," and he outlined the Usher proposition and the help he could be in scores of ways. "You'll both be worn out if you go on like that," he said severely. "Let me send Usher round at once."

But there were objections he hadn't thought about. A man in the house would have to be fed, whereas women could look after themselves and subsist on little. Also the flat was so small that three people would be tumbling over each other. And a final objection.

"You see I could have brought one of my own maids from Ripley, only I knew we could manage."

As she spoke, Franklin seemed to catch a sound in the bedroom. He listened. "Isn't that him moving?" She listened too. The sound, whatever it was, had stopped.

"I don't think so. He generally knocks when he wants anything.... He was asleep just before you came in." She laughed at the sudden thought. "So he actually doesn't know you're here!"

"Sleep's what he wants.... A pity you can't get him down to the country. Very charming round that way, I imagine."

"Ripley? Yes, it's still unspoiled. We're quite near to Wokingham, of course... but really delightful country. Kenneth spends nearly every week-end down there, when he's not too busy."

"Why don't you get him down there now?" asked Franklin. "It ought to put him on his legs in no time, getting out of doors for walks this frosty weather... and you to look after him." He smiled. "Do you know, the prospect almost makes me wish I had an illness—a very tiny one, of course—so that I could get down there myself!"

She began to smile, then couldn't resist the reproof. "We must all be thankful for the health we have given us." Then she rose. "Shall I see if he's still asleep?"

"I say, don't bother. I'll come round some other time when he knows I'm coming."

"I'll just give one little peep!" She smiled to him as she moved quietly out of the room. Franklin looked at his watch. Twenty minutes—and gone like five! Then he heard her voice in sudden alarm.

"Annie! Annie!... Come here, Annie!"

There was a scurry of the housekeeper's steps and the sound of quick voices. Then Mrs. Hayles came back to the room, all agitation.

"Oh, Mr. Franklin! He's gone! Whatever shall we do?"

Franklin sprang up. "Have you looked in all the rooms?"

Her face suddenly seemed very worn and helpless.

"Oh dear! I'm so frightened!"

Out on the landing the housekeeper was looking just as bewildered.

"What about his clothes?" asked Franklin. "See what's gone!"

He followed her into the bedroom and watched her search. The clothes he had last worn were gone, and his overcoat and a bowler hat. For a moment Franklin was puzzled; then had an idea.

"You'd better go and see how your mistress is. She looked to me as if she were going to faint."

So did the housekeeper for that matter. Franklin stood looking round the room, waiting for the sound of voices. Then he put his knee on the bed and leaned across. That bed—clothes still warm as he thrust his arm down—lay alongside the wall of the room in which he'd been talking. With his ear tight against it, he listened.

"He's only gone for a walk, ma'am. He'll be back again in a minute."

"Oh, Annie! You know how ill he was..."

He slipped quickly out of the room and taking his cue from the overheard conversation, added his assurances. Undoubtedly it was merely a walk. Mr. Hayles had suddenly felt better. He'd said nothing because he didn't want to alarm the women or hear their objections. Then another idea, which he was careful to camouflage.

"What about the doctor? When do you expect him?"

"He said about three, didn't he, Annie?"

"Then Mr. Hayles has probably gone round to see him himself! Shall I 'phone... or run round? I think I'll run round, if you give me the address."

Had the doctor been further away than the other side of Curtal Square, Franklin would have been too late. As it was, the conversation took place on the pavement by the side of the car. The doctor was decidedly perturbed. His patient had been in a highly strung condition; trembling, in fact, on the edge of a breakdown; all nerves and far too ill to be moved—at least for some days—or he'd have had him away to the country. What he feared now was loss of memory, or at the best some sort of panic, with the amnesia to follow.

"What's the best thing to do?" asked Franklin. "Those two women are nearly frightened out of their wits."

The other thought for a moment. "I think I'll slip round at once and talk to them."

"That's very good of you. And would you mind telling his mother that I'll be round later to see if there's any news."

Not that he was expecting any news. What was worrying him was what had been in Wharton's mind when he gave him that job of trying to plant Usher in the house. Extraordinary how the General would tell you so much and no more—till he made up his mind that the moment had come to let out another microscopic portion of news! Precautionary perhaps, but damn bad for results, that working for a man who merely let you catch glimpses of his mind. For instance, Usher had distinctly said that Hayles was suspicious of him—he was even positive about it—and yet Wharton was, as it were, deliberately irritating Hayles by what he couldn't fail to recognise as a barefaced attempt to have him spied on.

Still, that wasn't helping much at the moment. The thing was, where was Hayles likely to be? Suppose as soon as he heard through that flimsy wall a voice which he knew only too well, he stuck his ear against it, heart in his mouth and wondering just what was in the wind; then just what would he have heard? There'd have been the questioning of Mrs. Burgess, the announcement that the police hoped to have news; that Usher ought to be in the house... and that he (Hayles) ought to be got away to the country. Franklin grunted to himself. Suppose Hayles had really had a hand in those deaths at Regent View, what had his thoughts been like during the hours he had been lying in that bed? He must have been going through hell. There'd been the restlessness his mother had noticed; the waking up in the night and thinking about it all; the ever-present dread of the awful drop and the breaking neck; no wonder he'd panicked and taken to his heels! And where'd he gone? Surely to the place he'd heard suggested—his native village. If the panic and the illness both were faked, Ripley Norton would be a reasonable excuse if the law demanded one. In any case, Wharton had better be told at once. His idea had probably been that Hayles was curled up like a rat in a hole and that the presence of one man and the mention of another would be the pair of ferrets that would start him; and if so, Wharton wouldn't be surprised at the news and might even have laid his plans accordingly!

He looked at his watch. Better wait a little longer—say till two o'clock—to see if Hayles really did turn up again. Moreover, both Wharton and Norris would be away.

At the very end of his lunch, a newsboy came shouting along the pavement by the small restaurant where he sat over his coffee and he slipped out and bought a paper. There was the inquest—a verbatim report; everything smooth and according to the schedule Wharton had laid down. There were pictures that spoke of the enterprise of the press—crowds outside the court and—so abrupt as to be a shock—the face of France himself, with its gloriously alert and slightly supercilious expression. For the first time, Franklin felt a sudden surge of infinite pity. Life became for the moment a thing of unutterable sadness and a topsy-turvy business that led nowhere. There was France, with his happy-go-lucky acceptance of things and his cynical laugh that nobody could have taken seriously, and—strange shifting of thought—outside there that damnable mist that looked like becoming another fog. Then he caught the eye of the waitress, paid his bill and went round again to Curtal Square.

* * * * *

At the office he got going on some enlargements of Hayles's photos from *Two Years in the Ring*. Next he tried to get hold of Wharton and Norris, and finally, tired of his own introspective company, strolled along to the Financial Department.

"Hallo!" said Travers. "Come along in! Heard all about the inquest?"

"Only the report. Why? Did you go?"

"Managed to sneak in. Nothing particular—except the crowds. I couldn't help wondering what a hole-and-corner business it'd have been if it'd been only that poor old devil Somers."

"Human nature!" said Franklin laconically. "When's France's funeral? To-morrow?"

"I believe so. His uncle's former place, somewhere down in Berkshire. Probably be half London there. Still, there we are... as you say." He broke off abruptly. "How'd you get on with Hayles?"

"That's what I partly came along for," said Franklin; "to get it off my chest," and he gave an account of the morning's adventures. Travers had no advice to give and no solution to suggest.

"What I was wondering was this," said Franklin. "Should I send one of my own men down there—to that Ripley Norton place? It'd save time. You see, Wharton couldn't otherwise get anybody down there till to-night. The trouble is, it seems rather like butting in."

"Risk it! If I were Wharton, I should think you a most intelligent chap." He leaned forward with his elbows on the table and fumbled with his glasses. "Doesn't it strike you that Hayles is in a devilish awkward position and that this—er—breakdown has been rather in the nature of a godsend?"

"Rubbish!" said Franklin curtly. "He didn't make himself ill. You can't do a thing like that... at least, not without doping."

"I don't know. If you're ill to start with, you can let yourself go and make things much worse. But you haven't tackled the major proposition. He *is* in an awkward position. He's apparently the only one who knew all the circumstances and might have been in the house at the time you heard him. I should say that as soon as he heard you ask the housekeeper that question about when he came in on the Sunday, he shot out of that bed like a stoat."

"You're probably right there."

"I'd like to put something up to you." This very apologetically. "You and I were mentioning last night, the subject of psychology—the value of impressions or summing people up as we say. Let's have a look at something that might come under that heading—but which is a permanent and not a cursory impression, if there can be such a thing.... You've read that book —*Two Years in the Ring?*"

"Cover to cover."

"Then you know it's good—very good. Take some parts that are not directly connected with boxing—France's boyhood, for instance, his uncle, his mother and his holiday in Russia; all as interesting as a first-class thriller. Then the boxing chapters; really great as you'll agree. The way it gradually brings out his rise to recognition, his unorthodoxy in training, his dispensing with a manager and so on; all making for sympathy as it were. Then the fights; the sense of touch in the creation of atmosphere and suspense.... Still, there we are. I've praised it very lamely, but it's amazingly good. Don't you agree?"

"I do. It's absolutely great!"

Travers took off his glasses. "That's the very point. It *is* a fine book—and well written. Now who was responsible for all that? If two men ride on a horse, one has to go behind. You'd say, as I did, that France employed Hayles as his ghost; that France burbled and babbled while Hayles licked everything into shape... sort of gave it the local habitation and a name. As I said, that's what I took for granted—and that's the kind of obvious impression that might be loosely called psychology. Last night, all that occurred to me, and after you'd gone I made up my mind I'd have a look at those two novels Hayles had written, as I'd told Palmer to get 'em for me. And I had a go at 'em both. The idea was to see precisely how Hayles wrote by himself—to get his single value, as it were. We already have the double value in the partnership book *Two Years in the Ring*, and therefore if you subtract Hayles's single value from the double value, it must give you the single value of France. What happened? Well, there I have to go carefully, in case you should think me superior; however, there was something that rose up and smote me clean in the eye—as it will you, when you try it out."

Franklin smiled. "I rather gather that you didn't think a lot of 'em!"

"My dear fellow, they're the cheapest, crudest sensationalism I've ever been let in for—and I've had some bad luck in the old days on railway journeys. And there's something else that's intriguing—perhaps you'll pick it up as we go along. The first one is *The Madison Gardens Mystery*. Notice the name for a start. The title is a flimsy disguise for the famous boxing arena, and should have been *The Madison-Square Garden Mystery*. That's a clue to begin with. The book is naturally all about boxing. It's ill-written and obvious and it gave me the impression of clinging to France's skirts. It was written immediately after the partnership book, on the same subject, so as to catch the reflected glory, *only*—everything that's taken from *Two Years in the Ring* is not nearly so good, and what's new isn't worth tuppence. I happen to know it sold quite reasonably—and, as I said, owing to the circumstances and the title.

"But there's a more interesting proof. If the theory's right, then the further Hayles got from France, the worse efforts he produced. The second book —*The Fighting Chance*—has a misleading title, a catch-penny title if you like. It isn't about boxing. It's pure Hayles—and it's terrible stuff. It was badly reviewed and it sold as well as it deserved. In other words we've arrived at the value of France in the literary partnership." Franklin made a wry face. "You're trying to work out a jealousy motive for the killing of France? If so, remember that Hayles *didn't* kill him!"

"It's a good motive. And if he didn't kill him, at any rate you'll admit that somebody who might have been Hayles, tried to poison him... and got the wrong man!"

Franklin grunted. "Hm! And what about regarding France as a regular, up-to-date Admiral Crichton! Literary graces and all the tricks of the trade!"

Travers accepted the ironic challenge. "Why not? He did what he did because he *hadn't* any tricks. All he had was the knack of doing what all the big ones have—putting down simply and vividly what he felt. In any case, why regard the unusual as incomprehensible?"

Franklin said nothing.

"I hope it hasn't bored you too much," went on Travers, with no idea of irony. "It just happened to occur to me... that's all."

"It's sound enough reasoning," admitted Franklin. "The thing is, does it get us any farther?"

Travers smiled. "Why force me to platitudes? 'Every little helps,' and so on. But why not send your man down? Send Potter. He's a shrewd and tactful person."

"Doesn't seem reason enough for butting in," said Franklin. "Now if he could find out something about that poison which Wharton's keeping very quiet about, we'd be getting along. I don't think it was bought over the counter. No man'd be such a fool as to sign his name to that."

"There is a long shot Potter might try," said Travers. "What about the habits of the common wasp?"

"The common wasp! What the devil's that got to do with it?"

Travers told him.

CHAPTER XVI
MRS. CLAIRE TALKS

WHEN FRANKLIN GOT round to Regent View, he found Norris there.

"The General was worrying about you," he said. "He tried to get hold of you, but you'd started away. He's been suddenly called back to the Yard."

Franklin went over to the fire and warmed his hands. "How did he get on to-day?"

"Don't know a word," said Norris. "He hadn't been here a couple of ticks when he was rung up. How have you been doing? Hayles still alive?"

"That's more than I know," said Franklin, and told him what he knew. Norris looked alarmed till he heard that Potter was probably at Ripley Norton by that time.

"Tell you what I'll do," he said. "I'll speak to the General as soon as he gets in and ask him to ring you up. He's bound to be back soon. You've certainly done everything you possibly could."

"Right-ho!" said Franklin. "Then I'll be pushing off. How'd you get on yourself—at Royston?"

Norris tugged at his moustache. "Depends on how you look at it. From our point of view—not so well; from Claire's—very well indeed."

"His alibi was all right?"

"Beautiful. Leather bound and gilt edges. I saw that chap Utley; very nice fellow indeed—and keeps some damn good beer. I made out we had an idea that Somers had communicated with Claire—had to pitch him some yarn or other and we didn't want him communicating with Claire. However, he swallowed it all right. He said he had Claire under his eye from the time they left the club—and that'd be about seven-fifteen—till the time he went to bed, and that was well after midnight." He thought of something. "No, that's not quite right. He missed him for about five minutes, just before the train started at Liverpool Street. He rather thought he'd gone to telephone—and he thought he saw him coming out of one of those boxes. However, next morning they concluded the deal and as Claire said he wanted to get back to town, Utley said he'd drive him. It's only about an hour in the car and they thought it'd be as clear in town as it was down there. It wasn't so bad as it was later, but they had to crawl the last bit and finally Utley dropped him at Euston. He thought the time was about half-past twelve."

"Just what I was going to ask you," said Franklin. "Not that it makes any difference, provided he was in town during the afternoon." He looked rather questioningly at the other. "Do you know I've been wondering if we haven't made a mistake after all. Why shouldn't it have been Claire we heard in the house and not Hayles!"

"I don't mind telling you," confided Norris, "that I've been thinking the same thing myself. I'll tell you why. You see, my idea was this. As soon as Claire got out of that car, if he'd been mixed up with anything he'd want to see a paper to find out if anything had been discovered. Now the exact place Utley had dropped him was at the junction of the Euston and Tottenham Court Roads; so I asked the bloke who sells papers there, if he could tell me where to find the chap who had the Sunday pitch and he put me on to him on a day pitch at the corner of Gower Street. So I went along to see this chap and described Claire to him and, do you know, he recognised him like a shot!"

"Did he, by jove!"

"He thought the time was nearly one. And the first thing Claire said to him—that's what made this chap remember him was, 'Are these the ordinary Sunday papers? Got anything later?' or words to that effect. What d'you make of that!"

"Looks as if he was mighty anxious to know something! How many'd he buy?"

"A couple—low-brow ones. Reckon he had the rest at home."

Franklin grunted, then, "Let me see. Wasn't there something about France receiving a telephone message at about eight on the Saturday night? Any connection, do you think?"

"I was wondering about that myself," said Norris. Then he shook his head. "We'd never trace a call like that! You know what a place like the Paliceum's like on a Saturday night; telephone bells going all the time. For all we know, there might have been more than one from Liverpool Street. And they wouldn't know the words."

"Exactly! And you'd have only Claire's word for what was said. Not that that matters much—he couldn't have done anything. France was alive long after that call."

He moved off towards the door. "Then you'll tell the General as soon as he gets back."

"That's right. You get along home and have a meal in peace—and no tea with it!"

Franklin chuckled; then stopped suddenly. "By the way, I suppose you didn't make any inquiries at that Air Force Camp while you were down there?"

Norris shook his head. "Damn sight too difficult! Also, what was the use? Midnight's a good alibi... and you can add an hour to get to town."

* * * * *

What had happened to Wharton was that his hunch had come off. That sudden recall to the Yard announced that a lady wanted to see him and that she wouldn't come to Regent View but would wait for him there. A word to Norris and he was off. A minute or two at the Yard to see the room was suitably staged and the stenographer ready, and he pushed the bell.

There wasn't very much to be seen of Dorothy Claire's face as she entered the room. The toque hat was well over the ears, and the collar of the superb fur coat left the merest oval of nose and mouth. But the mouth wasn't smiling—and it wasn't petulant.

"Come along and sit down, Mrs. Claire," began Wharton briskly, and almost pushing her into the easy chair. Then he stoked up the moribund fire and, as he did so, noticed her eyes turned to the far corner.

"You mustn't mind that officer there. He's got a job to do... and he won't pay any attention to us. Won't you loosen your coat? You won't feel the benefit of it when you get outside." No sign of conversation forthcoming, he bustled back to his own chair—and waited.

As she loosened the collar of her coat he caught the faint smell of some subtle and attractive scent. And he noticed the heaviness of her eyes. There had certainly been more tears and no little amount of worry since he saw them last. Still, there was no emotion audible in the voice; merely perhaps a delicate suggestion of the pathetic—or was it regret?

"I've come to see you, Mr. Wharton, because... because I felt I was wrong this morning. I... ought to have told you the truth."

"It's the shortest way in the long run," said Wharton quietly. "I'm an old man, Mrs. Claire, but experience has taught me that you can't go very far wrong while you tell the truth—and the whole truth."

"You won't be angry about... what happened this morning?"

He waved his hand with a gesture of magnificent dismissal. "That's all over and done with. You found the truth a hard thing to face, so you..."

She gave a little smile at that, then bit her lip. "You'll believe what I tell you—now?"

Another magnificent gesture. "Provided you give me your word that it's the truth—and the whole truth—I'll most certainly believe you!"

She settled into her chair and let her hands fall to her lap. "What annoyed me this morning was that you were all wrong—"

"One moment!" smiled Wharton. "Don't let's hear about *me*. I *am* always wrong—where ladies are concerned. I admit that right away. Now will you start at the beginning and tell me everything that led up to last Friday night. Take your time and tell it in your own way."

"Well, it started over a night club where the police made a raid and Mrs. Carruthers, whom we know awfully well, was caught and her name was in the—er—papers, and I said—we were having dinner at the time"—she hesitated the least bit—"and Michael Franee was there, and my husband said how disgraceful it was and all that and—er—he got very annoyed!"

"And you disagreed!"

There was a flash of the old spirit. "Yes, I *did*. We both did. I said it was ridiculous and if I wanted to go to a night club, then I *should*. And then my husband said I was *quite* wrong about that and he was perfectly beastly over it! He said he *insisted* I shouldn't go to a place like that... and then Michael chipped in and said there were night clubs *and* night clubs and Peter—my husband—said he'd be the one to decide that, and then Mid— Michael said he was talking a lot of rot, and then... well, everybody started being very horrid."

"Exactly how horrid?"

"I... don't know. I got up and left the table. They were saying most unpleasant things to each other, and we—I mean Mr. Claire and I, haven't really spoken since... except when people were there and we had to."

"And that was how long ago?"

"Nearly a month."

Wharton smiled. "And everything's settled now? You're good friends again?"

She fumbled with her handkerchief and lowered her eyes. "No... not really."

Wharton heaved a sigh. "And then what happened?"

"Michael—Mr. France—told me there was a special show on at a night club—the *Dame Heureuse*—and he asked me if I'd like to go. He was very persuasive and I was... well, all furious with my husband, and I said I'd go like a shot... and then I wished I hadn't. You see... Michael did keep on about it and I was an awful coward and I wouldn't go back on what I'd said, and... and that's all that happened!"

Wharton left the desk and took a seat opposite her at the fire.

"All those preparations... that elaborate planning—were just to go to a night club!"

She looked at him for a moment, then her cheek flushed. "You mean... you still think—there was something else?"

Wharton's eyes caught hers—and held them.

"And was there... Mrs. Claire?"

She moistened her lips and he saw the warning signs in time to make a gesture of acceptance. "You tell me about it... in your own way."

She nodded angrily. "I *have* told you!" The outburst of temper went as quickly as it came. "Don't you see I'm telling you the truth? We knew Peter was going away for the week-end and I... I wanted to see my nurse. I do see her every year, so I was to pretend on the Saturday that I didn't know if I were going or not, and then I was to make up my mind, only instead of going, I was to... to go to the night club with Michael... from his house. I was to put on the frock I had in my bag—you know I *couldn't* have left my house with that on—and then we were going to the *Dame Heureuse*... and Michael said that afterwards we could go to a really nice place he knew where we could play roulette—for quite small stakes—and then we were coming back, frightfully late of course, and then Michael was to take me straight to Maidenhead in his car. You see, I told Mary all about it... in a letter!"

"And you did go round to his house?"

She bit her lip. The tears seemed very near. "Y-yes. I did go... but not... as you thought. You see, Michael did ring me up at my house earlier in the evening and he said I wasn't to go straight back there. I was to go to town and then cut back to Camden Town Station and he'd be there waiting for me and we could walk back... He said he didn't like me going about alone... in that fog."

Wharton believed it. Paradoxically, the very untruths he had heard the same morning, made him believe it. She was so utterly transparent. Each little inflection of the voice, each faint hesitation, each small insistence stood out like a direction post. Foolish perhaps, and obstinate, but just what that nurse of hers had said—straight in the big things and impulsive in the little. As for France's game, it was obvious; the return in the small hours, the excitement of the evening, the cups of tea... and the car that had gone astray in the fog!

"I see. Well, Mrs. Claire, I oughtn't to tell you so, but I believe you. But I've got to convince other people as well as myself.

Is there, for instance, any other information you can give me—
say about that night club?"

"I can't... Michael did everything. I left it all to him."

He made a mental note to see the manager of the *Dame Heureuse* that same night. He knew the place, and its conduct, pretty well—a little better perhaps than the average show but probably just as ready to evade the law. As for the private house where there'd be roulette, he paid little attention to that. Even if it existed, France would have made some excuse to get away early. The question at the moment was, would it be better to get at once to the climax before she lost what was, under the circumstances, a perfectly amazing fortitude, or approach it by such gradual steps that she'd reach it before she was aware? He decided on the latter.

"Well, we needn't worry about that... at the present. But, before you go, just a personal question or two—and, of course, confidential in every way. Tell me now; what was your precise opinion of... Michael France?"

"Well, he was... just what he was!"

"And that was what?"

"Well, he was... like somebody you'd been brought up with. I'd always known him... as I'd known my husband!"

"And, may I add, as you'd known Mr. Hayles?"

She smiled involuntarily. "Yes... and Kenneth Hayles. We were all together... all in the same county; the same dances and house parties..."

"*Only,* you happened to choose Mr. Claire!" added Wharton encouragingly. "Isn't that it?"

"Yes... perhaps it is."

"Just one other question between ourselves. What was Michael France's opinion of *you?* The same as yours about him?"

She looked up quickly, then her eyes fell again and she fumbled with the handkerchief.

"Just the same. I mean... they weren't any different."

"Quite so! And your husband; was he what you would call jealous?"

He read the answer, and in the same second the quick wonder how to avoid it. "Well, I don't know.... I don't think he ever had any reason to be jealous."

"Men are not reasonable creatures!" observed Wharton sententiously. "However, we'll leave that." His voice fell a pitch or two and became unconsciously dramatic. "Shall we go back to the time you left Camden Town. You were walking along by the side of the Park—in the fog... all yellow, choking; every step as if you were going into something unknown. And at last you got to the gate, and how pleased you were... and nervous. Then he opened the door and... then what?"

She went on, almost without a break, eyes looking into his, as if to avoid the sight of something she knew to be coming. "Then he undid the door and switched on the light and I came inside. He put the suitcase down on the table and began to look at the curtains and I remember I said how unnecessary it was to worry about the curtains with all that fog outside.... Then we went across to the fire and he turned it on... and he drew me up a chair."

The great thing was to keep her going. "Yes. What happened? What did you say, for instance?"

"He said, 'Isn't it fun! Just like playing at Indians!' and I said it *was* rather jolly, and then he said, 'Wait a minute! Something I've got to do!' and he went round the screen by the door and I heard him... I didn't hear him really—I was looking into the fire... and then I heard a shot and like something moving... and... oh! it was terrible!"

Her eyes filled with tears. Then she started to cry; quietly, like a child that sobs beneath the bedclothes. Wharton watched for a moment, then came over and patted her shoulder.

"Don't worry, Mrs. Claire. I know how you feel. I'm old enough to be your father... with daughters of my own.... Just tell me what happened. Ease your mind and don't keep it to yourself any longer!... You felt scared—frightened to death. You tried to call out."

"Y-yes."

"Then you plucked up courage and peeped round the screen and you couldn't see anything."

She looked up with eyes red and streaming. "Yes... I could see.... The lights were on.... I saw him lying on the floor and... the mark on his head. I didn't know what to do. It was... oh! it was horrible!"

It took another quarter of an hour to get the rest of the story, then Wharton made up his mind. He pushed the bell.

"Saunders! bring in some tea—for two!" and a whisper in his ear—"See the cups are clean!"

"I really couldn't—" she began.

"Now, ma'am, you allow me to have my own way," said Wharton oracularly. "A cup of tea never did anybody any harm." He gave his man a quick look. "Wilson, just hurry that tea along... and tell 'em not to sugar it!"

Between his scribblings, he spoke in his best paternal manner.

"I want to put two things up to you... that I want you to do... and both are going to need a lot of pluck.... And you *are* a plucky woman, Mrs. Claire."

She gave the ghost of a smile and shook her head.

"Well, I *know* you are... but not half so plucky as you're going to be!... I want you to come round with me to that house and show me just where... things happened. That won't take a minute and then you'll be finished with everything for good and all.... And then you must go to your husband and tell him just what you've told me. You promise that?"

It took her a good few minutes to decide. "That's right!" said Wharton benignantly. "You'll be laughing at yourself one of these days, when your husband has forgotten all about it. Ah! here's the tea!" He rubbed his hands as if it was the first cup for years, and himself the purveyor of some rare, incalculable delight. But he passed over to Wilson the pencilled slip.

i. 'Phone Norris, *urgent,* Regent View. Have lights on and fires going. Curtains drawn upstairs but *not* down.

ii. 'Phone Mr. Peter Claire to see me 7.00 p.m.*urgent,* at
    23, Regent View. If absent, have him informed.

After the tea there was another objection. Mrs. Claire had her car, and her husband might see it drawn up outside the house.

"We'll soon settle that, ma'am," Wharton assured her. "Leave your car here, and if you don't want it again you can 'phone your chauffeur here."

One other thing only, Wharton elicited during that ride to Regent View—what had happened on her return on the Sunday evening. In the entrance hall, she'd run full tilt into her husband, who told her she might be interested to know he'd bought those two yearlings off Utley. His manner was so friendly that she felt as if she wanted to cry—then he broke the news about Somers. After that she fainted; remembered coming round, and everybody very anxious, and then being almost hustled out of the house and down to Marfleet, where her husband said he'd be the following day. All that happened, however, on the Monday, was that he rang up early with the news of France.

As they drew in at the main gate of the house, the lighted windows of the ground floor looked cheerful in the November mist, and the sight of Norris and the fires, more reassuring still. Then in a very few seconds the ordeal became a painful one, and the business of reconstruction almost unbearable. Where Wharton had anticipated fifteen minutes, over an hour was necessary before he and Norris had any clear idea of what had happened. Moreover, the fact that Norris with bag and coat, acted the part of France, made the climax for her even more horrible than Wharton had contemplated.

The position of the body, on its back just clear of the chair; her approach—the chesterfield well back since it hadn't even been noticed; all that grizzly performance had to be gone through. And there'd been no sign of a pistol, though the lights were full on. Then she'd shaken him—told him to speak—then felt his head—and his heart—and almost fainted when she saw the tiny, red smear on her fingers; and all the time the house as still as death as she knelt there; no sound whatever after that first curious shuffle as if feet were moving rapidly over the floor. Then lastly Norris lying down and Wharton chalking an outline on the parquet flooring.

Wharton led her away to the dining-room. "There now! that's all over. You're a plucky woman, Mrs. Claire!"

She tried to smile but the effort was pathetic. Wharton got into his greatcoat and adjusted his muffler.

"Now we'll go along and hear what your husband has to say."

"Oh! but you're not—"

He smiled reassuringly. "Only as far as the house. You won't mind an old man like me going as far as that!"

He paused for a moment.

"When you got into that panic and seized your bag and ran out of the house, you're sure you didn't turn down the fire—and the lights?"

"I don't know.... Don't ask me any more... I'm very tired." Then at the door, a sudden recollection. "No... I remember now. I took the bag but I didn't... touch the fire... or the lights... I just ran."

And then again, just outside the door.

"I remember I shut the door ever so quietly.... It was just as if... as if somebody were looking at me!"

CHAPTER XVII
WHARTON IS ANNOYED

"WHAT'D YOU THINK about her, sir?" asked Norris. "Think she was telling the truth?"

Wharton glared. "Didn't you?"

The other saw which way the wind lay. "Looked like it to me, sir—though I didn't know anything about it, except what you've just told me."

Wharton nodded towards the dining-room. "Come along in and let's make a start on that reconstruction."

A detective must necessarily have a considerable deal of the histrionic in his make-up; all the same, an onlooker might have wondered at the antics and the absence of self-consciousness of two sober and reasonably mature citizens.

"We'll start from here," said Wharton, after the preliminaries. "I'm the murderer and you're coming round the screen. No! you be the murderer. Where are you going to be?"

"I'll try the chair, sir." He crouched behind it, and as the other approached sprang up with an imaginary pistol. Wharton ducked instinctively.

"Damn it! I can't get out of my head the idea that you're there. Try it again!" A little more successful this time but Wharton was even more dissatisfied. "Absolutely impossible! How could you shoot me through the left side of the forehead unless you're on my *left?* And you've got to get that pistol so close that it blackens the skin. What did they say? Six to eight inches, wasn't it?"

"Why shouldn't he have been coming between the chair and the chesterfield?"

"If he had, how could his feet have got there? Shoot me! Where do I fall?" He frowned and looked round. "That bullet got him ponk! like that. He couldn't have wriggled an inch. Very well then. I'll put my feet just in front of his. Now then; where are you?"

"Inside the last fold of the screen, sir."

"Right-ho! Get there then!"

Back went Wharton to the dining-room, then appeared round the screen. "No use! No use at all! You stick out as big as a house!" and he grunted.

"Couldn't we assumed the body didn't fall there naturally?" asked Norris. "I mean, why shouldn't the murderer have pushed it as it fell?"

"Then it must have fallen against the screen—or farther back in the room. The head went backwards. Very well then! Whoever pushed it must have been between the body and the door—and there isn't room!... Wait a minute though. What about that door—to the cloak-room?"

Both felt in the suggestion the approach of something strangely significant.

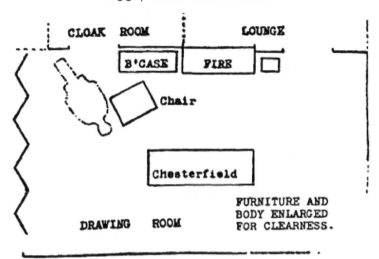

CLOAK ROOM   LOUNGE

B'CASE   FIRE

Chair

Chesterfield

FURNITURE AND
BODY ENLARGED
FOR CLEARNESS.

DRAWING   ROOM

"Try it!" said Wharton. "You get inside the door, with it just ajar. By the way, would she have noticed whether the door was open or not?" He shook his head. "I doubt it. Still, we'd better try that first. Open it the merest crack and I'll kneel here and have a look.... Hm! You try it!"

Wharton opened the door in his turn. The handle lever hampered him for a moment. "Why the devil do people have a craze for these new-fangled ideas? There's some sense about a knob!" He grunted again and opened the door a good three inches. "See anything?"

"I don't think I would, sir, unless I knew beforehand. That dull, black paint sort of mixes with the shadows."

"That's what I thought. Get inside... and open it just enough to keep your eyes on me."

As he came sauntering towards the cloak-room, his hand went out to the lever handle and his head turned instinctively to the right.

"Got you, sir!"

The General nodded. "Seems all right. You have a go at it!"

The second experiment seemed certain proof. In that cloak-room was undoubtedly where the man—or woman—had been hidden. Precisely why France had gone there couldn't be determined; indeed the cloakroom might have been a secondary thought, and the sight of its door have given him a new idea as he went along to the *lounge* to get something—perhaps the drink he never had!

But one other thing had to be tested—the falling of the body. Every available cushion was piled up for Norris to fall on and every trial showed the feet as too near the door.

"He hit the chair!" said Wharton. "That's what it was! It broke the fall and that's why there was only a small contusion at the back of the skull. As he hit the chair he'd be jerked sideways. Try it slowly, Norris!"

That seemed to be the solution, at least Wharton rubbed his hands and gave a sideways nod of satisfaction. And he produced his pipe.

"Put that chair on one side. There might be a blood spot or two on it—and on the floor. We'd better keep pretty clear of all this area."

"Just one thing, sir," said Norris. "What was that noise Mrs. Claire heard—like somebody moving?"

Wharton got the pipe going. "Probably the chair moving. It'd sort of ruck up the carpet when he hit it. I don't think it'd do more than that—it's too heavy. However, you try it, Norris, while I listen."

"Doesn't sound right," he said, coming back from the dining-room. "Mind you, she was in a state of tension as soon as that shot was fired." He thought for a moment. "Did the murderer come out and hunt for something in France's pockets? Was that what he was after?" Then he answered his own question. "No! damn it all, he daren't have done that! France had his dinner jacket and overcoat on. It'd have taken too long." He thought again. "Could he have gone to the lounge this way, and not through the cloakroom. Did she hear his feet scurrying past the fireplace here to get to the lounge?"

"Or to get up the stairs!"

"We'll try 'em both," said Wharton.

That took another ten minutes and both decided that with the speed necessary for a quick getaway, the feet would have made a clearly audible and identifiable sound. Moreover, the top of the stairs was visible from the dining-room over the top of the screen.

"Very well," said Wharton, "we'll leave it like that. He—or she—shot from the cloakroom and went out from there to the lounge direct and so out by the lounge window. The noise she heard was the moving of the chair and the body slithering off it—or both."

"But, excuse me, sir," put in Norris. "If he went out by the window, then he couldn't have fastened the catch—and it *was* fastened when Usher and Mr. Franklin came in on Sunday."

"As you say, *he* couldn't have shut it. I know that. It was the man they heard in the house who shut it. Therefore he knew it was open. Therefore he had something to do with the murder."

Norris opened his eyes. "But that cuts out Hayles and Claire!"

"Well, why not? You can't get away from facts."

"Yes, but there's something else, sir. We decided—or I thought we did—that the man who came in on Sunday did all that business of faking Somers's murder. If he faked France to look like a suicide as well, then he must have done it pretty quickly. And what about the woman in the bedroom?"

"Gawd knows!" said Wharton curtly. "Patience is what we want. Eliminate! Get rid of the rubbish—then concentrate! You want to concentrate too early." He warmed to his theme. "Let ideas float round in your mind—the more the better; otherwise you'll have nothing to test or eliminate. Somebody did all this. He isn't going into air. If we take our time we'll know who he is and when we want him he'll still be there." He regarded ruefully the pipe he'd been waving about and stamped out the sparks on the floor. "Our best clue is the one we haven't tried out yet! When we've—" He listened as a step was heard at the door. The bell rang.

"Sh! Claire! I'll let him in. You get in the background by the fire!"

Claire, in the thick blanket overcoat, looked beefier than ever, but if Franklin had been there he'd have noticed that much of that brutally healthy look had gone. As it was, Wharton noticed the dark under the eyes and the puffiness. Claire's voice, drawling and rather high pitched, sounded shrill and annoying in the immense room. His manner was just the least bit superior.

"Evenin', Wharton! They told me—er—you—er—wanted to see me about something."

"That's right!" snapped Wharton. "Come along in. Take a chair, Mr. Claire, will you."

Claire leaned well back in the chair and his eyes blinked under the light. Wharton made play with his notes and his glasses, then fired his question.

"Well, what have you got to tell us?"

"I! But I understood... that is—"

"Sorry!" said Wharton magisterially. "I can't help what you understood. I want you to make a statement. Begin where you like—*only* begin!"

"I see. May I ask—a statement about what?"

Wharton was beginning to lose patience. After the reaction from his experiences with Mrs. Claire, this cool assumption was the last thing he was inclined to tolerate. Moreover, the expression of the face, with its blond, close-clipped moustache, was putting his back up in quite an unreasonable way. Claire looked too comfortable; too well fed; too much on a tuppenny pedestal.

"A statement about what!" He laughed. "Mr. Claire, I admire your innocence! Well, shall we say, about Usher. Why you planted him here—in this house."

Claire, for a moment, looked decidedly less complacent. He resorted to a mild sort of bluster.

"Surely you don't intend to... to butt in on my private affairs!"

Wharton put down his pencil and made a wry face. "Look here, Mr. Claire; we'd better get this thing straight. You have two chances. One is to tell me here and now, everything you know. The other... to be taken elsewhere—"

"But you can't do that!"

"Can't I?" The General got to his feet. "You refuse to speak? Very well then"—and he looked round at Norris.

Claire raised his hand. "Just a moment, Superintendent! Perhaps I shouldn't have said that. You want to know about... Usher."

Wharton sat down glowering. "Why did you put him in this house? To spy on France and your wife—wasn't that it?"

"Well, not exactly. I thought... I had good reason to think that France was going beyond—er—what I might call the very wide license he had with my wife."

"But you suspected her too?"

Claire thrust out his chin. "You be damn careful what you start insinuating! It was to protect my wife... *against* France; that's why I had him here."

"Precisely what I say. You didn't trust your wife!"

Claire's eyes narrowed. Norris, glancing round, thought there was going to be a scene.

"If you like to put it that way—yes! I wouldn't trust any woman where Michael France was concerned." He stammered out something as if finding it difficult to express himself, then, "What you don't see is, that as soon as he started his tricks with my wife I determined to step in."

"Why didn't you speak to France direct? He was a friend of yours. He was more than a friend—ostensibly."

"Why didn't I? That's my business. You wouldn't understand in any case... I knew *she* was all right... that is to say, I knew she wouldn't go wrong. I knew it when Usher rang me up on Friday."

"How'd you know it?"

"I guessed it was that night club business... that's why I called him off. I decided to chuck the whole thing—very liable to be misinterpreted, as you see—and I did call him off and, as far as I was concerned, that was the end of it."

"And you spoke to your wife?"

"Why should I? There was nothing to it. I thought I'd let her have her fling, then talk afterwards. As a matter of fact, since you *must* know, I'd decided to thrash the whole thing out with

France on Monday. That's why I stayed in town. You don't think I spend my Sundays—er—mooning about alone, do you?"

"I see." Wharton nodded to himself once or twice. "As you say, most of that's your own business. However, you've put yourself in a hole of your own making and whether we can save you any inconvenience, entirely depends on yourself. We know your movements, over the week-end—as we do those of everybody even remotely connected with the case—but we want your own statement about one or two things. What did you do, for instance, after Captain Utley dropped you at Euston?"

"If it interests you, I came direct to my house by underground."

"And the time you got in?"

"Can't say. Wish I could! My butler probably knows the time, and Utley might know when I left him."

"What did you do the rest of the day?"

"Oh—er—just loafed round. I shouldn't have been there at all if I hadn't expected the chance of seeing France. However, my butler knows what I did. He fed me... and so on."

"Quite so!" He blew his nose unnecessarily. "Your alibi—I'm glad to say—is perfect; and that's a good thing considering the grudge you had against him. However, you're out of it.... Know anybody who might have killed him?"

Claire shook his head. "Not a soul."

"Hm! You showed no surprise at my statement that he *was* killed. How'd you know he was killed?"

Claire's eyes narrowed. "What's the idea? Trying to catch me out?"

Wharton waved a deprecating hand. "Not at all!"

"Everybody says he was killed. He couldn't have killed himself. Why should he?"

"I don't know," retorted Wharton innocently. "All I know is that I made a misstatement which you accepted for gospel. *Who* exactly says he was killed?"

"All the papers hint at it. People at the club all talk about it, and other men tell me the same thing. You see they talk to me because I'm expected to know."

"Exactly! And the best thing you can tell 'em, is that you *don't* know. You can take it from me, Mr. Claire, that whatever I may have said, we hint at nothing of the sort. Michael France committed suicide. Is that clear?"

Claire shrugged his shoulders offensively. "If that goes with you, it goes with me."

Wharton nodded. "One other thing. I may have to question your butler—entirely your own fault, by the way. I shall do that myself—as discreetly as I can. That, I hope, will be the full extent to which we shall worry you.... Oh, yes! Just one little thing. Did you happen to telephone to France on the Saturday night, from Liverpool Street?"

"Good lord, no!"

"Did you telephone at all?"

"I wanted to." He laughed. "I left rather a good pair of gloves on the porter's seat as I left the club. Only I couldn't get through in time."

"Exactly!" He shuffled the papers as if the business were at an end. Claire made as if to rise. "One tiny point, and we're finished. Mr. Hayles is, as you know, unwell, and we can't question him at all. Tell me, why exactly did he have to go to Martlesham?"

Claire frowned. "He was seeing the vendors over the purchase—my own purchase really—of the cottage adjoining Low Farm. We wanted it for extra quarters; rather a bit cramped as things were."

Wharton rose. "Thank you, Mr. Claire. We're very grateful to you for your help—"

Claire's eyes narrowed again. "Don't I have to put my signature to all—er—all this confession... and so on?"

"Confession!" Wharton appeared tickled to death. "My dear sir! This is only a friendly chat. You'd know the difference if it weren't!" He changed the subject with extreme agility. "I suppose you're going to the funeral to-morrow?"

"Naturally!"

"Of course," added Wharton lamely. "Well, that is all, Mr. Claire. If your butler is questioned it'll be more painless than the dentist's. He won't know the tooth's out."

But at the door he had to impart his little homily. "You'll think me rude—and perhaps I am, but I can't help it. Your wife made a certain—intimate confession to you to-night?"

"Possibly!"

"Go gently with her, Mr. Claire. I'm an older man than you and that's why I take this liberty. She's had a terrible shock—her own fault perhaps, but there we are. She's a fine woman that... and a loyal one!... Good night!... *Good* night!"

He watched the departing figure to the turn in the road, then shut the door. The glare he gave Norris made that gentleman think he must have put his foot in it.

"Did you hear how he spoke? 'Evenin', Wharton!' As if I was a bloody footman!" He glared again. "What'd you think of him?"

"Not much, sir. I wouldn't have minded putting my foot into his stern."

Wharton was mollified—then decided to be generous. "Mind you, Norris, we mustn't be prejudiced. He knew he was going to cut a pretty poor figure so he had to brazen it out with that God Almighty air of his. Only he's lying! Mrs. Claire promised me she wouldn't say she heard a shot—only that she found him dead—and that's a subtle difference. Also when I asked him how he knew that France was killed, you noticed that he didn't say, 'My wife told me,' as he'd have had a perfect right to do.... And he's a liar on another count. He couldn't have guessed from that telephone message of Usher's on the Friday that it was about a night club. Even Usher didn't guess that—and it bamboozled *me!* And if he wanted to get annoyed about anything, why wasn't it when I deliberately ticked him off—and asked him those alibi questions?"

"You remember Mr. Franklin said the same thing, sir—how it struck both him and Mr. Travers that Claire *wanted* his alibi inquired into... and that means there's something wrong with it, sir... and there isn't!"

Wharton went off at a tangent. "We'll never prove he was the man in the house here. No one can prove how long he took over that journey from Euston. *He* wasn't, in any case, the man Franklin heard in the house. He's invited us to ask his butler about that, and he daren't risk it if there was any flaw.... However, let's go on with those experiments."

The object of the new inquiry was soon apparent. Precisely how long had it taken to do *all* the camouflaging necessary to conceal *both*murders? Norris, as the more active of the two, tried it out. Wharton was lifted, carried into the bedroom and suitably arranged. The decanter used by Somers was washed out, the sink doped with the chloride, and the drain flushed. Then the decanter was refilled with whisky, the poison bottle placed and the window catch fastened. Everything took under ten minutes. Let five more be allowed for things which might have had to be done but were not apparent at the moment, and that gave fifteen minutes as a basis.

Wharton rubbed his hands. "Looks as if Hayles could have done the whole lot while he was here. *But*"—the General looked really pleased with himself—"now for *the* clue. Franklin was absent forty minutes from house and grounds, therefore, if the murderer had been watching him, he had forty minutes available. But he didn't *need* forty minutes—he needed fifteen—and therefore he didn't watch him! But the murderer was in the house when Franklin returned, and as he needed only fifteen minutes, and as he hadn't finished, he hadn't been there for fifteen minutes. That fits Hayles to a second."

"You say he hadn't finished, sir. Hadn't finished what?"

"What he had to do," said Wharton. "He hadn't had time to think of that murder confession, or if he thought of it, he hadn't time to find it and put it where it ought to have been found—by France's body—upstairs!"

"That's right enough, sir."

"Not only that. He didn't move France's body at all! If he had, he'd have thought of the confession the very first thing instead of leaving it to the last! However, we'll try to prove that in another way—by the clue."

Norris still couldn't see it. "What clue's that, sir?"

Wharton preferred to be mysterious. "Did Usher leave a tray out for us?"

"Yes, sir—in the kitchen."

"Then bring it to the lounge. And you'd better make a pot of tea to go with it. First of all I'll put out this fire. Open the windows and leave the front door ajar. Let the air blow through the room!"

He fussed round while that was done, then pulled out his watch.

"You bring that supper to the lounge. I'll try to get Franklin and tell him I'll be round in an hour."

During that small meal, he left the subject of the case absolutely alone. Norris went out and got a couple of evening papers and they read them over their pipes. Finally the general looked at his watch.

"Forty minutes since we put the dining-room fire out. It's a cold night—quite as cold as it was on Sunday afternoon. Come along to the dining-room.... Now then, do you feel the room to be what Franklin described as 'icily cold'?"

"It isn't all that cold," said Norris.

"That isn't the point. Is it cold or not?"

"Well, it isn't cold, sir. You'd know the fire had been on."

"That's the clue!" exclaimed Wharton triumphantly. "Mrs. Claire left the fire on. If nobody had been in the house till fifteen minutes—or even forty minutes—before Franklin entered it, Franklin wouldn't have noticed any clamminess. The fire must have been put out earlier in the day! Therefore there were *two* entrances made—one before half past two when Franklin first came and the other after three when he went away!"

"Yes, sir; but couldn't this man have been lying doggo all the time till Mr. Franklin went away, and have been the same man he heard when he came back?"

Wharton shook his head. "As soon as Franklin finished knocking at two-thirty, he'd have assumed he'd gone away and he'd have started to move about again. But Franklin hadn't gone! *He sat on the step with his ear virtually against the door.* He'd have heard the least sound." He pushed his pipe almost into the other's eye. "I tell you there were *two* entrances made—and by two different people—or my name's not Wharton. You and I were testing two processes done by the same person at one time. What happened was two processes done by two independent people at two different times."

"If I understand you correctly, sir," said Norris, "what happened is this. Sometime early on the Sunday—or it might have been late on the Saturday—somebody came in and camouflaged France's body, and turned out the lights and fire. Then on the Sunday afternoon, while Mr. Franklin was marking time, somebody else entered—"

"*Not* while he was marking time! After Somers entered—and that wasn't before half-past three."

"Quite so, sir! After Somers came back, this other party entered and camouflaged his body and it was him Mr. Franklin heard in the house."

"That's it! Take the first man as X. He might have been Claire, entering on his way from Euston to his house. Call the second Y. That might have been Hayles—entering after his arrival at St. John's Wood. That's where we might start to concentrate—on the problem of X and Y." He glanced at his watch. "Gone half-past nine. Franklin wasn't in but I left word I'd be round. When's Usher due in?"

"I told him ten, sir—and to get some supper out."

"Right! Keep his hoofs off that space round the door there. I'll send round for that chair—and I'll have Pryor come himself and look at the floor. You get on with Hayles's workroom and I'll make a start on Mrs. Claire's times to Maidenhead…. And I must see the people at the *Dame Heureuse* to-night. Think of anything else?"

"Did you think of sending a man of our own down to … that village where Hayles might have gone?"

"Potter's a good man. He'll do till I've talked it over with Franklin."

"Then is it any use going through the list of window-cutting specialists? It might have been a pro."

"Don't you believe it! No pro would have shot France for fun. It isn't as if there was a struggle. And there wasn't a thing touched. However"—and the General got on his greatcoat and muffler and stamped off.

But what he was thinking of as the car moved along to St. Martin's Chambers, was not that elimination on the value of which he had so much insisted to Norris—or even the fact that, but for Lucy Oliver, precious little *had* been eliminated. What was worrying the General was two things that up to then had scarce been mentioned—the confession in France's writing, under the body of Somers; and the long, silky hairs on the settee in France's bedroom.

CHAPTER XVIII
POTTER STRIKES OIL

HAD POTTER BEEN a golfer, his description of his day's doings might reasonably have been "a perfect round"; every drive clean away, approaches bang up and putts well in—until perhaps at the eighteenth. He started off well by getting clear of town in his little two-seater before the dusk ended, and Ripley Norton was reached by teatime. At the "Hound and Huntsman" he ventured on his first question—to the ostler.

"I suppose you haven't seen anything of Mr. Kenneth Hayles this afternoon?"

To his enormous surprise the answer was in the affirmative. The chase, in other words, seemed to be over.

"Yes, sir. He came along past here about an hour ago."

"Good!" said Potter. "Where's he live?"

Ten minutes later he drew in the car alongside a trimmed thorn hedge that fronted a rambling, white-walled house whose white gate was plain in the darkness. Moreover, a few yards ahead at the end of a paved path, a light showed clearly in a downstairs room. Potter knocked.

The light went out as though his knock had been a conjuror's pistol shot; there was a sound of shuffling and finally the door was opened by a middle-aged woman in what might be called "civilian" costume. She put out her head like a hen from a coop and said nothing.

"Is Mr. Hayles in?"

"No, he isn't. He's away."

"But I just inquired at the 'Hound and Huntsman' and they told me he was in the village this afternoon!"

"They must have made a mistake. He's in London... he's very ill."

"Curious!" said Potter. "Might I come in for a minute? You see, I've come down for Mrs. Hayles. Mr. Hayles got a bit light-headed this morning and got away from the house and nobody knows where he is. We thought he might have come here."

She waited for a moment or two, making up her mind apparently whether or not Potter was a specious and dangerous character, then, "Would you come round to the back door?"

Potter moved off gingerly as directed. Through the side gate was a kitchen garden with fruit trees that came as far as the door itself. In the large kitchen was a fire and a light, and a girl of under twenty was laying a cloth. A quarter of an hour later he was joining them at tea and, thanks to a homely recital of his private affairs, was hearing those of his fellow feeders, and the Hayles family in particular.

Mrs. Burgess, he learned for instance, was an old family servant. Mrs. Hayles was a good mistress and had the money. Mr. Hayles was regarded as delicate. He had definitely not been there that afternoon—the light Potter had seen was that of the housekeeper "getting something." Moreover, he heard news of the rest of the triumvirate. Peter Claire had strains of the stand-offish and the cruel in him. As a boy he'd been inclined to give himself airs and once he'd tied together a cat and dog by the tail, with horrible results. He was described as rolling in money. Michael France had been of the mischievous, lovable, forgivable type—with a tongue like July butter.

Potter prepared for his long shot. He waved to the window. "I see you've got some nice young fruit trees out there. My sister usually sends me some fruit from the country every year, only she couldn't this year. The wasps got most of it."

"We had a big nest up the garden, didn't we, Florrie?" said the younger Mabel.

The older woman nodded. "I hate the beastly things all over the place! Can't keep 'em off the food, and every minute I think I'm going to get stung."

"What's the best way of getting rid of the nests?" asked Potter.

"I don't know what they do. Young—the keeper here—he kills off all the nests. Mr. Kenneth spoke to him about ours. Some kind of poison, wasn't it, Mabel?"

"I don't like poison," said Potter with a shudder. "Always reminds me of weedkiller." He explained the mystery. "You see, my wife might get tired of me one of these days!"

She gave him a waggish look, then side-tracked to the latest arsenic *cause célèbre*. Five minutes of that and Potter rose to go.

"I suppose Mr. Hayles wasn't here last week-end?"

"Oh, no! When was he down, Mabel? Week-end before last; that was it."

A final giving of instructions and he was off again. Not far down the road, he asked a passer-by where Young the keeper lived and found he was close by his cottage. Furthermore he was in—and alone.

"I suppose you haven't seen anything of Mr. Hayles?" began Potter.

The other apparently misunderstood the question, but the answer was electrifying.

"Oh, yes! He came round all right." A pause while he examined the stranger. "Was it you he wanted it for sir?"

"I expect so," said Potter, sparring for time. "When did he come?"

"It'd be about half after four."

Potter made a gesture of annoyance. "Then I just missed him!" He clicked his tongue and racked his brains for a further opening. "May I come in a second? Thank you... I'm a friend of his—as you probably gathered.... What did he tell you exactly?"

"He just said he wanted a little more of the poison... for a friend to kill a dog with, so I give him enough for a dose."

"That's right.... What did you give him? The cyanide?"

"That other ain't much good.... Only don't you go saying anything, sir, or you'll get me into trouble. I ain't supposed to let any of that stuff out of my hands—or the rat poison neither—only I obliged Mr. Hayles once afore."

Potter nodded, then produced a shilling.

"Which way did he go when he left you?"

"Turnpike way, sir. You might of met him if you come that way."

"I came the other way," explained Potter. "Oh! and by the way, Mr. Hayles was rather queer when I saw him this morning and the doctor said he wasn't to go out—that's why I came round myself." He shook his head. "I can't understand him coming out a night like this. Did he look ill when you saw him?"

"Well, I can't say I noticed anything, sir. He was in a rare hurry—and a bit fussy, but that's his usual way, sir, as you know."

Another question or two and Potter was off again. Not far down the lane was the main road where Hayles might have caught a bus for Reading. In any case, Franklin's instructions had been that if he weren't at Ripley Norton, he was to push on to Marfleet Parva. But why Hayles had wanted that poison Potter didn't know. All the orders he'd had were to find out if he'd had a chance to get any, and—something he'd been unable to do—to discover if a bottle were missing from his mother's house. But Hayles had had poison from Young the previous week-end, on the plea of doing in a dangerous cat. Was the excuse genuine? The season for wasps was over and some sort of excuse had to be made, and as for the excuse given that day, it'd been that a friend wanted some to destroy a dog that was old and blind.

The moon was now up, and with an eye for the speedometer and then another for direction posts, he drove steadily along the frosty road with the sky above a mass of stars. Young's nine miles proved correct; more difficult was the finding of the private road to Marfleet Hall. As he drew in at the porticoed entrance he looked at the dashboard clock—7.15. If by a lucky chance Hayles had come there, he ought to be well on his heels.

"Mrs. Claire in?" he asked the footman.

"No, sir; she's in town. We expect her back at any moment."

"Mr. Claire in?"

"He's in town, too, sir. We expect him to-morrow, sir."

"What about the butler? Could I see him for a moment?"

"He's at the town house, sir."

"Hm!" said Potter. "Perhaps you could help me. Has Mr. Kenneth Hayles been here this evening by any chance?"

The footman's face took on an expression which was either interest or relief. "He called this evening, sir. He hasn't been gone very long."

Thereupon Potter introduced himself formally as the confidential emissary of Mrs. Hayles, and asked for details. They proved, as far as Potter was concerned, thrilling enough but utterly incomprehensible. Mr. Hayles had called at about 5.30, and on being admitted, seemed very odd and excited in his manner. He asked to see Mrs. Claire and on being told she might be late, said he'd wait in the drawing-room and there the footman brought him some tea. Some of this he drank but the cake was left untouched. He then rang and asked for a very small bottle with a cork in it, and this was brought from the kitchen. A minute or two later he rang again and said he wouldn't wait after all—he'd leave a note for Mrs. Claire. He then shoo'd the footman out and rang again a few minutes later, in order apparently to hand over a note concerning which he gave the most careful instructions. It was to be handed to Mrs. Claire, when she was alone, and to nobody else; and it wasn't to leave the footman's hands before then.

"He gave me half a crown, sir," said the footman, "and then what do you think he did, sir? He shook hands with me! Gripped my hand, like that! And he didn't say a word! I helped him on with his coat, just here where we're standing, sir, and I'm blowed if he didn't shake hands with me all over again! And he was crying—tears all running down his face!"

"Good Lord! What for?"

"Don't ask me, sir—unless it was the thought of Mr. France's funeral to-morrow."

Potter nodded knowingly. "Might be that. And you said he was odd in his manner. Just how?"

"Well, sir, he kept muttering to himself and acting sort of queer, as if he was the worse for drink; only he wasn't that, sir—or he didn't smell like it."

"Which way did he go?"

"Along the track road, sir."

"The track road! What's that?"

The footman led the way out to the porch. The moon was now clear of the trees and in the clear, frosty night a ribbon of pale road could be seen merging into the black of the far plantations. That was the track road, a private drive leading to the stretches of levels on the open park where Claire opened out his racing cars. From it a path led to the main road, on the London side, just short of where the Marfleet road branched from the main turnpike.

Potter couldn't make much of it. His first thought had naturally been that Hayles had put the cyanide crystals into the small bottle and had then filled it with hot water; the intent being to commit suicide away from the house, though why a man should come all that way to do himself in, Potter couldn't fathom. But that note with the secret terms of delivery, the lugubrious farewell of the footman, and the unstrung condition of Hayles generally, all pointed in that direction. But why had he gone off down that track road unless he wanted a short cut to the turnpike; in other words, to get back to London as soon as possible? And if so, he wanted the poison for purposes of murder, not suicide! Then another thought. Was Hayles going off to commit suicide—crawling away like a sick animal—to die in a corner? Or was the whole thing the result of a nervous breakdown? Was Hayles performing a series of strange actions, not knowing himself what they signified? In that case the note to Mrs. Claire would be the deciding thing—whether, for instance, it were coherent or gibberish.

"Look here!" said Potter, making up his mind. "As I told you, I was sent down here on behalf of Mrs. Hayles by Mr. Franklin, who's a personal friend of Mr. Claire. I'd better let him know what's happened straight away. Where's your 'phone?"

He tried unsuccessfully to get Franklin at his flat; then told house exchange to take a message for the hall porter. As a further precaution he got through to Durango House and left instructions there. By that time it was eight o'clock.

"I shall have to stop here till somebody turns up," he told the footman. "I think I'll have a walk down that road in case he's still wandering about—lost his memory or something."

The long, cross tracks, when he got to them, were as interesting as railway lines, and about as informative, and having gone half a mile along one and back on another, he had seen all he wanted. Another track, a rougher, unmetalled one, looked more inviting as it led away between the woods through a private gate. A few yards of straight track, a downward turn and he was on the edge of a great pool of water, acres and acres by the look of it, tree-fringed and gloomy at the banks, but out beyond the shadows silvery gray with the reflections of the moon. As the frosty air met him, he shuddered. A hell of a night that, to commit suicide by drowning! Then when he came to wonder why that thought had come to him, he didn't know. In the case of Hayles, with that small bottle of poison in his possession, the thought was utterly preposterous.

Then along the path that skirted the lake, he saw with the moonlight full on it, what was evidently a boathouse. He hunched his shoulders and trudged on. A mere trickle of a stream to jump over and he was on a raised platform that led to the boathouse side where wooden steps went down to the water. On that platform, by the steps, lay a newspaper, folded once, and on it a bowler hat! He picked it up carefully and flashed his torch. The hat showed no name or the shop that had sold it. But the paper, spread out as if to make a dry place for the hat, was a London *Evening Record*, 6.30 edition of that day's date and therefore purchased by Hayles on his way down, and after 3.30. Then he tried the hat on his own head; very small—probably a seven or less, and quite likely to be owned by a man of the physique the guv'nor had indicated to him.

He looked away to the indeterminate distance of the far shore, then back at the boathouse. Then an idea! At the bottom of the steps by the low, gable roof a flash of the torch showed two boats moving gently in the water; but the *third,* the one that ought to have been occupying the vacant space nearest the steps had gone, and on the mooring ring its rope was still hanging!

He flashed the torch round again and this time found a boat-hook in its slot under the eaves—the very thing for testing the depth of the water. But when he thrust it down all round the boathouse, the depth was nowhere more than three foot, and that slanting! Then if Hayles had drowned himself, it had been out in the lake, from the missing boat; and if so the boat would by then have come ashore. Where was the wind? Due north, behind the boathouse.

Five minutes later, he found what he was looking for—the boat sideways to a shelving bank of gravel under a thicket of young willows. It looked immovable and good for the night, and in any case Potter knew better than to run the risk of undue interference. There'd be the risk, of course, of the wind's freshening and shifting, but he chanced that and left it there, oarless and empty as far as he could see.

Back at the Hall, the footman had a message from Mrs. Claire which made things more difficult. She would not be returning that night. And that was the seventeenth hole of Potter's perfect round. In the smoking-room with a whisky and soda and a plate of cold beef, he began his wait for the men higher up—a wait that was to be well over two hours.

CHAPTER XIX
AND STILL MORE LADIES

IT WAS EIGHT O CLOCK the following morning when Wharton and Franklin returned to Marfleet Hall, to see by daylight what Potter had made out in the less revealing moonlight. Potter had spent the night with them at Reading, and even after a night's sleep on his story, Wharton refused to commit himself to a definite statement of opinion. Hayles might have panicked himself into suicide—and then again he might not.

The ground was hard with frost till they reached the cutting between the woods. From there to the boathouse, the trees had kept off most of the wind and that was distinctly unfortunate as far as the boathouse platform was concerned. No sign of a footprint, even Potter's, was visible in the hoarfrost which didn't exist. However, Wharton had a good look round, noted the position occupied by the folded newspaper, then turned his back on the boathouse.

"Show us where the boat is, Potter, please."

The three of them moved with care down the gravelly bank. A few feet away, Wharton went on alone to examine the ground. Then he shook his head and motioned them forward.

"There aren't any footprints—and there ought to be!"

"Potter's?"

Wharton shook his head again. "You didn't come so far, did you, Potter?... I thought not. What we ought to see are Hayles's footmarks—as we should have done if it hadn't been for this shingly gravel."

Franklin looked surprised.

"You see those patent rowlocks? Whoever took the boat out must have had the oars in them or he'd have had no fulcrum for leverage. Only, once the oars were in, they couldn't *slip* out. And if they didn't slip out, then the boat couldn't have drifted dead straight with the wind. Look at that long stretch of weeds between here and the boathouse—regular semicircle of 'em, all round the middle. Now you see the point. If the oars didn't slip out, they were lifted out; probably just before the boat came ashore. Where are they, Potter? Pretty close?"

"I didn't see 'em, sir. It was too dark for that."

"Never mind! You go that way, and you try that, John. Look well under the bushes."

In five minutes both were found, one on each side of the boat; Potter's six foot beyond the bank and Franklin's rather more—but with a damning piece of evidence. The blade of the oar rested clear of the water on the stout twig of a submerged branch!

"There you are!" said Wharton triumphantly. "They were taken out after the boat had grounded. He slewed her round and threw back the oars at convenient places. Both blades outwards?... I thought so! That's the natural way to throw an oar—by the shaft, if that's what they call it. Only, unfortunately for him, one rested on that branch; the water couldn't have lapped it there."

He gave a quick look round. "Mind you, I don't see the point of going over all this for footprints. We don't know the exact boots he was wearing—and they wouldn't add to the story if we did. We'll haul the boat up the bank and when we get back, find out if it was really fastened in that boathouse yesterday afternoon."

He set off again for the road as if the whole episode had been forgotten. "Funny, leaving that hat!" he said. "And all nicely on the paper! Still, we're told to expect eccentricities from suicides. Wonder if it *was* his hat. And will his mother know?"

"When are they 'phoning you up?"

"I told them, at once. And not to scare his mother—poor old soul!" He stopped short in his tracks. "Curious sort of idea I had running through my head after breakfast this morning. Jacob and Joseph, wasn't it? 'Tell me whether this be thy son's coat or no.'" He tossed his head and moved on again. "Still, hats are different."

"What on earth was he doing with that poison?" asked Franklin. "Trying to obscure the trail?"

"I've got an idea," said Wharton. "So have you, probably; but whether it's worth anything is quite a different matter. I should say he panicked badly as soon as he heard your voice in the flat. He'd worked himself up to such a pitch that he imagined we were on his heels, so he got the poison because it's a sure thing. One gulp and you're holding a harp. But he wanted to see Mrs. Claire first, and get the last ounce of the pathetic out of it. He was disappointed when he found she wasn't in, so he wrote the note instead. When he got away from the house—looking for a place to die in—he felt somehow he wasn't getting a square deal. Dying was a bad business—especially alone! And he was going to miss a good deal—the comfort, for instance, he'd just seen in the Hall. And he began to feel most damnably cold. All the same, he wandered on, putting it off till he got to the boathouse—the scene, I should imagine, of some pleasant doings in the past. There he funked it altogether and decided to fake a suicide instead. When we see that letter he left for Mrs. Claire, we ought to be able to fit in the pieces."

"You don't think he was really unstrung, as the footman told Potter?"

Wharton gave a snort of derision. "He was playacting—or my name's Walker. I believe he was scared the first time I clapped my eyes on him at Regent View, and that's why I tried him out with that... that ambiguous accusation you were so indignant about." He cut short Franklin's protestation. "He's always been sheltered—sort of mother's white-headed boy. France and Claire kept him as a kind of odd man, because they'd always been together. I dare say he was useful and had a certain amount of brains, but they didn't take him any too seriously. This time, I think he took himself too seriously by biting off a man's ration which he couldn't chew. You couldn't call him a murderer. Doping that whisky wasn't real murder. It was a kind of sneak-thief murder. He stuck the poison in, then sneaked off. If the whisky hadn't been touched, he'd have poured it away as soon as he got back, and thanked God for a lucky escape. As it was, he lost his nerve on the Sunday night and behaved like a child. A man would have faced what we had to tell him, without all that swooning business. And I believe he's been building on that swoon ever since. He's frightened to death and he's remarkably sorry for himself—and he didn't want to die in a corner. He wanted the footlights and the orchestra." The General shrugged his shoulders. "I may be wrong, but that's how I sum up Kenneth Hayles."

Franklin agreed. "I think you're right... but I'd rather like an opinion from somebody else—and that's Travers. He's been making quite a study of Hayles."

Wharton shot his head round. "What's *he* know about it?"

Franklin smiled. "Now, George, don't keep up that pretence! You know as well as I do—and you've said so—that Travers is a long way short of a fool. To-day for instance, he's gone with Claire to the funeral. I'll bet you he finds out something that you and I have missed."

Arrival at the Hall put an end to that argument.

"Wait a minute!" said Wharton. "Before we go any farther, we'd better decide who's to see Mrs. Claire. I think I'd better, don't you? Then will you find out about that boat. And ask whoever's in charge of the boats, if Hayles knew the lake pretty well. Also... what's the breeze like, Potter? About the same as last night?"

"Just about the same, sir."

"Right! Then you might try out those patent rowlocks and test that point about the oars not slipping. Tow out another boat if necessary, and see if it'd move by itself through the weed patch. And Potter might have a general hunt round for anything suspicious."

He left the others at the garage turn, and entered the Hall.

"Any message from Mrs. Claire yet?" he asked the footman.

"Yes, sir. She's on the way now."

"Good! And now I want to use your telephone."

What he had in his mind may be gathered from the sequence of telephoned instructions. Detective-inspector Eaton was to be at the junction of the Ripley Norton and main roads at 10.30. The man who'd done Hayles's alibi at Chingford was to go at once to the garage and find out if the car was still there. Norris himself was to see the bank manager and find out if any large sum of money had recently been drawn out. Then Wharton rang up Mrs. Hayles. Everything, he assured her, was going fine. Did she think it was his hat?... It was! Splendid! Then they'd traced him as far as Marfleet and in a few hours he'd probably be found. There was, of course, the chance that, having lost his memory, he'd go somewhere else where the subconscious prompted him. Where'd he usually gone for his holidays, for instance? Always in the country? Never abroad? Oh, twice at Dijon! Michael France had once trained there. Well, the great thing was to keep cheerful. Just a little patience and everything'd be all right.

Mrs. Claire arrived a little before time and Wharton, with his door ajar, heard her enter.

"Morning, Bissett! What's all this trouble about Mr. Hayles?"

"They think he's lost his memory, madam, and is wandering about the country."

"He was here last night?"

"Yes, madam."

"Where'd he sleep, Bissett? Have they found out?"

Apparently she moved away without waiting for an answer. Then came Bissett's voice. "There's a gentleman—a Mr. Wharton, madam, in the lounge. He's been waiting some time." Then Wharton heard him move away—to do the job Wharton had rehearsed with him.

He himself made up his mind that his attitude towards Mrs. Claire should be one of utter forgetfulness of the past twenty-four hours. His manner, as he came forward, was a delicate blend of the solicitous and the gratified.

"Good-morning, Mrs. Claire. Too bad of us dragging you down here so early. You see, we're rather worried about Mr. Hayles."

She was looking rather subdued; at least there was none of the quickness of movement, the haphazard cheeriness, and that pleasant recognition of the obvious admiration she was causing, that usually marked her. The scene with her husband must have been a frigid one and at the moment she was probably still resentful, though far too shaken to think of obstinacy or reprisals.

"You see," Wharton explained, "we want his help very badly. And his mother's dreadfully worried. Have you heard all about it?"

In any case he gave her a hasty and much edited account of what had been happening. When he got to the discoveries at the boathouse, she closed her eyes wearily and Wharton got to his feet; then, as he came forward concernedly, she opened them again and gave a wan smile.

"Isn't it all dreadful! And all happening at once!"

"Don't you worry about Mr. Hayles," said Wharton. "There's a good chance he may be alive after all. Will you excuse me a moment?" He pushed the bell. "There's just one little thing you can do for us. Mr. Hayles left a note here for you. Ah! here's Bissett with it. What we think is that it may have some sort of a clue as to where he is. Will you read it?... and then let me see it?"

She slit the envelope mechanically and ran her eyes over the note. Then her face coloured violently. Then she went deadly pale. As she leaned back in the chair, Wharton motioned to the footman and took the note from her limp fingers. Bissett beckoned outside, and Warren—the maid with the medieval hair—came in quickly. Wharton took the note over to the writing table.

Dorothy my dear, when you get this I shall be dead. You have never understood, but now you know. Everything I have done has always been for you, even when I listened at the top of the stairs last Friday night.

Think only the good things about me and may you always be happy. Burn this and forget it, just as I shall soon have forgotten it.

Kenneth.

In the holder on the table was paper of the same make and he quickly made a copy. Behind the chair, Bissett was standing, self-conscious or anxious, and the maid was kneeling with a bottle of smelling salts. Mrs. Claire seemed to be slowly recovering. Wharton placed the copy on the table within reach of her hand.

"Good-bye, Mrs. Claire! Don't worry! Everything will turn out for the best. The next time I see you, there'll be some good news." He gave a cheerful smile, then moved out to the lounge hall with Bissett at his heels. A questioning look and the footman handed over an envelope.

Franklin and Potter were waiting outside and Wharton's deductions had been correct. The oars did not slip out, and the boat, of its own volition, could not move through that weed belt. The boat used by Hayles had been laid up as late as two days previously. Further, Hayles had spent a good many hours on that lake, fishing and experimenting with a mainsail. He and Mrs. Claire had often gone down there on a summer evening with a gramophone, but lately the weeds had got too trouble-some and in the summer Mr. Claire intended to set a gang to work to clear them. Nothing whatever in the nature of a further clue had been discovered by Potter.

* * * * *

At the Ripley cross roads, Eaton was given his instructions. Young was to be questioned most carefully on his dealings with Hayles, and dates were to be obtained if possible. After that, the Ripley Norton household was to be interrogated as to the use of the poison and a missing bottle. Any general gossip might also be useful.

Up to then on the homeward journey Wharton had been, for him, remarkably taciturn. The talk with Eaton seemed, howev-er, to have cleared his mind. Franklin also had felt little desire to talk as he sat puzzling his wits over that final note Hayles had written. One coincidence did strike him.

"That's the second confession in this case," he remarked, "and both a bit wide of the mark. One for the wrong man, and the other for a non-starter."

"Now what about my theory of Hayles?"

"Dead plumb right!" said Franklin. "He certainly wanted an audience—and soft music. All that part about Mrs. Claire—per-fectly nauseating! Whines and forget-me-nots and... treacle!" He gave a nod of satisfaction. "Somehow I never quite cottoned to Hayles."

Wharton raised his eyebrows at that but made no comment. His remarks about the note, however, were much more to the point. "It gives a motive—that's the big thing! He suggests to her that he heard all that Usher heard... and what it implied. Then he hints that he did something for her sake—removing France, shall we say? Finally the request to burn the letter, shows her he did something that nobody must even suspect."

"Yes—but he didn't kill France."

"I know he didn't... but it's all there, if we can join the piec-es together. The connecting link is that confession in France's handwriting. If Hayles wrote it—as you suggested he might have done, after that autograph album practice—then it should be plain sailing. That report'll be in when we get back. And that reminds me. Would you mind going over again what happened that evening you were with the Claires?"

That recital was ending as the car pulled up outside the cottage at Maidenhead.

"Got to have another word with that nurse," explained Wharton, as he got out. When he returned, five minutes later, he was obviously satisfied.

"Just had to make sure about that—er—intimate confession of Mrs. Claire's. The nurse says it's positively all correct."

Franklin, as a non-family man, saw nothing of any importance in the assurance. What interested him was the General's very definite relief.

"More elimination, George?"

"Only Mrs. Claire." He shook his head with the portentous gravity of the much experienced. "Funny how you come back to the old lessons you learned in the nursery! Women—*cherchez la femme,* and so on. Mrs. Claire gets her back up, snaps her fingers and says she *will* go to a night club in spite of the sudden and curiously puritanic views of her husband. The sequel is you and me... here in this car!"

"You're getting a regular dramatist!" smiled Franklin.

Wharton chuckled and dug him in the ribs. "You'll see my name in the West End one of these days. What's the time?"

"Just gone half past."

"You going to the office?"

"Must. Unless there's something frightfully important you want done."

"No, it's all right. There'll be a conference tomorrow, early. Just ourselves. However, I'll let you know about that." He blew his nose while Franklin, out of his experience, waited for what was coming next. "And by the way, if Mr. Travers should have any news about Claire, you might look it over. Very impressionable—those amateurs... but you and I might find something to get our teeth into."

Franklin nodded comprehendingly. The General produced an envelope from his breast pocket and passed it over.

"I got the footman to get me these—from her dressing table or whatever she uses."

Franklin fingered the long, silky hairs.

"Whose are they?"

"Mrs. Claire's maid's. She's got a head like Joan of Arc's in the picture books... and a voice like a dairy maid."

Franklin frowned. "Without being in the least degree lascivious, George, what's her *body* like?"

"You mean—er—what might *France* have thought of it?" He shrugged his shoulders. Franklin tapped at the window for the car to stop.

CHAPTER XX
THE TALE OF A CLOAK-ROOM

FRANKLIN KNEW that conference of Wharton's reminded him of something and suddenly remembered what—a distribution of Sunday School prizes without an audience. The General himself at the lounge table, with his old-fashioned glasses drooping nearly to the walrus moustache, looked beneficent and just the least bit obvious. On the table were assortments of notes, a pile of autograph albums, and still in its gaudy wrapper, a copy of *Two Years in the Ring*. Less pious were the pistol that had shot France, and the decanter and siphon. At the ends of the table sat Franklin and Norris—appendages that rounded off the whole.

Wharton peered round benignantly over the glasses. "Mr. Franklin might like to know where we stand with regard to Hayles. On the Saturday morning early, he withdrew from his private account at Baker Street the sum of one hundred and five pounds, leaving a balance of five pounds only. The day he disappeared from his flat, he went straight to Chingford, where he sold the proprietor his car for less than half what he gave for it a year ago. Details don't matter at the moment." He peered round again. "I think that leaves no doubt as to the intentions of Mr. Hayles. However, we're looking for him, memory or no memory. A good man—Prentiss—has gone to Dijon, via Paris. If necessary we shall give information to the Press, but between ourselves I don't think we ought to scare him just now. We'll let him think he's genuinely dead."

"Why not tell the Press he's dead?" suggested Franklin.

"Well, I've rather suggested it already," said Wharton apologetically. "Now to the case proper—from the beginning. First the anonymous letters and who sent them. I'm absolutely satisfied the real Lucy had nothing whatever to do with it, and France himself was satisfied about the same thing. Now then, who wrote them?"

"The man who made the entry."

"Very well. Then who made the entry? Not a confederate of either Hayles or Claire, because either of them could have provided him with a key. Certainly not a professional housebreaker; he'd have run like hell as soon as he heard voices. Who could have done it? And have we got to enlarge the circle of inquiry? And if so, in what direction?"

"Any professional enemy of France?" suggested Franklin. "Say somebody in line for the title with him out of the way."

"Don't think so. We've talked that over with those in the real know. There's nobody—at least in England. I may say we're still making inquiries in that direction.... Nothing to suggest? Very well then; we'll leave that for a bit. Something may lead back to it, then perhaps we'll see it from a different angle. Now we'll go on with France's movements on the day of the murder, after Usher saw him last.

"He lunched in Coventry Street and on his way to town called up at Willaments of Baker Street and ordered those roses, with very strict instructions that they were to be delivered at the front door between half-past five and six—which they were. While the boy was there, another delivery was made, probably the biscuits. The ordering of those we haven't traced. As he was alone in the house, we might assume he didn't give a damn for the anonymous letters. He watched another man eat at the Girandole, as Franklin told us, and just before eight was at the Paliceum. The entry to the lounge must therefore have been made after he left the house and before his return. That's all plain sailing. Now let's review the situation in the light of what Hayles wrote to Mrs. Claire in his dying confession.

"Hayles definitely states that he did something for Mrs. Claire, on the strength of what he heard upstairs on the Friday night. Our other evidence shows that he'd been suspicious of France's attitude towards Mrs. Claire, and I suggest therefore that what he heard on the Friday, merely crystallised what he'd brooded over in his mind for some days before. He got the poison some time before, for instance. He got it from Young on the plea that he wanted to do away with a dangerous cat. The cat at Ripley Norton did actually die of poison the week-end he was down there, but the servants say it wasn't dangerous or bad tempered. We're practically agreed that Hayles put this poison into the decanter for Hayles to drink. When he put it, we don't know. It might have been before he left on the Saturday morning, or he might have come back later and done it."

"By the way, sir, if he heard those arrangements on the Friday, he must have taken into account the fact that Mrs. Claire might have come round to the house *before* he'd taken that drink. Then why shouldn't he have poured her out one?"

"He wouldn't!" said Wharton quickly. "Mr. Franklin told me she never touched whisky—and Hayles knew it. However, to go on. The poison in the decanter involves the certainty that Hayles'd have to return in sufficient time on the Sunday to fake the suicide. That would need new whisky, and needless to say, we haven't been able to trace the purchase by him of the particular proprietary brand required to refill the decanter. But we do know that he wouldn't let Usher unpack his bag at Martlesham, and when Usher went into the room while Hayles was out, the bag was packed again—and locked! And remember that Hayles denied that he was in a desperate hurry to get back to town.

"Now to the crucial point. When he did get to number twenty-three on the Sunday, he expected to find the body of France. Suppose the body had been discovered before he got there—and he had to allow for that—he'd have had to leave nice and handy the confession France was supposed to have written, so that whoever discovered the body might think it was suicide. *Where* did he leave it?"

"Personally," said Franklin, "I regard it as vital that Hayles should have got back in time to fake the suicide; otherwise he'd have to face a nasty inquiry as to why a man who wanted to poison himself should dope the whole decanter, and not the tot he was going to drink."

"That may be so—but it's begging the question. Shall we say he put the confession on the mantelpiece where France wouldn't notice it. If the death were discovered prematurely, then on his arrival Hayles would have 'discovered' the confession himself. Let's take that as hypothetical. But there's something else. There was on the desk of the secretaire bookcase a blotter, which—the experts are positive—was actually used for blotting that confession. You'll say that Hayles put it there for the sake of creating verisimilitude but—"

"That blotting paper had no other marks on it?"

"None. It was a virgin sheet except for the reverse marks of the last few letters of the confession. And now you're going to be very annoyed with me! I wanted to talk about all this to see where we stood, assuming certain things. But all that house of cards falls to the ground. *The confession was actually written by France, and so, of course, were the marks on the blotting paper, in the strictest sense!* The experts refuse to consider any other suggestion!" After that, Wharton took off his glasses and leaned back in the chair.

"Do you know, I rather anticipated that," said Franklin. "It looked too easy the other way." He hook his head. "All the same, I don't see any sense n France writing it. Did he really intend to commit suicide or did he—I've got it! Do you think he wanted to convince Mrs. Claire that he did intend to commit suicide. He definitely intended to induce her to spend the remainder of the night with him. Could the confession have been a species of blackmail?"

"I don't follow," said Wharton. "Make it more concrete."

"Well, France says to Mrs. Claire: 'If you don't agree to this, I've made up my mind that life isn't worth living any longer. I'm going to do myself in and here's the note to prove it!' Crude, I admit, but there it is. He had that note all ready in the secretaire. He was shot against the secretaire, mind you! And that's what he left Mrs. Claire for; to get it or see it was handy. Now when Somers came in, he had some reason to go to the secretaire and there he saw the confession, which he took with him to the lounge to puzzle over. The rest we know."

Wharton shook his head dubiously. "Ingenious! Very ingenious! Still, it's a suggestion, and that's more than I've had. However, we all agree that Hayles tried to poison France and got Somers instead, and that he was the man you and Usher heard in the house. Is that so?"

"I'm agreed," said Norris.

"And I," said Franklin; "at least as a working hypothesis."

"Right! That eliminates the Somers murder, and Hayles. It becomes a separate and clean cut affair of its own. Now to the murder of France, and before we go on to that, we've got to go back to those specimens of writing and the anonymous threats. Why did France suspect the three people in his house?"

Franklin smiled. "Suspect! What of? A genuine desire to murder—or a practical joke?"

"Not a joke," said Norris. "He wouldn't have consulted you if he'd thought that."

"We're wandering from the point," said Wharton. "Why should he suspect them at all? My own idea is that this was a single occurrence out of many. He may have suspected Usher, and he may have had his ideas about Hayles—"

"Just a minute!" broke in Franklin, and related the affair of the man in the taxi—the man whom Travers suspected of being Hayles.

"The very thing!" said Wharton. "France suspected espionage and that scared him. He thought, when he saw the word 'Lucy,' that somebody knew about that establishment at Harrow and would split to Mrs. Claire, and so spoil what looked like a promising intrigue. He decided not to risk anything. Somebody was trying to frighten him away from London over the week-end, when he'd planned to consummate that delightful affair; therefore he decided not to take any chances. While he was sending specimens of writing of the two men he most suspect-ed, he threw in a specimen of Somers's writing for luck. *And* he made sure by sending the whole three of those people away for the week-end."

"That sounds logic," said Franklin. "By the way, has Dyerson any ideas?"

Wharton grunted. "He's got ideas—but nothing much else... at present. He says the threats were written in two processes; first crudely with the left hand, then the paper was turned up-side down and a copy made, still with the left hand. That's what France got.... And he's inclined to Hayles; *inclined,* mind you."

"Hm!... And was Hayles the only one who knew about that Cambridge affair with Lucy?"

"Somers probably knew—who else we don't know I think Hayles *might* have written them. Claire *couldn't.* He didn't know anything about the week-end till Usher 'phoned him on the Friday, whereas the first anonymous threat arrived early in the week." He reached over to the pistol, balanced it in his hand, then passed it over to Franklin.

"Perfectly ridiculous—and a tragedy! A toy like that... to kill a man like him!"

That was the first time Franklin had really seen that pistol. It looked of the size to be carried unobtrusively in a lady's hand-bag, and there was something effeminate in the apricot-colour-ed enamelling of the stock.

"Looks foreign!"

"Yes, it's French. Garnier-Lafitte's the make. We think it's a war souvenir. And it's the one that killed him all right. Here's the diagram of the path of the bullet; report in medical language underneath."

He passed the diagram over. "Notice anything peculiar about that pistol?"

Franklin tried its weight, then the pull of the trigger. "Good God! It goes off at a touch! It's been tampered with."

"That's right. A woman, for instance, could fire it as easily as dab her nose."

Franklin looked at him, then back at the pistol.

"Take those hairs," went on Wharton. "A woman, alone or with a confederate, enters by the lounge window. She goes over the house and enters the bedroom, which she may have known from experience, and sees the roses and other preparations, which give her information or inflame her jealousy, or both. She sits on the settee and waits for France, then decides to give him a surprise. She waits in the cloakroom, sees the entry with another woman, and that decides her. When the time comes, she shoots!"

Franklin nodded. "Then according to this diagram of the path of the bullet, she must have been a tall woman—or have stood on something, and I'm damned if I see why she should have done that."

"There are a couple of hassocks in the cloakroom she might have stood on…. But that maid of Mrs. Claire's is a tallish woman—best part of five foot nine!"

"And what about the hairs?"

"All I can say at the moment is that apparently—almost certainly—*those hairs found on the settee were hers!*"

Franklin gave a whistle. "Interviewed her yet?"

Wharton shook his head. "I only got the news this morning. Also, between ourselves, I can't credit it. She isn't the type; I don't mean the sex appeal business, I mean for the shooting and so on. That woman's not an actress; she's immature—no, that's not the word; she's transparent, unsophisticated; that's it; pretty face and empty head—except at her work probably."

"Well, you know best," said Franklin. "It's a pity, that's all."

"You're right there!" added Norris. "That woman'd fit like a glove. She knew all Mrs. Claire's movements; she knew Mrs. Claire daren't say a word about having been in the house, and she could have slipped back at any time to have shifted the body."

Wharton waited with exaggerated patience till they'd finished. "I know all that—but there's a snag you haven't seen. At the present moment I don't want to worry Mrs. Claire again, and I don't want to set Claire thinking too much—as I should do if that maid were questioned. I may say, however, that a little diplomatic work is being done. Now where are we?"

"We've got France killed."

"That's it. The rest I told you down at Marfleet and you agreed with how Norris and I worked it out. Two different entries, you remember, at two different times by two different people—the first probably Claire and the second Hayles. The Claire one now suggests that he and the maid were in collusion and that'd be a satisfactory solution. It seems to me, therefore, the best thing we can do is to leave that till we've got her alibi."

In spite of that they spent a good half hour re-traversing the ground; going into minor details and shying down the coconut theories that kept popping up. As for the immediate points of concentration decided on—other than the maid's alibi—they were the possibility of an intrigue between her and France, the tracing of the ownership of the pistol, and the finding of Hayles. With regard to that last, however, Wharton produced a bombshell.

"There's something unusual I'd like to ask you and Norris to do. Imagine I'm Hayles. I've just been found by you two and I know as much as you. You ask me if I'd care to make a statement or answer any questions. Got that? Right! Now you two fire away with everything you want to ask!" and he leaned back in the chair with a look of pleasant anticipation.

Franklin. "Why did you ask Young for poison to kill a cat which wasn't dangerous?"

Wharton. "In my opinion it was—and cats are unhealthy things in a house. I didn't want to hurt my mother's feelings, so I naturally mentioned it to nobody but Young."

Norris. "Doesn't it strike you as peculiar that you and Usher were the only ones who could have doped that whisky, and you should have been in possession of the very poison that was used?"

Wharton. "Not in the least! The person you say broke into the house, he's the one who doped the whisky. As for it being in my possession, that's nonsense. It's used all over the country for destroying wasps' nests."

Franklin. "Why were you listening in on Friday?"

Wharton. "I wasn't! Everybody thought I was out, but I happened to be working upstairs and heard voices."

Franklin. "In your note to Mrs. Claire you say you did something as a result of that listening in. What was it you did, exactly?"

Wharton. "I had a confidential word with France the following morning and he threatened to abandon the attempt on Mrs. Claire. I threatened, if he didn't, to go straight to Claire. Only when he'd promised did I consent to go to Martlesham. I thought afterwards that France had been so upset about this, that he'd committed suicide."

Norris. "In your note to Mrs. Claire—"

"You can hold on there!" said Wharton. "Whatever you ask me about that note I shall deny—or accept—as it happens to suit me. Remember, the doctor will be prepared to swear I was suffering from loss of memory, and the doctor'd have the whole of the Medical Association behind him. I can get that memory back just when it suits me—and *vice versa.*"

That was enough for Franklin. "I see your point. If Hayles has his case all ready, we've a very flimsy, circumstantial case against him; not enough to proceed with, shall we say."

"That's just it. He may even decline to make a statement at all, then we'd be still more in the dark. Now if he'd forged that confession—which he didn't—he'd be a goner! That's why I'd like you and Norris to make a special attack on Hayles's position from the point of view we were just rehearsing."

Franklin glanced at Norris. "We'll have a shot. By the way, what about France's will? Any motives disclosed by legacies?"

"None at all. Mrs. Claire and Somers were down for souvenir legacies, and Hayles for the sole rights of the partnership book. Lucy gets the house at Harrow and a sum of money which doesn't exist. There's nothing to incite murder in any of that. I ought to say, however, that in view of the big fight where he'd have made an enormous sum—win or lose—he'd expressed to his solicitors the desire to make a fresh will at once."

That was the virtual end of the conference, except that as the three of them were on the point of leaving the lounge, Franklin suddenly thought of something.

"Would you mind if I had a look round that cloakroom by daylight. One or two things I don't understand."

"Come along!" said Wharton, and led the way through the lounge door. "Here are two lavatories. That, as you see, is the twin wash-basin with towel rack," and so on from the tiled floor with its rugs, to the stands for sticks and umbrellas, and the row of pegs for hats and coats.

"And this is where the shot was fired from!" said Franklin, opening the door and looking out to the drawing-room. He seemed to imagine himself as firing the shot, for he closed the door gently and drew back quickly to one side. As he did so he caught his head a nasty jab against a coat-hook set in the up-right of the panelling.

"Blast the hook!" He started to rub his ear. "Why the devil did they want to plaster that door with pegs? The room's full of 'em already!"

He looked round. "By the way, wasn't this Usher's headquarters for spying? The two doors are nice and handy. Wonder if France ever caught him here—you know, that question we were discussing of France being suspicious."

"He's in the kitchen. Bring him here, Norris, will you?"

Usher's contribution to the part played by the cloak-room, proved to be unexpected. As Franklin had said, it had been his headquarters for espionage. On occasions when he'd been on hand at the entry of Mrs. Claire, he'd retired to the kitchen and so into the cloak-room by the lounge window—his entry being screened by the tall out-houses. Once France had al-most caught him and he had to make a quick pretence of wiping the wash-basin.

He had been rather annoyed, with a "What the devil are you doing here?" whereupon Usher had explained and withdrawn.

As for the other special advantages of the room, as Usher pointed out, with the door slightly ajar a conversation could be heard in either of the main rooms. Moreover, an eye could be kept on the end of the screen and even the staircase, and surprise be guarded against.

"Then I discovered this knot-hole, sir," said Usher, in the manner of one who approaches his *chef d'œuvre*. He indicated what would certainly have passed unnoticed—a knot-hole clean up against the side of that coat hook which was nearer the lock.

"How it happened, sir, was that one day the door slammed and I found a knot on the floor and wondered what it was; then I found the hole and put the knot back, and it stuck all right. Then I saw it might be useful, sir, and as there were plenty of coat-hooks about I put these two up here on the door munting, sir—"

"Door what!"

"This upright, sir; muntings they call 'em. Well, sir, as I was saying, I put up the two hooks. I knew they'd never be noticed; also I kept a coat hanging on this particular hook so that the knot shouldn't be seen. Also I dabbed the hole and the knot with black enamel. After that, sir, I could prise out the knot with a pin and keep an eye on the end of the screen without having the door open. Also the coat being there kept the knot from falling out."

"Let me have a look," said Wharton. Usher felt for a pin. Franklin anticipated him with the blade of his knife but found the knot difficult. Finally it levered out.

"The resin must have exuded," said Franklin, making a face and wiping his fingers.

"I'm sorry, sir! I ought to have remembered," said Usher hurriedly. "I put a dab of seccotine on it."

"Why?"

"Mr. Claire told me to, over the 'phone that Friday evening, sir. He said the whole thing was a wash-out, and I was to close up this hole as he didn't want anything suspicious left about; especially if I could induce Mr. France to give me the sack straight away."

"I see." Wharton, shorter than Usher and Franklin by two inches, tiptoed and peeped through. Franklin and Norris had a look. Through the hole, thanks to the angle at which it was set, was a good view of the approaches to the door itself.

Wharton stood back and surveyed it, then turned to Usher.

"You had a pretty low-down game to play but you certainly kept an eye on the main chance. Still, that was not your fault." He frowned. "Suppose he couldn't have been shot through that hole?" He approached it again and squinted through. "Of course he couldn't!" He turned round to the others and made a gesture of explanation. "You can only shoot what you can see, and this hole was barely big enough for a pistol, let alone a look through at the same time. Also it'd have been burnt round the edges."

"That's right enough," said Franklin. Norris had another look, then agreed. Wharton replaced the knot, then turned to Usher.

"Inspector Norris will be here till tea time, Usher, and I shall be in later. You can take the afternoon off if you care to."

Wharton and Franklin parted company at St. John's Wood Station, the latter going back to town and the other to Harrow—at least, that's what he said. But under cover of his train that came in first, Wharton made his way up again to the street. Five minutes later he was back again in the cloak-room of Number 23.

CHAPTER XXI
TRAVERS MAKES A SUGGESTION

WHEN LUDOVIC TRAVERS was excited, there was usually nothing in his face to show it. If anything, his manner on such occasions was slightly more diffident; a hesitancy to admit—not that he *was* excited, but that what he was anxious about should really be of the importance he imagined it. True, there was that trick of polishing his glasses, but that was rather an inherent, general nervousness which might mean anything.

Still, all the signs were there when he came, extremely apologetically, into Franklin's office just after an early lunch. His "Busy?" for example, was for him very off-handed, and his acceptance of the answer before it came, more casual still. Franklin watched him amusedly as he took a seat and removed his horn-rims.

Franklin finished what he was doing, pushed the papers aside, found his pipe, then drew up the other chair.

"You want the full report of the France-Somers Case, up to date!"—and regarded him ironically.

"That's very good of you," said Travers mildly.

"Moreover, you've got an idea!"

Travers blinked up at him. "No, honestly! I mean it isn't an idea. It depends exactly on what's been happening."

Franklin couldn't keep back a blast on the trumpet. "Ludo, I can read you like a penny tract!" He took the seat. "However, I'll tell you what happened at the conference and that'll sum it up."

It didn't quite do that. There was so much that Travers didn't know that the recital was constantly switching off into details and byways; as Travers remarked, it was like one of those exasperating, eighteenth-century novels, and yet the whole thing could be summed up in a paragraph.

"If I take it right," he said, "the case against Hayles having murdered Somers, lies in the establishing of more evidence, while the affair of France is all in the air except that Mrs. Claire's maid would be a pretty solution."

"That's it. If you like, you can call it—confession, pistol and hairs."

"Quite!" Then off came the glasses. "I do happen to be working up an idea, but it's very nebulous at the moment. I'd better own up to that much in case you claim any further psychomantic powers. Now—er—have you read those two novels yet?"

"Damn it! I haven't had five good minutes to myself!" remonstrated Franklin.

"I rather guessed that," went on Travers, exceedingly placatingly. "I know you've been frightfully busy. Still, you remember what we were discussing in the matter of those two books of Hayles. Now don't misunderstand me. I know that what I'm going to say will carry very little weight with Wharton; it wouldn't convince a jury, as he'd put it. But you're different."

"Thanks very much!"

Travers ignored that. "We proved, I think, that France was responsible for the really excellent work in *Two Years in the*

Ring, He had the art of writing naturally, of seeing where his colleague was writing unnaturally, and he had sufficient control over the partnership to take final charge. Let me add that no other partnership book has been begun; that's so, isn't it?"

"I've heard nothing about a manuscript."

"I think you'll find there isn't any. Parrys say they put the case to France for a new book—*The Fight for the Championship,* and he suggested to them that *if* he did it, it'd be called *My Fight for the Championship.* You see the subtle difference? Also we agree that Hayles's first story hung on to France's skirts. The second one—I really wish you could have read it!—is exceedingly informative. It tries to be independent of boxing, or shall we say, France. It's dedicated to 'Dorothy,' by the way. What you and I got out of it was that it must have showed Hayles he wasn't the last word in mystery stories. It sold badly. We agreed, therefore, that it gave Hayles one motive for wishing France out of the way."

Franklin smiled. "I rather fancy those were *your* conclusions. Still, I don't mind your roping me in—as it's confidential!"

Travers looked rather hurt at that. Then he fished a paper from his pocket and passed it over.

"There are the summarised motives I think Hayles had. What do you think of 'em?"

1. Dislike of France's attitude towards Dorothy Claire.
2. Dislike of patronising attitude of France and Claire towards himself.
3. Recognition of his inferiority as an author and the hope of recovering that position by being, on his death, the chief authority on France—the greatest phenomenon British boxing had ever known. He could write two or three books that would be bound to sell.
4. Generally a hysterical desire for the limelight—a position he was never allowed to occupy.

"I'd like to make a copy of that," said Franklin, and went back to the desk. Then came various disjointed comments. "As you say, they don't help with a jury.... And it wouldn't get

Dorothy Claire for him... unless of course he intended to pol-ish *him* off afterwards! ... And what about his losing a good job when France died?"

Travers explained that latter objection. "His mother's very frail and he'll get a good bit when she dies. Also she'd look after him if he hadn't a bean. And the new books on France'd help."

He waited for Franklin to resume his chair.

"What I wanted to put up to you was this—to do with that second book, with the hopelessly misleading title of *The Fight-ing Chance.* I've been told you can see an author in his books—see him infallibly, that is. I've been told so about myself, though as an author I've been inclined to resent it—rather foolishly per-haps. Then what exactly do we see in this shocker of Hayles, the one he wrote independent of France? I'll tell you. All the preposterous and creaking machinery from every shocker ever written! All the cliché and outworn flourishes! We get rooms that descend bodily, sliding panels, a vanishing corpse, dope dealers, an opium den, a mysterious poison, a Chinese villain, and a heroine—black-haired, by the way—who's abducted and rescued. The Chinaman turns out to be a detective in disguise, and the hero's a quiet little chap who might be Hayles himself. And there's yards more of it. It's as full of lumber as a tenth-rate antique shop. Now then; what's all that suggest to you?"

Franklin frowned, then owned up. "Not a damn!"

Travers seemed perfectly reconciled to the comment. "Well, perhaps you're right!"

"Yes, but what was your own idea, Ludo?"

"A foolish one... that depended on your answer. Let's leave it alone for a bit and give it time to settle down. If I can put it more clearly, I'll do so—later."

Try as he might, Franklin couldn't budge him from the deci-sion. As Travers had put it, the merit of the theory lay in its easy comprehension. Franklin made up his mind to get it out of him by less obvious methods.

"How'd you get on with Claire—at the funeral?"

"Oh—er—had a reasonably dismal morning. Crowds af people, celebrities by the score and photographers by the hundred. Then we went on to Claire's place—"

"Marfleet Parva?"

"That's the place—and had lunch there. I went over his garages and repair shops—extraordinarily up-to-date places. I tried one of his supercharged Bentleys on the track. He's got a couple of those, by the way, and he's having a new Mercedes over almost at once. I rather gathered he does a lot of his own tinkering and experimenting, and so on. He's got one frightfully ingenious idea for lagging the exhaust as a foot-warmer for passengers—quite a new dodge."

"What's lagging?"

"Covering a tube with asbestos cement to prevent local loss of heat. He lags the tube on one side—the bottom—and allows radiation at the top which acts as a foot warmer. I'll tell you about that later. Then on Saturday he's due at Brooklands for an attack on the world's 200-kilometre record, if the weather's all it should be."

"But isn't that rather callous, after France's death?"

"Oh, I don't think so! It's a long-standing engagement, as it were. These things have to be planned months ahead. However, I was going to tell you about that footwarmer—"

On the subject of cars, Travers was likely to be too communicative. Franklin cut in with a hasty question.

"Tell me, Ludo; what's your idea about Claire himself?"

Travers hesitated somewhat. "That's a bit difficult. You see, I'm rather prejudiced. I've known him for some time, and we've got things—and acquaintances—in common. On the whole I should say... I don't like him at all. Tremendous admiration for his skill and so on, but... well, there you are. I just don't like him. And, of course, I'm a much older man than he is."

"Find out anything interesting about him?"

"I did rather—at least I pretty well bludgeoned it out of him by alluding to his heirs in a rather blatant way. He mentioned, as between the two of us, that he was hoping to have a son, and all that, to carry on things. Most unusual I thought it—I mean for him to refer to it. I felt a bit of a fool, but he seemed quite bucked about it; sort of assumed entire credit!"

Franklin laughed. "And why shouldn't he!... And so you don't think very much of him. What would you say his real character is?"

Travers smiled. "That's a tall order. If I were making a rapid pot-pourri, I should say he's got too much money; has an exaggerated idea of his personal caste; is drawlingly polite to his equals and as drawlingly rude to his inferiors. He has the meretricious polish of his particular breed, only he remains quite obviously a merely magnificent specimen of an animal.... I should say he'd prefer the furtive in direct attack—paradoxical, but I mean that he lacks *moral* courage. He's not generous minded.... In other words—since I can read you as easily as a Bovril advertisement—I should say he funked tackling France direct; employed Usher, as we know, instead, and if he'd made up his mind to do so, would have doped France's whisky with a perfectly good conscience!"

Franklin roared with laughter. "Good for you, Ludo! And that's Claire, is it?... And what about his wife?"

"She was in to lunch. Naturally she hadn't the least idea I knew anything about the case; all the same, judging from what you told me, I should say she'd sobered down enormously. She was watching him with big, spaniel eyes."

"Claire still behaving like a pig?"

Travers shook his head. "I wouldn't go so far as that. Of course, we know he's been pretty rotten about things. All I could feel was that he'd given her the hell of a thin time, and was being frigidly polite in that infuriating way such people have."

Franklin nodded. "And going back to that matter of Claire and the whisky. Was that your big idea?"

"You're trying to worm that book business out of me? Well, I'll have another shot.... If you know a man thoroughly, say by personal acquaintance or by reading his books, couldn't you try to work out for yourself how he'd commit a murder? Take that little, snivelling Hayles, for instance... or Claire. Take you or me, driven to committing murder. Since you lured me into crime,

I've sat dozens of times wondering how I could kill a man and get away with it, and every time it had to be a series of steps, perfectly timed and involving no physical courage. Take yourself; you'd do something physical. I know you would—it's in you!"

"I don't know so much about that," smiled Franklin. "However, where's it all lead?"

"To this. I've been trying to put myself into the skin and mind of Hayles; from what you've told me, from what I know, and from what I've got out of his books. I ventured yesterday to make one experiment and it turned out rather well, thanks to a lot of luck. I told you about the man in the taxi and how I thought it was Hayles. I remembered the number of the taxi because I couldn't very well forget it—3003. I'm now prepared to swear the man was Hayles—though he wore glasses."

Franklin looked up. "I say, that's good! Wharton'll be pleased to know that's definite."

"Well, it is," went on Travers. "I rooted out the driver and recalled the occasion. He said a gentleman—an American—hired his taxi and drew it up short of France's car with instructions that the car was to be followed discreetly. The excuse was that he—Hayles, shall we say?—was France's private detective. There was a lot more to it, but there you are. Hayles was tracking down Claire in the best, Haylesian, detective fashion. As a matter of fact it appears to have been a perfectly harmless dinner engagement, since they went to the Cholmondely."

Franklin was disappointed. "Yes, that's all right, but how's it help?"

Travers made an unusual sort of grimace. "Help?... Well, it sort of gives one encouragement! You'll find that taxi incident, or something very much like it, in *The Fighting Chance,* for one thing. But what I want to get out of it is something that isn't in the books. Something he might have used, if he wrote another!" Then the glasses came in for a really magnificent polish. "I want you to send a man to Dijon—if you've got a suitable one—at my expense."

"Dijon! That's where Hayles may be!"

"Yes, I know. Only I don't want him to be there." Franklin couldn't see it. "But you didn't know anything about Dijon till I told you last night!"

"Oh, yes I did. I had an idea of the sort so I ventured to ring up Mrs. Hayles—on your behalf of course—to ask about his holidays. I've got the address where he stayed—74, rue Prieur. I'm sorry about that, but I knew you wouldn't mind. The thing is, have you got a good man—tactful and a good French scholar?"

"I've got the man all right. What d'you want him for?"

"I want him to catch this afternoon's train to Paris; fly from there to Dijon—I've got the times all worked out—and call at the place in the rue Prieur and ask if Hayles has written there recently and if so, about what. Hayles is to be announced as dead; drowned if you like. As soon as anything's known, whether favourable or not, your man's to wire you—or me—and then get back here at the double. If the wire's what I hope it is, then I'll tell you all about it, and the Government, or Durangos, can pay expenses. If it's a wash-out, then I'll apologise and pay up... and shut up."

* * * * *

Two things of consequence arose out of that conversation, and later that afternoon, something really thrilling was to happen. First of all, Franklin went off at once to give instructions to his agent, then sat thinking things over in his office; trying, in fact, to get against Hayles something of the nature Wharton had suggested and far more definite than the ingenious and rather amusing theories which Travers had propounded.

Then the first, faint idea. Was there, after all, anything in them? Those ideas about Hayles's tortuous ingenuity, for instance? What about Dyerson's opinion that Hayles had written—with laborious and elaborate precautions—those anonymous threats? Wouldn't that be, according to Travers, the very kind of thing he'd do?

Just then Cresswold came into the room with some papers, and as he went out Franklin had a further idea—Hayles, if it *had* been Hayles, and his glasses and his American accent, calling at the Air Ministry in his anxiety about the weather and then successfully pulling the legs of Cresswold and his brother with fantastic tales about an aeroplane dash for America! The thing was, had that fog really been so desperately important for Hayles, assuming he'd played that part in the tragedy which Wharton's hypothesis had assigned to him? With that house screened from the road, and its private back entry, was fog absolutely necessary for escaping observation? Franklin couldn't quite see it. The fog admittedly made assurance doubly sure, but that was hardly the point.

Then another idea which seemed to show that Travers and his theories were scarcely as nonsensical as they first appeared. Hayles *might* have done all that business with Cresswold's brother. It was in the best detective vein. There was a certain real-life kick to it. It satisfied in a small way that desire of Hayles to *do* something, and to do it in that furtive way that seemed characteristic. The times for the Friday afternoon fitted in as far as was known. The pseudo-American had presumably left the Air Ministry building well before five. Hayles had rung up Durango House about that meeting at St. John's Wood at about ten past five, presumably from the box opposite France's house, and had then entered the house surreptitiously before the arrival of France and Mrs. Claire.

All that produced the course of action which would have saved time at the beginning. From a drawer he took a couple of those enlargements—pictures of Hayles from *Two Years in the Ring*—profile and full face. With a piece of charcoal he added the glasses and then chalked a film over the eyes. Then he pushed the bell for Cresswold.

* * * * *

How Travers actually spent his evening was to be told later by himself. His idea, originating in the smoke-room of the Scriveners' Club between tea and dinner, was merely the remembrance that in that very room a few days ago he had heard Hayles prevaricating about his presence in the Hampstead Road. The thought produced another—then a third; then he suddenly hoisted himself out of the chair. A quarter of an hour later he was strolling along the Hampstead Road with an eye on the windows.

As for the third episode, it deserves a chapter to itself.

CHAPTER XXII
WELCOME WANDERER!

NORRIS WAS OUT and Franklin had just come in. At the moment he was talking nothings to Wharton and watching his workmanlike attack on a late tea. Then the front-door bell rang and various things happened simultaneously. Wharton, with an instinctive curiosity, opened the lounge door, still grasping the remnant of buttered toast, and peeped out; Usher appeared from nowhere, and the sound of a key was heard in the lock. Then came Usher's exclamation.

"Mr. Hayles, sir! Excuse me, sir, but you gave me quite a shock!"

Wharton shot the toast into his mouth, waited the necessary second to give a final gulp and wipe his lips, waved frantically for Franklin to get into the cloakroom, then went to greet the wanderer; his expression a mixture of intense gratification, concern and disarming friendliness. He thrust out a welcoming hand.

"Well, Mr. Hayles! This *is* a pleasure! What on earth have you been doing with yourself? You've had us all scared to death!"

Hayles, looking more fragile than ever, gave a tremulous smile. Wharton flashed a look at him; clothes clean and hat new; his face shaved, pale and purple-patched under the eyes. But the eyes themselves were clearer than they'd been on that Sunday evening, and the voice was more alert. In some ways it was a new Hayles who began the explanation of his absence.

"I'm sorry about that. I'm afraid I've had—er—rather a thin time. All that worry—"

Wharton made a hasty gesture of comprehension. "I'm sure you have. Enough to worry anybody! But what about some tea? You look cold."

Hayles began slowly taking off his gloves. "It *is*... rather cold."

Wharton turned to Usher. "Get Mr. Hayles some tea and toast... straight away... in the lounge!" He helped Hayles off with his overcoat and led him away. "Come along into the warm and tell me all about it."

That seemed a very difficult thing for Hayles to do. His manner immediately became exceedingly nervous and the account itself elusive and vague.

"I'm afraid I—er—can't tell you very much. You see, I—er—sort of remember hearing a voice—I think it was Mr. Franklin's—and then I think I went to Chingford; at least I know now I must have done that because I just rang them up and they say I sold them my car. And then I think I must have gone straight down to Ripley and then after that... well, it's all a sort of dream and I was wandering about."

"You lost your memory!" put in Wharton heartily. "That's what you did!" He leaned forward inquiringly. "And where were you when you began to... remember things?"

Hayles's face lit up. "Do you know, it was most extraordinary! I was actually at St. John's Wood Station! I must have got out of a train because I was half way up the stairs when I sort of stopped short—and then I began to remember. Then I got a paper and found it was Thursday!"

Wharton nodded knowingly. "Just as we thought.... Of course you've seen your mother?"

"Oh, yes! I've just come from there—I mean I *was* there and I went out for a stroll to try to remember things... and that's why they've just started coming back."

"Hm!" went on Wharton. "However, I'm glad you've seen your mother. She was very worried—and no wonder." A nod from which he seemed to derive intense satisfaction. "And how are you feeling now? Fit enough to give us a little help?"

Hayles smiled bravely. "Oh, I think so! I don't know how long I'll be able to keep it up—but I'll do my best."

Usher, who must have sacrificed his own toast, came in with the tray. Wharton mumbled an apology and went out to the drawing-room; scribbled a hasty note and left it where the valet couldn't fail to find it. When he came back he gazed round approvingly and helped himself to another cup.

"This looks more comfortable! And now let's hear the wanderer's adventures! You haven't any idea what led you, when you lost your memory, to do what you did?"

Hayles sat there, plate at elbow, looking into the fire. He spoke like a man who has just arrived at certain convictions.

"Do you know, I have! I probably don't know half what I did, but I can see a perfectly good reason for what I remember. It's all absolutely logical, if you know what I mean."

"That's very interesting!" said Wharton—and meant it.

"For instance, I sold my car. I intended to do that in any case. Like a fool I went to the Motor Show the other week and immediately got dissatisfied, as I ought to have known I should. What I fell in love with was one of those S.K. sixes—the sports model—and I sort of put the idea on one side and then it kept popping up again, and finally on Saturday, when I knew I was going down to Martlesham, I got a hefty sum—for me—out of the bank. You see, I'd seen a car in a garage at Ipswich, so I thought I'd have a deal for my old one and pay the balance in cash.... Then the fog ratherspoilt that—sort of put me off it—and I thought I'd do it on the Monday when I was in town." He turned round and looked full at Wharton. "Now, do you see? I must have done all that mechanically, when I lost my memory!"

Wharton raised a comprehending hand. "Precisely what I guessed! The very kind of thing people do." He paused to wipe his fingers and set aside the devastated tray. "Anything else in the sequence? What happened at Ripley, for instance?"

Another flash of illumination lit up Hayles's face. "The very same thing! I remember I went to see Young. That was all the talk of poisons running through my mind. You see," he explained, "Young gave me some poison last autumn to destroy a wasps' nest in our garden at Ripley and I happened to be mentioning it to... Michael France and he asked me if I could get some for a friend of his—name like 'Field' or something like that—who had a dog he wanted to destroy. That'd be about a fortnight ago, so when I was down there I saw Young and made the excuse that I wanted it to kill off a cat of ours I didn't like—I did kill it by the way. It was a miserable little brute—and when Young gave it me, I handed the balance to Michael—"

"You gave the poison to France!"

Hayles looked surprised. "Yes! I just told you he asked me for some. It was in crystal form but I filled a bottle with water and made a solution."

Wharton disguised his feelings admirably. "I see. As you say, it all works out. That poison business was on your mind and you went over it all again." He went on as if in reminiscent vein. "Mr. Franklin was very upset about your mother's distress and did his best to find you. He seems to have found out all that business you've been telling me." He leaned forward again. "And then you went to Marfleet. Remember that?"

Hayles looked up at the ceiling. "Yes... I remember going to Marfleet... now you come to mention it."

"Hm! And that's where you scared us.... And Mrs. Claire. That letter of yours nearly frightened her to death."

"Letter? What letter?"

"The letter you wrote her, saying you were going to commit suicide!"

Hayles started, then frowned. "I wrote Mrs. Claire a letter! What was in it? What did I say?"

Wharton wasted no time over finding his notes. "I think I know it by heart. This is how it went—

My dear Dorothy,
   When you get this—

Hayles leaned forward, head between his hands. Wharton started again.

When you get this I shall be dead. You have never understood me but now you know. What I did was for your sake, even when I had to listen last Friday evening at the top of the stairs. I hope you will always be happy. Burn this note and forget it, as I shall.

A good half minute elapsed and when Hayles raised his head, to Wharton's surprise and no inconsiderable relief he was smiling—a bit dazedly perhaps, like a man who understands only partly.

"You frightened me when you said that—about Mrs. Claire. May I say something in confidence, but—er—perhaps you know it already. I—er—thought a good deal of Dorothy Claire"—he looked away to the fire—"and your mention of a letter, well, it was like visit to the dentist when you have gas and wonder what you've said when you come round again, in case you've... you've said what you shouldn't. When I lost my memory it was—er—like having gas. I wondered what I'd said." He looked up anxiously. "Did Peter Claire see that letter?"

"Oh, no! Only Mrs. Claire—and ourselves."

Hayles nodded. "Not that it matters much.... But what else did I do? Could you tell me?"

Wharton told him—at least he gave him a subtle version that included more than one error of fact. Hayles, however, never turned a hair, even when Wharton arrived at the lake.

"What else could we think after seeing that boat? There didn't seem a ray of hope. However, we decided to give it another twenty-four hours, so as not to distress your mother." Then casually, "You remember nothing about that?"

Hayles screwed up his eyes as if looking back into the inscrutable past. "Not a thing. I just remember going along the drive to Marfleet Hall... then everything's a blank."

"Quite! However, we'll leave that. You don't want to be reminded of it, that's a certainty!" He pulled out a species of notebook. "Now let's see what you can do for us. Oh, yes! What's your exact opinion of Usher?"

"Usher! You mean his spying on Mrs. Claire?"

"Mrs. Claire! My dear fellow, you've got it all wrong! However, you found out that, did you?"

"Yes... by luck really. You see, the windows of my room upstairs look out over the back, and one morning—Mrs. Claire happened to have come in at the time—I looked out of the window for something or other and I saw this chap Usher actually getting into this room by that window there! After that I kept an eye on him; then I laid a trap—pretty shrewd one—and he fell clean into it."

"Good work! I'll have to talk to you about that some time soon. But you're really all wrong about his spying on Mrs. Claire. It was everybody *he* was keeping an eye on! Didn't you tell us about France getting some anonymous letters? Well, France got Usher into the house to act as a sort of bodyguard."

Hayles looked startled. "Yes, but those letters arrived only last week and Usher was here a fortnight and more ago!"

Wharton shook his head and smiled patiently. "Oh, no! There were others before that! They reached France privately—so you didn't know anything about them."

Hayles frowned and went laboriously through the orthodox motions of a man in a mental morass; all the same, Wharton could see he'd tied him in the devil of a knot.

"Tell me," he went on. "When you overheard France and Mrs. Claire on that Friday evening, where were you? Upstairs at work?"

"That's right."

"And you thought they were making arrangements for—what we might call bluntly—an adulterous rendezvous—in this house?"

Hayles glared. "And weren't they?"

"Good heavens, no! Ask Claire and he'll tell you! They were making arrangements to go to a night club without Claire knowing it. That's the only deception there was practised on *him!*"

Hayles blinked rapidly, made as if to speak, then looked miserably into the fire.

"Two questions, Mr. Hayles—and one answer will do for both. You *were* desperately anxious to get back to town. Also, when you got to this house, you were scared stiff. Exactly why?"

Hayles looked him straight in the face and fairly snapped the answers at him. "I thought Usher would tell Claire all about it and he'd kill France—I mean, that's what I thought he'd done when I came in on Sunday and you said he was dead. All the time at Martlesham I kept worrying what had happened. I even

206 | CHRISTOPHER BUSH

thought France had wanted the poison to get rid of Peter Claire. I tell you I was in a state of collapse before I got here. That's why I rang up Claire when I got back—to see if he was all right."

"But you took your time over that!"

"I know I did. I sort of... didn't like to dive in. I was afraid something had happened."

"But you didn't come round here when you got back?"

"Why should I? France told everybody he was going to be away all the Sunday."

Wharton shook his head. He daren't let himself go, but a mild relief *had* to be given to his feelings.

"One of these days, young man, you'll land yourself in queer street! You were asked certain questions on the Sunday night and you chose to prevaricate. Oh, I'm not questioning the chivalry of your motives! The trouble is, the law doesn't take much stock of chivalry, as an answer to plain questions." He watched the other with a careful eye and saw the danger signal in time. "However, that's all over and done with. You've let a flood of light on things—and we're much obliged to you." He shook his head consolingly. "You've had a very bad time of it. Rest'll soon put you right. And just a second, if you don't mind."

When he returned to the room he was holding the poison bottle.

"Is that the one you brought from Ripley, with the poison for France?"

Hayles examined it carefully. "Looks like it. I'm practically sure it *is* it!"

"You couldn't swear to it?"

"Well—er—I couldn't, but I'm sure it's the one—if you know what I mean."

"I think I see." Out of his pocket came the pistol. "And what about this? Ever seen it before?"

Hayles undoubtedly had; his eyes showed that. "It's Michael's!" Then he looked startled. "Is it—er—"

"It is," said Wharton. "It's the one... he killed himself with. And you're sure it's his?"

"Absolutely! I was with him when he got it. It used to be Dunally's. He got it in the war."

"*Dunally* did! I didn't think he was as old a man as that!"

"He's over thirty. We saw it in his quarters one day and Michael took a fancy to it."

"Where did France keep it?"

"In a drawer of the secretaire out there—at least, that's where I last saw it."

"When was that?"

Hayles frowned. "I don't know really, but Claire'd remember it. One day last week, I think it was; we were all out there having an argument about the calibre gun it'd take to drop a man clean in his tracks—size of bullet and so on—and Michael got out this pistol. Claire laughed at him, you know—'You don't call that damn thing a pistol!' sort of thing; then we all laughed, and, as far as I remember, Michael shoved it back in the drawer again. That's the last time I saw it—till you just gave it me."

"Why exactly did France take a fancy to it?"

"I think he said it was unusual. Also I remember how he laughed about it. Said it'd make a charming present for a lady."

"Did he!" said Wharton. "Well, that's been a great help to us. But just one other question and I think that's the lot—and it's about Michael France. Had he, do you know, been carrying on an intrigue with a woman? the sort of woman who might come here?"

Hayles was quiet for a moment. "That's a rotten sort of question to ask—"

"I know it is—but it's a necessary one, and in confidence between you and me."

"Well, the trouble was you never knew when he *wasn't* carrying on with some woman or other. Two things used to pull him together. He loved boxing more than he did women. He'd never do that sort of thing when he was in training or semi-training—"

"You mean doing a music-hall show?"

"That's it; as he was at the Paliceum. I don't think he ever fooled about then... but you couldn't have been sure. Once he used to bring... well, some pretty warm people round here, till

Claire made a fuss. Also since he—er—well, I don't think he'd have risked Mrs. Claire seeing anything of that kind."

"Puritanic, was she?"

"Not at all," said Hayles frigidly. "There must be limits, you know."

"Exactly." Wharton had another peep at the notebook. "By the way, one thing's just occurred to me. Why didn't you refuse point-blank to go to Martlesham?"

Hayles turned his head away and looked rather ashamed of himself. "To own up, I suppose... I was a coward. And I kept on hoping something'd turn up.... Also I couldn't very well refuse because I hadn't a reason... and it was really most frightfully important—on the face of it—for me to see this chap... I had to see."

"Precisely! You were in a difficult position." He rose, took off his glasses and put them ceremoniously away in the battered case. Hayles rose too.

"Now if I were you, Mr. Hayles, I'd see a doctor. If he orders it—and I think he *will* order it—get back between the blankets for a day or two. If we should be in a muddle, perhaps you'll help us."

"Oh, most decidedly!" At the door he paused. "I wonder if you'd mind telling *me* something. If—er—Michael France committed suicide, why was he buried in consecrated ground?"

Wharton gave the high-sign of secrecy. "There wasn't a verdict brought in! Besides"—and the rest was whispered into Hayles's ear. He nodded as if he understood; then a further question.

"Yes, but why are you keeping Usher on?"

"He had a week's notice to run," explained Wharton airily. "And he was our only evidence till to-day. Now you're back he can go at any time."

"What do you mean 'evidence?' If you don't mind me being rather rude, why is everybody still here?—yourself, for instance?"

"Heaps of things to clear up," said Wharton enigmatically. "We have to know *why* people commit suicide! it isn't enough to know they've done it. France, for instance, why should he?"

Hayles looked at him oddly. "Haven't people—people like Michael France especially—all sorts of things in their lives that none of us will ever find out?"

Wharton led him adroitly to the front door. "True enough! But we're the servants of the law—not its masters. All the same, everything's practically cleared up.... And now you get away to bed!"

Hayles smiled wistfully. "Well, I'll go home... and I think perhaps I'll see the doctor, only, if I'm fit enough, I'd better come round to-morrow. There must be an awful accumulation of work."

"Work be damned! It's rest you want—not work!" The remainder of the conversation lost itself on the porch and Hayles's footsteps had died away before Wharton came quickly to the lounge. He rang up Claire.

"Hallo!... That 3, Regent View?... Mr. Claire in?... Tell him I want to speak to him very urgently, please.... Never mind the name."

As he stood there, receiver at ear, Franklin came through from the cloak-room. "You heard everything?" Franklin nodded. "Norris in?" Franklin nodded again.

"Hallo! That you, Mr. Claire?... Wharton speaking from number twenty-three. Hayles has just turned up!... Yes, loss of memory.... You might let Mrs. Claire know, will you? I think she was rather worried.... I'm just coming round to see you about that. If he gets to you first, I don't want you to see him. Leave word you're out.... Yes, in ten minutes or less.... Good-bye."

Norris came in. "Everything all right?" asked Wharton.

"Yes, sir. He won't give us the slip this time."

Wharton gave a dour look. "If he does, I pity the bloke who's responsible.... You heard everything all right, John?... What'd you think about it?"

"Damned if I know," said Franklin. "I couldn't see his face. From what I could hear, I should say you d have a stiff job in fastening anything on him. He might even be genuinely innocent!"

"Almost thou persuadest me!" drawled Wharton with what was meant to be a sneer. Then he let himself go. *"Might* be innocent! He *might* be the Archbishop of Canterbury!" He snorted again. "What he's done is just what I told you two yesterday. He's been in retirement in a desert place, thinking things out. He's got a cast-iron set of answers and reasons... and it's our job to find a hammer to smash 'em! He knows his principal witness—France—is dead. I'll bet he's hunted every newspaper through, since he's been away, and had a pair of earphones glued on, listening for his name in an S.O.S.... Now he crawls back with a yarn that'd break a jury's heart.... And he's gone home to think of some more!"

Norris put in a consoling word. "You did get that news about the pistol, sir."

"I'm going to check that now. John, would you mind going back to your place and I'll call up there later. Write up all that conversation, if you can. Norris, you'd better tidy up Hayles's room in case he decides to turn up to-morrow.... As a matter of fact I think I'll call up the doctor and tell him he's pretty bad. And you might get hold of likely spots and see if you can find anybody who knows where Dunally's hanging out, and then check up on that pistol. I'll see Claire about it now... and I'll give him the tip about those lies I had to tell Hayles."

"By the way," said Franklin, "has Claire attempted to communicate with Usher?"

"Devil a word! However, I'll make some excuse to refer to it. I might ask him what he wants done... about notice and... a reference."

"Reference!" said Franklin. "That's damn good!" Norris caught his eye and winked. Wharton tucked the ends of his muffler into his coat and trudged off.

Franklin got on his own coat and squinted at himself in the glass. "What's your own idea, Norris? Think he's innocent?"

"I didn't hear all of it," said Norris. "And, as you said, I didn't see his face. Still, the old man seems pretty sure he's not.... However—"

Franklin caught his eye again, and laughed. "As you say, *however—*"

* * * * *

It was very much later when Wharton did roll up at St. Martin's Chambers, where Franklin was still brooding over the intricacies of the case and feeling decidedly egg-bound. His face lit up as he let the General in.

"Just popped in for a second!... Just the tiniest spot!... Got any more ideas about your friend Hayles?"

Franklin handed over the drink, then looked thoughtful. "I don't know that I have... except that things rather fit in with a theory Travers is rather keen on."

Wharton took a deliberate look at the drink, nodded, then took a first pull. "Travers, eh?... What's *he* know about it?"

Franklin told him the case as presented by a study of the books. The mysterious mission to Dijon he kept to himself, seeing that it rather looked like an attempt to check Wharton's official arrangements.

"Do you know, there's a lot in it!" said Wharton, uncommonly graciously. "As I've always said, Mr. Travers has got a head on him. My own opinion is that Hayles'll make a slip sooner or later. Either he's innocent and knows who did it, or else he's what we've made him out to be."

"What about the pistol? Claire confirm it?"

"Absolutely! He said he didn't notice exactly which drawer France put it back in, but he saw it all right. Norris got hold of Dunally at a big boxing show at Blackfriars, and he confirmed Hayles's story—over the phone, of course."

"News about the maid in yet?"

"Some. I had to go very carefully. She had supper in the servants' room after Mrs. Claire left on the Saturday, and was under observation till half-past eleven when she went to bed. As she shares a room, I may get that later. On the Sunday morning she was allowed to go to her home at Marfleet by Mrs. Claire's special permission, as she was to be away herself. That end's being gone into now."

Franklin nodded. "And what's the next move?"

"Trace Hayles after he left Marfleet—every inch till he got back to town. Interview everybody with whom he came in contact and find out if he was playacting all the time or not. Also I'm still hopeful of finding something against Claire. He's got too strong a motive to be let out easily."

He finished off the drink. "No, not another! I've got a lot of work to do to-night. And that reminds me. To-morrow—say at half-past eight, which'll give you aristocrats time for your coffee and cigars, come along to twenty-three and see if there's any news.... Perhaps you might bring Mr. Travers along... if he cares to come."

Franklin forebore any leg-pulling.

"Eight-thirty to-morrow. Right-ho, George! We'll be there!"

CHAPTER XXIII
TRAVERS FINDS A HAMMER

THE WEATHER REPORT for the following morning, as far as concerned the three professional upholders of the law, was "most unsettled." Wharton had already set in motion the machinery for following the course of Hayles's erratic pilgrimage. Then he saw the doctor, on the question of the advisability of relying on his patient for information immediately necessary. What he learnt was disquieting. The doctor was not only in perfect agreement with his patient's account, but feared a recurrence of the amnesia. The nerves were in such a condition that one too tragic reminder and he'd be off again.

In spite of that, Wharton chanced his arm and called round at the flat. Hayles was asleep and his mother was of little help. As far as he could gather, the patient had had no further revelations from the subconscious. Complete amnesia began with him at Marfleet and ended at St. John's Wood Station, and Wharton, suavely sympathetic, cut short his visit.

Then that alibi of the maid had turned out exasperatingly right, as far as concerned the Sunday. She *had* spent that day at Marfleet, and couldn't therefore have been in the house in

Regent View; moreover, as she had not left Claire's house on the Saturday evening before eleven-thirty, he decided on elimination. Those hairs, therefore, that had been found on the settee in France's bedroom were either not hers—in spite of what the experts said—or had got there by other than the obvious means.

Thereupon Usher was hauled upstairs again and shown the position where the hairs were found. Wharton even placed them cunningly and told the man to find them—which he did.

"You see, sir," explained Usher, "if they were short hairs, it'd be different. These curl up and catch the light. And the vacuum couldn't have missed 'em, sir."

Wharton saw all that for himself, but still stubbornly refused to admit that the hairs were not there on the Saturday morning after Usher had done the room.

"If you don't mind me saying so, sir," said Usher frankly, "I'm afraid you're wrong. In the first place, sir, I was in all day on the Friday and I'm dead sure nobody called—at least, with hairs like those. And I shook those cushions out on the Friday morning. And then they had to dodge the vacuum on the Saturday. I tell you, sir, those hairs got there after I left the house."

Wharton had an idea. "But why did you do the bedroom at all on the Saturday? If Mr. France was going away, why not have left it for the woman on Monday? And you wouldn't have wanted it *then*. You were all going away!"

"As a matter of fact, sir," said Usher, "Mr. France told me specially to do it. If I might say so, sir, there seems to be a connection with the—er—roses and the biscuits."

"Hm! And did Mrs. Claire ever come up here?"

"Never, sir—not to my knowledge."

"Then they couldn't have come off her clothes after contact with the maid," said Wharton, thinking aloud. He moved off down the stairs with Usher at his heels.

"You sent Mr. Claire about five reports in all?"

"Yes, sir."

"And you told him everything?"

Usher ventured on a smile. "If I hadn't done that, sir, there wouldn't have been anything to report at all."

"Hm! Suppose not. You had to earn your keep. Mr. Claire was here on the Saturday?"

"I told you that, sir. And he was here on the Friday."

"Hm! So you did. Came on the Friday, did he? Well, come along into the lounge and tell me just what happened."

* * * * *

Franklin, pausing in the middle of his ordinary work for a pipe and a pull up at the fire, soon found himself in all sorts of difficulties. Upon whatever mental path he felt his feet going, there was soon a snag in the way to hit his feet against, and the logic began to halt. The fact that France had been shot with his own pistol and that Hayles and Claire knew where it was kept and had easy access to that place, seemed certain proof that one or the other had shot him. And yet neither had! Then had either of them given the pistol to the murderer? Surely not, or they'd have given him a key at the same time and made that forcible entry unnecessary. Or had that entry been merely a blind in order to suggest a murder? If so, why go to the trouble of staging a suicide?

Franklin wriggled in his chair and told himself the thing must be reasoned out carefully. France *had* been shot, and only Mrs. Claire knew he'd been shot. Then why pretend it was suicide? Mrs. Claire had only to open her mouth and everybody'd know it was murder. Then the murderer must have known that she *daren't* open her mouth, and therefore the murderer must have been one who had that information—in short, either Usher or Claire or Hayles. And neither of the latter could have shot him because they were scores of miles away!

Franklin wriggled again, relighted his pipe and set off once more. That confession, found under Somers's body; why hadn't the General questioned Hayles about it? Surely one of the most vital pieces of information and one that shrieked aloud for exhaustion. And then that business of Travers and the man at Dijon; twenty quid it'd probably cost him! He glanced at the clock. Word might come through at any minute... and what sort of word? What was it all about?

Then his mind went back to that couple of photos of Hayles which he'd touched up. Cresswold's brother was sure the man had been Hayles and he'd be prepared to swear to it. But just how did it help? Wharton had hit the nail clean on the head when he'd said that everything Hayles had asserted could be proved *wrong* by one person, and one person only, and that person—France—was dead. Would it sound too preposterous, for instance, if Hayles said that in following France's car and posing as a detective, he was merely following France's instructions, in view of the threatening letters? As for that visit to the Air Ministry's building, why shouldn't he say again that he was under France's orders? After all, France's plans were likely to be very considerably affected by the fog.

Franklin wriggled once more in his seat, bit hard on the cold pipe, and began all over again.

* * * * *

Norris, in a car travelling from Chingford, was wandering about in the same hypothetical circles and was finding hypothesis exceedingly remote from lucid reality. For all that, he was to arrive at much the same conclusions which were at that identical moment forcing themselves on Wharton and Franklin.

Norris had precious little use for the wide net and gradual elimination of his immediate superior. In his younger days he had been taught reliance on the ready-to-hand; in other words, motive makes crime and, except in cases of mental derangement, there's no crime without motive. The motive of Hayles, however high-falutin it might seem to the uninformed, stuck out like a barber's pole. And as for the motive of Claire, Norris was damned if he knew what the old General was up to. "A man rings me up," he said to himself, "and tells me on first-class authority that my missis is putting in the night with another man. What do I do? Go away and let her get on with it? Just buy a couple of extra racehorses? Do I hell!" That statement of Claire's about knowing it was nothing but a night club frolic was all flapdoodle. Claire *must* have done something! Was his alibi as tight as it had appeared when he'd tested it at Royston? Norris felt a cold trickle down his spine.

A minute's hasty recalling of the details for his own reassurance, and Norris was off again. What would be the ideal solution? Two people involved, almost certainly; therefore Hayles and Claire. Hayles made his low-down, back-stair attempt and got Somers instead. Surely that other affair—the shot in the dark—looked like Claire? It was a sort of direct levelling up of the grudge right in the place where the adultery was going to take place. But Claire wasn't there! Yes, but suppose he *had* been there! How beautifully everything would sort itself out! Even that confession might have been forced out of him and.... Then Norris frowned once more as he found the alibi be-straddling that too convenient exit.

* * * * *

Ludovic Travers, also presumably on the side of law and order, was, in a subdued sort of way, quite pleased with himself. Thanks to the last night's investigations, whatever the report from Dijon, the point he'd set out to make was proved. The thing was, would Wharton act before the whole case was complete? Had he anybody—the other man, for instance—in his mind? If Franklin's accounts were complete, the General was, for him, remarkably quiescent. All the more reason therefore for something being up his sleeve, ready for production at the auspicious moment.

The latter half of his morning was spent at Brooklands. Except for a couple of cars and a motor-bicycle or two, the track was deserted and he sauntered casually round by the garages till he found one open. Inside were two mechanics, listening to the ticking over of a Sunbeam.

"Seen anything of Mr. Claire?" he asked.

The dungareed mechanic came over, wiping his hands on a piece of waste.

"Mr. Claire, sir. He'll be here this afternoon, so one of his men told me."

The Sunbeam raced noisily and under cover of the roar Travers plucked up courage to ask his question. "Suppose you haven't any asbestos tubing about?"

The other motioned to throttle her down. "Asbestos tubing, sir? What bore?"

"Oh—er—about three-quarters of an inch."

There was a look of amazement. "Three-quarter-inch! Never heard of it. What's it for?"

"To kill a man with!" was on the tip of Travers' tongue. Instead he produced a crumpled note from his trouser pocket and began to smooth it out.

"Fact of the matter is," he said, "I don't actually know what the chap wants it for. What would you do if you wanted any asbestos tubing of that bore? Take a piece of ordinary piping and lag it round with asbestos cement?"

"The very thing, sir. It'd be the simplest way. Thank you very much, sir!" He nodded back to the other to let her out and Travers slipped away. On the whole he was not dissatisfied. It certainly had been asbestos cement Claire was using at Marfleet.

It was just after his usual lunch hour when he drew the Isotta into the kerb outside No. 23, and in the second or so that elapsed between the ringing of the bell and the opening of the door, removed his gloves and rubbed his hands on the grimy surface of the wall. The gloves were replaced.

"Morning, Usher!" said Travers genially, and stepped into the dining-room. He peeped round to the drawing-room, then began to move over to the fire. "Tell Mr. Wharton I'd like to see him a minute, will you?"

"I'm afraid he isn't in, sir," said Usher, fluttering in his wake. Travers was now at the fire, removing his gloves and warming his hands. "As a matter of fact, sir, there's nobody in but myself."

"Dear oh dear!" said Travers, and continued to chafe his hands. "Devilish cold to-day!" Usher was looking as if he'd let a python into the family hen-run. Then to his relief, the caller got up.

"You don't know when he'll be in, I suppose?"

"I don't, sir."

"Well, I'll just push off again." He suddenly caught sight of his hands. "I seem to have got myself into the devil of a mess. Is there anywhere I could wash? Sorry to—"

"In here, sir." Usher opened the cloak-room door, saw to the towels and set the water running.

"Capital! Any chance of a spot of paraffin to get this grease off my hands?"

Usher bustled off to the kitchen. Travers, like an exceedingly active mosquito, nipped across the room.

* * * * *

When Travers finally returned to his office, it was to find Franklin's chit about that night's conference with Wharton. Then, just after five, came the telegram, and Franklin with it.

"Here's your wire, Ludo. Something's happened, though I'm damned if I know what it is."

Travers gave his glasses a quick polish, then had a look.

Requested post letter self Wednesday last. Full statement taken. Returning as arranged.

He contemplated it for a moment, then, "Don't you think you'd better see Wharton at once? This rather alters things."

"I say!" expostulated Franklin. "What the devil do you think I am? A thought reader?"

"I'm sorry!" said Travers with his most apologetic smile. "I'm getting rather flurried. But it's really frightfully important Wharton should know. Will you try to get hold of him and say you're coming round at once?"

Franklin located him first time—at his room at the Yard. The General would see them immediately.

"I say, you shouldn't have said anything about me!" said Travers, genuinely alarmed. "I'll tell you just what happened and then you can slip round and pass it on to Wharton."

"I'm damned if I do!" said Franklin. "Get your hat and come along and tell me about it on the way. Wharton might want to ask you half a hundred questions for all you know, and a pretty fool I'd look then. It's got to come out sooner or later."

"So it seems," said Travers mildly. He reached for his hat. "Truth will out—as they say—but that's no reason why I should be made to shout it through a megaphone."

Franklin took his arm. "Now, what's the yarn?"

"Well," began Travers, "it was like this ..."

*　*　*　*　*

Wharton popped up all smiles and affability.

"Come along in! How are you, Mr. Travers? Take a seat. And what about a cup of tea?"

"It's more like cocktail time," said Franklin. "You won't want any tea! Travers here has got something for you that'll cheer— and inebriate. All alone he did it!"

Wharton smiled tolerantly as he swivelled round the desk chair, but his tone was anxious beneath the geniality.

"That's good news. We always expect something original from Mr. Travers. And what is it—er—this time?"

"He'll tell you!"

Travers gave him a look, then cleared his throat. "Well, it was like this. By the way, do you want me to start at the end or the beginning?"

Wharton shrugged his shoulders humorously. "Either end— so long as we get the whole of it."

"Good! I only asked because I may be a bit long-winded and—er—unnecessarily mysterious. The start was that Franklin and I had been interested in Hayles before all this business be- gan, owing to certain peculiarities of conduct. Early last week, for instance, we caught him out in what looked to be an unnec- essary lie. That, of course, is nothing at all. We all have to tell 'em occasionally; even you and I and Franklin here. The bigger you are, the bigger the stretch as it were; publicity the mother of mendacity and so on."

"Quite so!"

"The actual facts were that Hayles didn't seem any too keen on anybody knowing he'd been in the Hampstead Road at a certain time. I should say we weren't interested in that to any great extent, only when this murder business cropped up—and

Hayles with it—naturally that cropped up too. Still, that's hardly the point. The whole thing is that suicide confession in France's writing. The way I thought about it was asking myself a question. If I wanted France to write it, how should I proceed? Or, if I'd put myself sufficiently into the hide of Hayles, how would he have proceeded? Certainly by some far from dangerous means; by what we might call the safely spectacular or the furtively safe. He's that sort—and his books show it. Then naturally I thought of a method and Franklin sent a man of his to Dijon to prove it. He couldn't tell you about it because I was his client. What I thought of was this.

"Hayles would have a letter sent to himself from abroad, from people he could trust. The letter, written in, say, French, would contain a certain passage he might ask France to translate. Later on, I saw the flaws in that. It was, very frankly, extremely crude. In the first place France, for all we knew, had no better acquaintance with French than Hayles had. Then I thought, 'Why not Italian—or German—or Spanish—or—?' Then, of course, I had it. The passage would have to be in Russian—the language which France spoke like his own and which Hayles certainly wouldn't know. You see that?"

"Yes, yes! Go on!"

"If I may, I'll now resort to a kind of hypothetical narrative. Hayles had written a letter, very shrewdly disguised, in what we might call pidgin Franco-English. He displays the letter to France—foreign postmark, stamp and everything—and says, 'Look here, France—or Michael or whatever he called him—I wish you'd do something for me.' I ought to have said they're in Hayles's room. 'There was a girl I got to know at Dijon. I didn't tell you about it because you'd only have laughed. Well, she started to get a bit of a nuisance pestering me and so on—so I had to write her a pretty stiff letter telling her I was through. This morning I got this from her and there's something in it—Russian, I think; she's a Pole, by the way—which I can't make out. I wonder if you'd tell me what it is.' Thereupon he passes the letter over to France, making pretence of covering everything except the paragraph in question. Then, of course, we imagine a bit of leg-pulling on the part of France and blushes from Hayles. France takes the letter and gives a free translation. The girl is taking it rather badly; threatening in fact to commit suicide! Hayles is scared stiff. 'I say,' he says, 'that's pretty bad for me. I'd better have that translation in case anything happens. Would you mind writing one out, there's a good chap. And for the love of heaven, don't say a word to a soul!' Thereupon France sits down at the desk, takes the sheet of grey notepaper which Hayles hands him, and writes—boldly and fluently as the writing shows. He blots it on the beautiful new sheet of blotting-paper... and that's that! What were the words exactly? Do you remember?"

Wharton repeated them from memory—

> *This is really the end of everything. I can't go on any longer with things as they are. And they say life is worth living! Good-bye.*

"It does sound rather affected," added Franklin.

"You're being wise after the event," said Wharton curtly. "Carry on, Mr. Travers!"

"Well Hayles takes the note and when France goes out removes the blotting-paper and on the Saturday shuts it in the blotter case in the secretaire. On the Sunday afternoon when he slipped into the house expecting to find France's body, he got a shock. The confession he'd placed, say, on the mantelpiece, had gone. We assume, of course, that he looked for it last, *after* faking the suicide, so as to take it away. Then he was disturbed by Usher and Franklin and had to give up the search. And now you'll want the proof."

Wharton's eyes never left his face. His look was so concentrated that Travers thought he needed placating.

"I do want you to understand something and that is that I had a short cut. Given the idea I've just outlined, you could have got the information in twenty-four hours through other channels—the press, for instance. What I mean to imply is that the apparent coincidence is of no real value. Still, here it is.

"As Hayles didn't know Russian, he'd have to get somebody to write that paragraph for him. First I thought of the people at Dijon, but that appeared too much of a gamble. Then that Hampstead Road business cropped up again and I wondered if he'd consulted a regular Russian of some sort. Then I remembered a place I'd seen there—one of those schools of languages—so I called up and made inquiries. Hayles had been there. He'd asked to see a Russian expert and he'd seen one—a Pole called Barinski. By the way, I've got Barinski where Hayles can't get at him, supposing he gets suspicious.

"This chap's prepared to swear that Hayles told him he had a Russian girl who was threatening to give him up and he wanted, therefore, to scare her badly—to show her he was serious, if you like—that Barinski should write for him a paragraph in which he threatened suicide. Barinski's English is poor but his French is perfect, so I imagine Hayles wrote down the paragraph he wanted in both languages. Barinski did what he was asked. Then suddenly Hayles thought of something he hadn't thought of till then. Since it was supposed to be a woman writing *to him,* endings and so on, would have to be feminine! He got out of that by asking Barinski to transcribe it as if a woman were writing it. He was a fool there. He ought to have gone to another firm for that. As it was, the double translation fixed every word in Barinski's mind. He's prepared to go through the whole business with you whenever you care to see him. And, by the way, you'll have to square his absence with his employers. And—er—well, that's everything."

"Thank you, Mr. Travers," said Wharton quietly. He sat there a good minute, thinking it over, then got to his feet. "I think that accounts for Mr. Hayles!"

"Travers thinks Hayles cut the hole in the window," said Franklin. Wharton sat down again.

Travers dissociated himself forthwith. "Nothing of the sort! All I'd say is that it'd be absolutely consonant with what we know of him—personally and from his books—and his amnesia." There Wharton grunted. "I should say he faked the burglary so that, if France's body were discovered before he got back to fake the suicide, then there'd be a further red herring. It might have been assumed that whoever broke in did so in order to lay the poison trap."

"I quite agree," said Wharton emphatically. And what about the letters? He wrote them?

"I should say he did. It's all part of that mysterious stuff he revelled in. Only, if I might venture to say so, I don't think there was any idea of scaring France out of London. For one thing, he didn't know anything about that Mrs. Claire business till long after that. What I think is, he wrote them as another stand-by. If it had been thought that France *didn't* commit suicide, then he was killed by the chap who wrote' anonymous threats—same chap who broke into the house, if you like."

"Quite so! But just one little point—about the placing of that confession. We assumed it was on the mantelpiece, under a vase. If the body were found prematurely, that confession had to be found too. Yet it had to be where France couldn't see it! And in spite of that, Somers saw it!"

"I think," said Travers, "that's a case of rather subtle psychology. I thrashed that out with my own man—you know him—Palmer. We experimented and agreed that if the note were placed with the corner protruding from under the vase, France wouldn't have paid any attention to it. It's not his duty to see casual things like that. He always had things *given* to him. But Somers—he'd be very different. The first thing he'd see—being trained that way—would be the untidy corner of paper protruding. And he *did* see it."

"Sounds all right," said Wharton and got up again.

Franklin turned to Travers. "About that visit to the Air Ministry. Don't you think Hayles had to know for certain about that fog? For all he knew, France might draw the blinds back when he entered the house, and he'd be bound to leave the lights on after he was dead. A policeman might have gone round to inquire into that."

"What's all this about the Air Ministry?" asked Wharton.

"Only another small theory," smiled Travers and nodded over to Franklin.

Wharton sat down again.

CHAPTER XXIV
TRAVERS IS WORRIED

AS SOON AS Travers opened his eyes on the Saturday morning, the first thing they fell on was the door leading to the bathroom, with its brand-new, oxidised silver, lever handle and the coat-hook fixed in the munting. Invisible at its side would be the hole Palmer had bored for that reconstruction they'd tried out the previous night. At the same moment Travers knew just what it was that was on his mind; what had woke him up twice in the night, and what looked like providing a worrying morning.

It was the previous evening that had started it. The conference had, of course, been washed out; the new disclosures for one thing and Norris's absence for another. "Where's he gone?" Franklin had asked, and "Marfleet!" Wharton had replied, and had left it at that. "Marfleet," of course, might have meant anything—following up the trail of Hayles, for instance—but Travers, with his mind on the final elucidation of the case, was little disposed to think so, especially in view of what happened later.

"There's something I've thought of," Wharton had said, "which, if he doesn't mind me saying so, might absolutely clinch Mr. Travers's story. I put it to you now. You both tell me, and so did Usher, that Hayles was a sort of perennial joke with the others; not joke in the unkind sense perhaps, but someone they refused to take very seriously and who was always exciting risibility. Mr. Travers had that idea in mind when he said that as soon as he broached to France the matter of a girl in Dijon, France'd have started pulling his leg. We'll assume that Hayles told France to keep it dark. Even then my suggestion is that France couldn't resisted the temptation to tell it to the others, especially to Mrs. Claire—on that Saturday night."

Travers had seen the point; that Saturday night—the walk in the gloom from Camden Town—a time for delicious confidences. Wharton took off the receiver and got his long distance call through to Mrs. Claire. His shrewdly guarded question and his answers told the result.

"Oh, he did!... Any mention of locality?... I see. Merely abroad.... Oh, yes! I recognise that it's confidential." Then he glanced at Franklin. "Oh, just one other thing, Mrs. Claire! Did Mr. France, after you met him on the Saturday evening, say anything about a telephone call?... Nothing whatever! Thank you. How are you keeping, by the way?... That's capital! Well, thank you, Mrs. Claire. Good-bye!"

He replaced the receiver with a nod that had considerable meaning. "Just one thing occurred to me as I was talking. Can Mrs. Claire be kept out of it?"

"It'll depend upon Hayles," said Franklin. "If he makes a clean breast—"

"I wouldn't rely on him," said Wharton. "He's the sort that wriggles like an eel on a fish-hook."

"What was that telephone business?" Franklin asked.

"Oh, that!" with a perfect air of matter-of-fact. "I just wondered why France should go straight to the cloak-room when he came in. Did Claire telephone him to go there, when he made that call at Liverpool Street?"

Franklin apparently had no desire to press the point, and that had ended things till the very last moment when Wharton was seeing them out of the door. Then he'd called Travers back with an, "Oh, just a minute, Mr. Travers! Aren't you a great authority on cars?" Travers, as he lay there, could recall the very gesture that accompanied the remark.

"I wouldn't go so far as that!" he'd said.

"I suppose you know all about the modern use of asbestos tubing?" Wharton asked, disinterested as you like.

Travers determined to draw him out. "Asbestos tubing! What on earth's that for?—outside a kitchen." Wharton had laughed genially, made a doesn't-matter-a-damn gesture and ended with a sorry-you've-been-troubled sort of dismissal.

"What was that idea about the telephoning?" Franklin had asked when he rejoined him. "Does that imply that Claire called France up and reminded him of something connected with the cloak-room so that he should go there?"

"Lord knows!" Travers had answered. "It seems rather elaborate."

"Elaborate! It's damned ridiculous! Claire couldn't have had a confederate waiting in that cloak-room. We've already knocked the bottom out of *that* argument."

* * * * *

That was what was weighing heavily on Travers's mind. In the matter of the death of France, Wharton, in the words of the children's game, was getting very warm. The arrest of Hayles was being held up only in view of that further development. At any moment Wharton might swoop down on the murderer of France, *and the reason Travers felt the certainty in his bones was that he himself knew, not only who did the killing, but the circumstances in which that killing had been done!*

At breakfast, Palmer noticed the unusual preoccupation. Travers, as a matter of fact, was getting more and more anxious. Then over the morning papers came the first consolation. Dare Wharton make an arrest? Where, unless he had got hold of some vital evidence of which he himself was unaware, could he produce sufficient to justify a warrant? He could neither force a statement nor run the risk of exposing his hand in a coroner's court. Thereupon Travers's outlook became temporarily less cramped—he actually read a column of his favourite financial leader-writer—until it occurred to him that a shelving of the main problem wasn't the same as abandoning it. Sooner or later Wharton would succeed, as he always had done, in worming his way into some subterranean and buried essential.

Palmer was still more intrigued when he was ordered to ring for the Isotta. It looked as if the week-end in Sussex wasn't coming off after all.

"And the arrangements stand for twelve-thirty, sir?" he asked.

"Don't know. Don't pack anything... yet. I really can't say. *And will you order that car!*"

Palmer, looking as if his pet canary had suddenly savaged him, bobbed, and bolted for the phone.

At Durango House, Travers went in search of Franklin. Cresswold reported that he'd come in early and had gone out after receiving a telephone call—where he couldn't say. Back went Travers to his room and started the daily round. Then he suddenly thought of something else. Was it, or was it not, at midday that Claire was starting on that attack on the record? He ran the answer to earth in the Sports' Diary column.

> MOTOR-RACING. Brooklands. 11.0 a.m. Attempt by
> Peter Claire on the 200 kilometre record.

At that very moment, fortunately for Travers's peace of mind, the telephone went—Franklin ringing him up from the-Lord-knows-where, and positively spluttering with excitement. He'd just left No. 23, where he'd been with Wharton. The old General had turned up the ace of trumps as usual! Perfectly astounding!

Travers cut in quickly. Wharton definitely knew who did it? Franklin chuckled. Did Wharton know! and in a sentence gave the game away. Travers cut in again.

"Hallo! Are you there?... I say; come along and tell me all about it!" He slipped the receiver back, then stood thinking for a good half minute before pushing the bell. "Find out the next train to Weybridge... or better, bring me the Southern time table!"

He looked at the clock—just gone ten. He'd never do it in the Isotta. Might take most of that time to get clear of London, if traffic blocks went wrong. In came the time table with a train leaving Waterloo at 10.20 and arriving 11.0. If he remembered rightly, there'd be plenty of taxis at the other end outside the station. And Claire would almost sure to be late in starting. A hasty order that if Mr. Franklin looked in, he was to be told that he'd been suddenly called away, and where nobody was to know—and he was off.

A minute before that train left, he was in it and with a scribbling block on his knees, was wondering to just how much he dared commit himself. The train arrived dead on time and he hopped into a taxi—"Brooklands—and drive like hell!"

The driver set off with apparently that object in view, and they shot away up the hill through the woods. If Travers had had eyes for it, he would have seen the leaves a golden yellow, the road a brilliant carpet, and the distant hills warm with the November sun. As it was he caught the sharp tang of the oak leaves—a smell he was never likely to forget.

They swerved round the bend and shot wildly along the drive—Travers flourishing his member's ticket as they passed the barrier. Just short of the members' bridge he tapped on the window and the car drew up. He stuck his head out of the window and listened. In the air was a hum; the hum became a snarl, then a raucous sort of grind as a car roared towards the bend. A quick pop-pop! from the exhaust as it checked below the bridge—the roar became a snarl—then a hum that receded.

"Someone travelling down there, sir!" remarked the driver of the taxi.

Travers grunted. "Hm! Push on to the Paddock!"

The car ran through the tunnel and drew up inside the enclosure. Travers, putting out his head, caught sight of a yellow-capped paddock attendant and motioned him over.

"Is that Mr. Claire on the track?"

"Yes, sir. He's going round now."

"Where's he being timed from?"

"Fork Timing Box, sir; up there—opposite Vickers!"

"Am I allowed to take the car up?"

"Certainly, sir!—as far as the Fork."

Travers signalled to his driver and the car shot off again. Exactly what the plan of campaign was to be, he hadn't much idea at the moment; all he did know was that it'd be a remarkably awkward business. Then the car drew up at the Fork and he waited for the Bentley to roar by.

Under the timekeeper's window, Claire's two mechanics were watching. One of them recognised him and flicked his fingers to his cap.

"Morning!" said Travers. "How's he going?"

"Not too well, sir. Air's a bit heavy this morning. Track's pretty good though."

Travers smiled. "You can't have it all ways. Also he's not warmed up yet. What time'd he start?"

"This is the sixth lap, sir."

Travers nodded. "Then it won't matter so much if I get the timekeeper to flag him—"

"Flag him, sir!"

"Yes! Something most frightfully important and private. As the Bentley hurtled by, he hurried in to make his request. By the time he was out again it was checking towards the Box. Thirty yards past it, it drew up. Travers sprinted towards it.

* * * * *

Five minutes later, as the taxi breasted the hill at the end of the tunnel, Travers stopped the car and again went up the bank to the members' bridge. He looked at his watch. Plenty of time to catch that 11.35 back to town. He ran up the steps and as he got there, heard the roar of the racing car as it approached the Fork. It came round the bend, hugging the line, and as Travers peered below and saw it like a momentary, clamorous beetle, it was gone by the railway embankment. He watched it out of sight round the far banking, then took off his glasses and shook his head perplexedly. Then he felt a trickle of moisture down his cheek, and the handkerchief, as he mopped his forehead, came away wet.

An hour later he was back in his rooms at St. Martin's Chambers and Palmer was announcing lunch. Travers ate little and what he did eat was mechanically. Palmer cleared away, then came cautiously back for instructions. He was hustled off at once for an evening paper-far too early, as Palmer reported— then was told the week-end was probably off. Then Travers changed his mind. He didn't know. He'd decide definitely later.

Just before three, Franklin came breezing in. "Hallo! Where'd *you* get to this morning? Hunted all over the place for you."

"Sorry!" said Travers, with his most disarming smile. "Unpardonably rude of me, but I had to go out—privately—and I couldn't very well let you know."

Franklin, apparently on pretty good terms with himself, took it very well. "That's all right. Only you're a damn nice detective! You sweat blood and hunt round and when the rabbit bolts out of the box—"

"Bolts! Who's bolted?"

"Nobody! Merely a figure of speech." He drew himself up a chair. "Get ready to be thrilled! It's the most ridiculously easy thing you ever saw—if Wharton's got it right... and I think he has."

"I expect it's right enough," said Travers.

Franklin looked at him. Some strangeness of expression on the other's face prompted his own sharp question.

"What *d'you* know about it? You've seen Wharton?" Travers shook his head. "No!... I've seen nobody... and heard nothing." He waved his hand towards the far door. "Have a look in my bedroom... and tell me if I'm right!"

CHAPTER XXV
THE MAN WHO KNEW

FRANKLIN HAD one look at the bathroom door, then came back.

"How on earth did you find that out?"

"Don't know," said Travers. "It just... sort of came!"

Franklin was still puzzled. "Damned if I know how you did it! It took Wharton and Norris best part of yesterday."

"It took me more than that," said Travers. "Even then I think there's a good deal left out."

"Yes, but how'd you do it, Ludo?"

"By exhaustion—elimination, if you like—as you fellows did. Claire must have done *something*—but he wasn't there to do it.

Therefore he did it without being there—by some simple mechanical device."

"I know. But what about details?"

"Those came last night, after Wharton had made one or two remarks which weren't nearly so casual as he'd meant them to be." He glanced at Franklin. "You'd really like to hear how I fitted it all in?"

"I certainly should!" He laughed. "It'd be damn funny if old George had got something wrong after all!"

"I'm more likely to be the one who's wrong." He went over to the bureau and came back with a bundle of notes. "Here's my material—what I remembered of the accounts you gave me from time to time, and what little I managed to glean for myself. And here's the diagram I made last night before I tried it out."

Franklin had a look at it. "It's practically the same."

"As for details," went on Travers, pushing his long legs towards the fire and leaning almost out of sight in the backward depths of the chair, "we might take Hayles first. You probably won't agree with me when I say that I don't really consider Hayles a murderer. What I mean is that you wouldn't put a first-class burglar in the same category as an inferior pickpocket. However, all that melodramatic machinery was his; the faked burglary, the anonymous threats, the confession, and everything as we imagined it—only he got Somers instead. Hayles seems to me rather like a—er—creeping sort of thing; something you ought to put your foot on and crush. Still, there we are. The rest is Claire's; working independently of Hayles, of course, and thanks to the fog or because things in the mind of both men had got to an unbearable climax, working at the same time and in the same place.

"Usher gave Claire the idea through the knot-hole. Claire had got tired of France. He was naturally selfish and now he was furiously jealous. Think of what Usher must have told him in at least one of his reports—that *France meant business!* His immense dignity and beefy importance had a tremendous shock. You can imagine him—smooth and sleek—not man enough to tackle France chin to chin; hunching those slab shoulders of his and scowling it all out. He's a long way from a fool, and he's got a certain inventive talent, as I saw when I was down at his place.

"Very well then. He went round on the Friday—or maybe earlier—when he had the chance to go to the cloak-room—and that wouldn't be very difficult. I should say he had the pistol and he had in his hand a lump of softish putty. Into this he squeezed the knot from the door, and so got an impression of it. All he had to do then was to put the barrel of the pistol into the mould in the putty and fill in with asbestos cement. The pistol was then embedded in what might be called 'an asbestos knot.'

SECTION OF
MUNTING,ETC..

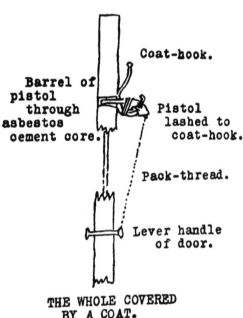

Coat-hook.

Barrel of
pistol
through
asbestos
cement core.

Pistol
lashed to
coat-hook.

Pack-thread.

Lever handle
of door.

THE WHOLE COVERED
BY A COAT.

"He knew, moreover, that France was to be alone in the house on the Saturday; he knew it before Usher rang him up on the Friday evening. Also he took good care to let everybody know that, fog or no fog, he'd be away himself over the Saturday night. Before ever he knew a word about what his wife and France had planned, he'd therefore intended to kill France in any case.

"Usher's message meant little modification of plans—except that Claire made one big mistake. He thought the arrangements made by France and his wife were final—but they weren't. France rang up Mrs. Claire and what he said made all the difference. France should have been killed before Mrs. Claire got to the house. Claire expected she'd knock at the door, get no reply, then go away in a huff. Even if she had a key and went in and found France's body, he knew she daren't say a word.

"However, what Claire did was this. As soon as France left on the Saturday evening, he nipped in. He had plenty of time before going to the club to meet Utley. Palmer and I worked it all out and found he needn't have been in the house more than ten minutes all told. He slipped the pistol, with its asbestos cement end, into the knot-hole, which it fitted to a hair's breadth. Most important that, for fear of a blowback. Then all he had to do was to lash the pistol to the coat-hook by its magazine or stock or both. Through the swivel on the handle he attacked a piece of stout thread—black of course—to the trigger at one end and to the lever handle of the door at the other. The asbestos knot had already been well blacked so as to be invisible. Then he probably had a rehearsal to see it went all right; covered the whole thing with a coat and a hat on the coat-hook, *locked* the door and left the cloak-room by way of the lounge. Next he slipped upstairs and deposited those hairs he'd got from the maid's bedroom.

"What happened, of course, was that France—not alone as Claire expected-having been rung up by Claire to go to the cloak-room for something urgent—that can be worked out later—went straight to the cloak-room door. His hand went out to the handle and, as the door was locked, his body followed. The knothole was the height of his head—Claire knew that through his own height and Usher's—and as soon as he depressed that lever handle the merest fraction of an inch, he was dead!

"Now what about risks? In the first place, suppose the preparations had been discovered by France—gadget didn't work, or something. France wouldn't be sure it was Claire, but under the circumstances he'd have a thundering good idea. In any case you can bet he wouldn't have gone to the police. If he tackled Claire direct, he hadn't much of a leg to stand on—on the face of it. Also Claire might have said the whole thing was a joke—*that the pistol wouldn't kill a man in any case.* Hadn't they all laughed about it when discussing what sort of gun would drop a man in his tracks? In any case, you can bet your life there'd have been no scandal. In other words, it looked for Claire like 'heads I win; tails you lose.'

"Again, suppose the body was discovered by an outsider—police or who you like. Do you think they'd start looking under coats and hats in the cloak-room? Not they! They'd look for the man who bolted after firing the shot. Even if they did look round, what might they have seen? If they had eyes like gimlets, they might have seen a piece of black thread hanging from the handle lever inside the cloak-room. There wouldn't be any mark on the door—burning or anything like that—the asbestos lagging made that all right. The pistol shot out of a kind of second tube. The only thing unusual was the hole in the munting on the drawing-room side where the bullet came through, but that was above the level of the eyes of an ordinary man and it was all black.

"Of course Claire made a slip about Usher. If he'd had any sense, he'd have seen Hanson and Maude and got him away at once. The trouble was that Claire imagined himself of such importance that the law would only approach him with considerable circumspection. Remember Mrs. Claire's similar attitude towards Wharton? Curious how people like that imagine themselves as immeasurably out of the reach of the law. Even Lecoq, you remember, couldn't bring himself to think that a Duke had committed a crime!

"However, Claire was fairly lucky. His wife kept her mouth shut—if she hadn't, there might have been complications. Then on the Sunday, all he had to do was to face the suicide, dismantle his apparatus and—*voilà!* Placing the body with that bowl of roses as a background might have been a sardonic sort of gesture. Probably, too, he rumpled the cushions, and of course he had to fetch the hat and coat. He must have felt pleased. France had committed suicide. If that didn't seem likely, or if Mrs. Claire said anything, then he'd been killed by the woman who'd left those hairs in the room.... I think that's everything. Does it agree with Wharton's version?"

"Almost word for word—except that he didn't think of the black thread. He thought it was silk. Still, that's nothing. What gets me is why Claire should have been such a fool as to cut off his nose to spite his face. He'd have made a fortune over France's American trip!"

Travers shook his head. "What did he want with more money? He's rolling in it. It was his personal dignity that counted—nothing else." He got up and sauntered over to the window and looked out at the mists that hung over Covent Garden. "After all details don't matter—not a hoot either way. The telephone message doesn't matter; black thread or silk, asbestos cement or asbestos tape; nothing matters... except whether he did it nor not.... Er—what's Wharton going to do?"

Franklin wasted a shrug and a shake of the head on Travers' back. "Do! He can do nothing for the moment. There aren't any marks on the coat-hook, or if there were, Claire got them off. And he replaced the knot with seccotine, as we know. All George can do is to have a microscopical examination made for the asbestos cement—traces of course." He leaned forward and lighted his pipe. "Between you and me, Wharton's going to have the hell of a time fastening anything on to Claire. The beauty of it is he doesn't know it!"

Travers looked round quickly. "What do you mean exactly?"

"Well, he didn't say anything, but I think he thinks he's got a brain wave. You know that chuckle of his? He gave me a special one as I came away."

"What about Hayles?"

"He hasn't decided... but I'll lay two to one he nabs him to-night—after he's had a word with Claire."

"What's he seeing Claire for? To spring the mine? Sort of show him how it was done?"

Franklin shook his head. "I can't say. All I know is the General's got something up his sleeve... and he's going to see Claire... this evening."

"And what's your own opinion."

"Mine?" He shrugged his shoulders again. "I don't know. Claire'll probably get away with it. He'd never be such a fool as to own up."

Travers sat down again. He leaned forward in the chair, fingering his glasses and staring into the fire with a fixity of gaze that was almost mesmeric. Neither he nor Franklin said a word for a good few moments, then Travers broke the silence.

"There *is* a way to find out if he did it or not... or there *could* have been a way."

Franklin looked up. "How?"

Travers shook his head slowly. "It's difficult to say." He fumbled again with his glasses, then put them on. Then he got to his feet and strolled quietly to the window. "Suppose... merely suppose . somebody who knew Claire had got wind of all this murder business and how it was done. This morning Claire was making an attack on the two-hundred kilometre record at Brooklands—smashing round and round at about two miles or so a minute. Suppose this chap merely hands Claire a copy of that diagram there on the table... with two requests—to look at it... and then destroy it. You can imagine Claire—I can—running those greyish-green eyes of his over it, giving it a bored sort of recognition, then shrugging his shoulders and lighting a cigarette with it. I can see his eyes narrowing—that horrible trick he has—as the chap moves away."

Travers turned round.

"If Claire didn't do it, then he'll go to Wharton... of his own accord, because he'll have nothing to fear. If he did do it, Wharton may never know... and the papers may tell him so... this afternoon."

"Good God! You don't mean—"

"I mean nothing," said Travers quietly. "Who am *I* to be any man's executioner?" He came back to the fire. "Er—will you—would you mind going to see if you can get a paper?"

Franklin hopped up like a shot. On the corner of Chandos Street, the newsboys were calling excitedly Franklin shoved out his penny and grabbed the paper almost before the boy had picked it out; then stood there—hatless, rigid—staring at the headlines and the photograph that looked at him.

TRAGEDY AT BROOKLANDS
FAMOUS RACING SPORTSMAN KILLED
CAR TURNS TURTLE

He took a deep breath, then bolted off with the paper. Outside the main entrance he stopped again and glanced at the letterpress—twenty lines or so of news and the rest a mixture of conjecture and biographical write-up.

"A terrible tragedy occurred to-day at Brooklands, involving the death of one of the best known of English racing motorists—Peter Claire, as he was affectionately known to every habitué of the world's racing tracks.

"Mr. Claire set out this morning in his well-known Bentley, to beat the world's 200-kilometre record, at present held by the Comte de Rigainville.

"Just after the start at 11.0 a.m. the attempt was temporarily abandoned, but shortly afterwards Mr. Claire made a fresh start in another Bentley, and at a hundred kilometres was very slightly inside record, which was flagged as he passed the timing box.

"On the very next circuit, immediately after passing under the members' bridge, the car was seen to be out of control and mounted the embankment by the railway bridge, crashing into the arches. Help was immediately at hand but the car was a mass of flames. The body of the unfortunate driver was lying clear, and it is presumed that he fell as the car turned turtle. His neck was broken and death must have been instantaneous.

"All that can be conjectured at the moment is that a speed wobble..."

Franklin didn't wait to read the rest. Upstairs, in the semi-twilight, Travers was still sitting where he had left him, looking into the fire. He turned his head as Franklin entered.

"It's all over!" said Franklin quietly. His car mounted the embankment.

Travers said nothing.

"Looks as if he turned it deliberately towards that banking.... His neck was broken, They say he was dead before he knew it."

Travers still sat there, elbow on the arm of his chair and hand shielding his face, and Franklin could guess what he was thinking. He sat quietly himself for a moment or two, then had an idea.

"Wharton'll never guess anything. He'll think... whoever flagged Claire did it for him to change his car." Then another idea. "And when you come to think of it, Ludo, it's the very devil! Just what Wharton said. Dorothy Claire stamped her foot and said she *would* go to a night club—and three men are dead... and another's due for it. And she'll go scot free! She's done nothing—oh, no!"

Travers shook his head slowly. "I don't know... She'll pay. At least they always do... in the long run. Mrs. Hayles will have to pay. The other'll pay too. Don't you think she'll remember for the rest of her life? Won't that be punishment enough?"

Franklin said nothing.

"I think it will," Travers continued quietly. "If Wharton had had Claire hanged by the neck till he was dead, that wouldn't have brought France back to life... or poor Somers either. But it might have marked the woman down for life... and not the woman only."

"You mean... Claire's child?"

"What else? Why should that child grow up knowing his father was hanged by the neck?"

Franklin thought for a moment, then looked up quickly. "Tell me, Ludo! Is that why... you—"

Travers leaned back and switched on the light. He looked at Franklin and gave a queer sort of smile.

"Don't ask me.... What is it they call it? Conspiring to defeat the ends of justice, or some such formula."

"Justice be damned!" was Franklin's contemptuous comment. Then he lugged out his pouch. "Try a fill of this, Ludo. It's something new." Then, as Travers took the pouch and felt the contents with his long fingers, he got up and pushed the bell.

"And what about Wharton's stand-by?—a nice cup of tea!"

THE END